THRILL
RIDE

THRILL
RIDE

J.D. CAROTHERS

Dreamlific Publishing

Editing by Cece Carroll

Cover design by Mayhem Cover Creations

Blurb by Deborah Dove, Polgarus Studio

ISBN: 978-1-957997-03-2

To my husband and my parents
for their love and unbounded confidence
in me and my dreams

For more information, visit
www.jdcarothers.com

CHAPTER ONE

CASSIE

S crolling through news on my cell phone, I gasp as the image of a wrecked, silver car with the cryptic caption "Chef Bernard?" pops up. Swiftly, I tap the image as my pulse quickens. A dark scene dotted with flashing lights fills the screen as an out-of-breath reporter explains, "This is Rob Ross of LV News reporting live from the scene of a serious car accident about 15 minutes east of the Las Vegas Strip. We've just made our way across this dimly lit parking lot to an area illuminated by the lights of emergency vehicles. Unfortunately, the police have roped off the area behind us, so we can't get any closer to the accident."

Catching his breath, the reporter continues, "We were told that the first responders arrived about 15 or 20 minutes ago. Behind me, they are working on at least one victim from a crumpled, silver Lexus. As you can hear, sirens are blaring in the background as additional police and medical support arrive. A medical helicopter is circling overhead in preparation for landing in the deserted parking lot to my left."

Sporting an out-of-place, plastic smile, the emotionless news anchor at the station calmly responds, "Rob, this is Adrian. Can you tell us what caused the accident?" Grimacing, I wonder how a news anchor can be so jaded and detached when viewing such a terrible accident. At least the on-scene reporter's furrowed brow and frown indicate he feels some actual emotion about what he's witnessing.

Rob responds, "It appears the Lexus swerved off the main road and ran full speed into the side of a pawn shop. We don't know if the driver was avoiding another vehicle or if something else caused the driver to veer off the road. But no other vehicle appears to have been involved in the accident."

The thought of crashing full speed into a building sends chills through me. Arms wrapped tightly around my torso, I keep listening as the anchor asks, "Rob, do you know who was in the car? What is the status of the victim?"

"We have not received word as to who was in the vehicle. We did, however, learn that the vehicle is registered to Allison Bernard. She is the well-known chef and owner of the Chez Bernard restaurant here in Las Vegas. As you may know, the Grand Athena announced tonight that Chef Bernard will be one of the judges for its upcoming Guest Chef Competition." No! The headline mentioned Chef Bernard, but hopefully, she is not the one seriously injured or worse. It sounds silly, but losing her would feel like losing a friend. Her energetic image fills my screen on so many weekend mornings. My mouth waters just remembering the recipes she demonstrated over the last few weeks.

"That's right. The Athena —"

Interrupting Adrian, Rob says, "Adrian, hold on a minute! It appears there is a major development. The helicopter is flying away without landing, and the emergency response teams have slowed their movements."

As his semi-permanent smile finally morphs into a frown, Adrian replies, "Rob, that doesn't seem like a good sign." My gut wrenches as I fear hope is lost. But my eyes remain fixed on the video, praying I'm wrong.

Sighing and lowering his chin, Rob's voice takes on a somber tone as he agrees, "It doesn't. An EMT is headed this way. Let me see if we can learn more. Sir, was that Chef Bernard in the car?"

Wiping sweat from his brow with the back of his hand, the exhausted, dazed EMT responds "Yes. We thought we had a chance to save her. Then she mumbled something about champagne and was gone, but don't quote me on that."

Without further comment, the EMT disappears off camera as Rob concludes, "Adrian, you just heard it straight from this dedicated, emergency responder. They tried to save Chef Allison Bernard, but she was lost in a tragic accident, apparently resulting from too much alcohol. Back to you."

Shaking my head, I let out the breath I was holding as realization hits that one of my favorite television chefs on the Food, Fun & Travel Channel died last night. Chef Bernard's show, "Cooking without Fear," taught me and millions of other fans that we learn and improve from both our cooking successes and failures. Sadly, Saturday mornings won't be the same without her.

While Googling for more information on the accident, I think I hear my name. Then a little louder comes, "Cassie, unmute. We can't hear you."

Drawn back to the ongoing Zoom meeting and attempting to cover up my distraction with a confused frown, I unmute my computer and ask, "Could you repeat the question? My Internet connection is unreliable today." After all, I can't let them know I wasn't paying attention. I'd intended to surreptitiously glance down at my cell phone for a quick look at the latest news, but I got caught up in the story about Chef Bernard and forgot to tune back into the Zoom meeting.

My boss, Jackson, responds, "Cassie, we keep reminding you to upgrade your internet service. Get that done this week if you want to continue working remotely on a regular basis."

"Will do." I guess I've used the excuse one too many times, but zoning out or getting distracted during these interminable video calls is inevitable when they usually have very little to do with my part of the project. Today is even worse because our old-guard boss made the whole California team wear business attire so he could trot us in front of the European client for this middle-of-the-night Zoom meeting. It gives dog-and-pony show a whole new meaning. I'm sitting at my kitchen table in a silk shirt, gold necklace, and suit jacket. At least my bare feet are comfortably propped up on another chair, and no one can see I'm wearing pajama shorts. Honestly, I could be naked from the waist down and no one would know or care. Except for the occasional "Will do" or "I'll have that done shortly," we are all just staring at our computer screens, watching the client and our boss debate the current deal for an hour or two. The client must be wondering why so many silent faces are staring at him during these calls.

Anyone would get distracted and glimpse down at their cell phone occasionally, right? At least, that's what I tell myself. After all, what's the harm in catching up on some news and gossip while we wait our turn to answer to our boss?

"Cassie, we were asking when you will have the memo on the licensing issues finished."

"I should have that done by close of business on Friday."

"Did we hear you say 'should' or 'will'?"

Ugh. What a jackass. He knows I've never missed a deadline, but he can't pass up the opportunity to crack his well-known, verbal whip in front of the client. This time his show of power is at my expense. But I need this job, so, gritting my teeth, I dutifully respond, "My apologies. I meant to say the memo *will* be ready by close of business on Friday."

James snaps back, "Speed it up. We need it by noon Friday to get this deal closed over the weekend." Wow, I'm usually not on the receiving end of that whip twice during one meeting. To make matters worse, he already emailed me a 50-page contract this morning that I have to review and edit by noon on Friday. That only gives me three days to get the licensing memo and contract done, which will barely be enough time, given we have two more Zoom calls scheduled between now and the deadline.

Biting my tongue yet again, I hear myself say the perfunctory "will do." But the most frustrating part is that everyone on this call knows this is a fake deadline. Even the client knows the finance guys won't have their numbers done until late Sunday. That means this deal isn't closing before Monday or Tuesday at the earliest.

I better hit mute again before I accidentally verbalize my frustrations. Not only do I hate fake deadlines, but I also know there will be hell to pay if I miss one — not that I ever have. Starting with the first homework assignment in elementary school, my parents drilled in the importance of taking responsibility. While at my age it shouldn't matter what my parents think, I still don't want to disappoint them, but I don't know how many more "will dos" I have in me when Jackson pulls this crap. Nevertheless, I have to suck it up, or he will use it as another excuse to delay my promotion yet again. His last excuse was that I needed to increase my billable hours by ten percent. When I did, he demanded another ten percent increase, which is crazy. No matter how hard I work, I'm chasing a dangling carrot that he keeps moving farther away.

Attempting to concentrate on the call, I lock my eyes on the computer screen, but I keep wondering about Chef Bernard's accident. After a few minutes, I give into my curiosity and am glancing down at my cell again to see the Google search results for Chef Bernard's accident. The first article's headline reads "Judge Killed in Grand Athena's Guest Chef Competition." If I hadn't already seen the video, I would have been completely misled by the headline. No one killed her, and it didn't happen during the cooking competition as the headline implies. I guess they rely on clickbait to grab attention one way or another, even if by stretching the truth.

Regardless, I can't resist reading the article, which explains that at a press conference late yesterday, the Grand Athena Hotel and Casino in Las Vegas announced the names of its judges for the upcoming Guest Chef Competition. Allison Bernard was supposed to be one of the judges. Hmm, that must be what the reporter in the video was talking about. My best friend Lowri and I are both avid fans of cooking shows and competitions, so it's surprising we haven't paid closer attention to this one at the Grand Athena.

The article goes on to quote Sean Cartwright, owner of the Grand Athena, as saying "This is a tragic loss for the culinary world, and for me. I have lost a good friend." In response to a follow-up question about the report that Ms. Bernard crashed after drinking too much champagne, Mr. Cartwright said "I've never seen Allison have more than one drink, much less get drunk. We should all wait for the coroner's report before jumping to conclusions and disparaging her reputation."

In answer to a question about the status of the Guest Chef Competition, Mr. Cartwright stated, "We will continue to accept applications on our website and announce further details as they become available. However, today we mourn the loss of a great chef, generous individual, and loyal friend." Bookmarking the competition's website to check out later, I wonder why they are accepting applications. Don't these shows usually just invite the famous chefs and celebrities to compete? Hmm. Maybe this one is different.

CHAPTER TWO

CASSIE

On Wednesday morning the alarm jolts me awake after only a few hours of sleep. Realization hits that I'll spend another 14 to 16 hours on one of Jackson's projects, as usual. For the last few months, my laptop has been my bed companion. Each evening it warms my outstretched legs as I type until my eyes droop and exhaustion pulls me into a late-night slumber. Then an early morning alarm signals a new day sooner than reasonable. In the waking hours, my goal is to survive work and life on the fast track to burnout while knowing I'm lucky to have a good-paying job.

A couple of years ago, however, hope bloomed for a better work-life balance when our firm offered the opportunity to work from home several days a week. That option sounded incredible, so I immediately signed up, thinking that jettisoning the daily commute would free up tons of time. The first few glorious weeks working from home let me catch up on chores and sleep a little later. It also didn't hurt to be away from the stress and politics at the office, which meant an unfamiliar weekday calmness flowed over me like a peaceful waterfall drenched in sunlight.

Sans the evening commute, I even had time for my real passion. After my grandparents sent me to a summer culinary program for my

16th birthday, cooking took up residence in my soul. It taught me not only how to express my creativity but also that sharing my creations with others almost always guarantees smiles in return. Positive reinforcement is a powerful drug. Later I learned that the concentration cooking requires also provides an essential escape from tough memories that too often take over my consciousness.

I used the extra time to experiment with new recipe ideas, create dinner or dessert from the random ingredients in my pantry and fridge, and post on a friend's food blog, PinotandPie.com. My neighbors and friends quickly accepted the text-message invitations to stop by for last-minute weeknight tastings and weekend parties. For an only child whose outer confidence masks her occasional loneliness and fear of not fitting in, little compares to the natural euphoria of watching friends and neighbors bask in food-induced ecstasy.

Unfortunately, Jackson interrupted those fun evenings and weekends when he realized we could work even longer days with no commute, reclaiming every waking minute by piling on even more work. We are now truly on call 24/7 under this new paradigm.

After a steaming mug of tea and a quick shower, I take my place at the kitchen table and get ready to start work but decide to first check out the website for the competition. After finding and clicking the link, daytime and nighttime photos of the Grand Athena Hotel and Casino pop onto the screen. The photos confirm the hype. It is the ultimate in upscale Las Vegas style and indulgence. Spectacular replicas of the white and blue buildings of Santorini and Mykonos surround a crystal blue lake with small, two-person sailboats. Walking bridges allow access to the grand entrance from the Strip. Wow! Transport me there right now.

Following a link at the bottom of the screen leads to more information about the competition and its rules. Apparently, they are accepting applications until tomorrow from professional chefs as well as talented home cooks with dreams of taking the next step into the culinary world. Huh.

Taking a minute to daydream, I wish that could be me, but my only "formal" training was the summer culinary course as a teenager. It's not clear I could compete in that world. I fantasize about walking away from my job at the Firm and following my culinary dreams, but such a move would be in stark contrast to the road my parents guided me down. Mom and Dad always dreamed of their only child following their footsteps into the legal profession and climbing the big-law-firm ladder to stability, financial security, and prestige. In their words, they made sure I had a solid foundation to make the "right" choices rather than pursue my culinary fantasies, which would clearly not comport with their aspirations for me.

Coming back from fantasyland, I read that the winner of the competition will be guest chef for a month at the Grand Athena's Trendz restaurant. Why does one of the Grand Athena's restaurants need a guest chef? I keep reading. Chef Maurizio, the former chef at Trendz, decided to go back to Europe to help his parents with their restaurant and doesn't plan to return, so the Grand Athena decided to hold the competition and let the world watch by video.

After clicking on an interview about the competition, the Grand Athena's owner, Sean Cartwright, appears saying, "We are looking for competitors who think fast on their feet and tackle unexpected challenges with a smile. They must share our belief that the impossible is possible when it comes to giving our guests the best experience imaginable. Most importantly, the winner must create beautiful, delicious food. Be sure to watch the four finalists compete on Athena's Culinary Video Channel."

Over six-foot tall with thick blond hair laced with whiskey-colored highlights and intense, sparkling, azure pools for eyes, Sean is one gorgeous man. Staring at the video, I can't help but notice his custom, charcoal suit hugs his perfectly toned body like a glove. He must put in some serious time in the gym. And his captivating smile hides a note of a smirk that remains welcoming but hints at a touch of arrogance, or maybe it's just confidence. Successful, steaming hot, and a little mysterious — definitely not like the guys on the online dating apps my friends and I have tried.

As the video ends, I notice another link about the rules and prizes.

It explains that four finalists will be selected based on the applications, and the winner will receive the following:

- The title "Grand Athena's Guest Chef" for a month, which will allow the winner to set the menu for the restaurant. (Note: During the guest chef's tenure, the restaurant's dinner service will be overseen by the restaurant's sous chef until a new Executive Chef is selected for the restaurant. The winner of the Guest Chef Competition will be invited to apply for the Executive Chef position.)
- The opportunity to rename Trendz for their month as guest chef
- A suite at the Grand Athena during their stay as guest chef
- An interview in *Cooks & Kitchens Magazine*
- A guest spot on the Food, Fun & Travel (FFT) Channel's *Cooking Class*
- $250,000 cash prize

Wow! Just wow! That would be the dream of my lifetime. A quarter of a million dollars would pay off my student loans and leave more than enough to cover my bills until I figure out what to do after the month as the guest chef! I could even afford a vacation to Cabo or Hawaii!

But the chances of making the final four, much less winning, are probably as low as the chances of winning the lottery, and I don't take chances like that. It's time to get back to the real work that pays my rent.

CHAPTER THREE

CASSIE

While grabbing a quick lunch at my computer, Lowri's name lights up on my phone. Answering, I ask, "How's it going?"

"Good. It's been forever since we talked, so I thought I'd give you a quick call. Do you have a minute?"

With Jackson's deadline looming, stress instructs me to say no, but our friendship deserves better, so I say, "Sure. Jackson piled on again with two deadlines for tomorrow, but I could use a short break."

"Awesome. I've been super busy too but have a breather this weekend, so I'm throwing a party at my place Saturday night. You have to come. Jerry's bringing some friends we want you to meet."

Ugh. That's code for she wants to introduce me to yet another of her brother's friends, but her track record for picking matches is abysmal, so I hesitate before responding, "I'm probably going to need to work."

Calling me on my attempt to sidestep the invitation, Lowri chastises, "You just said your deadlines are tomorrow. No excuses. Be at my place Saturday night at 7. Most people are bringing drinks instead of food, so please do your magic in the kitchen and bring a couple of appetizers. I'm counting on you."

With the projects done tomorrow, Saturday night would be the perfect time to let off some steam. God knows I need to. And who knows, maybe her brother's friends won't be so bad. "Ok. I can bring lasagna dip and roasted veggies. Will that work?"

"Perfect. By the way, did you see what happened to Chef Bernard?"

I shudder at the recollection of the video. "I saw a video of the accident scene, and it haunted my dreams last night. It's hard to believe one of my favorite TV chefs died like that."

"I know. I wonder who will replace her as a judge for Athena's Guest Chef Competition."

"Your guess is as good as mine. Maybe another Las Vegas chef. By the way, did you know the competition is open to home cooks as well as professional chefs? I couldn't help daydreaming about applying. Crazy, huh?"

"No, not crazy at all! You're an amazing cook, and in college, you always shined in front of an audience. You'd be perfect in front of a camera. Why don't you apply? What do you have to lose?"

Striking up conversations with strangers at parties is not so easy, but she's right. Speaking or performing in front of an audience is no problem for me, probably because of all the dance recitals and plays my parents signed me up for as a kid. Whether or not my cooking would be competitive — that's the unanswered question.

"You know I have huge student loans to pay off, and my parents would not approve," I remind her.

"Cassie, you need to quit trying to guess what your parents would think or want. As sad as it is, they've been gone since your last year of law school. Big-law life was your parents' dream, not yours. It's past time for you to start following your dreams."

With tears threatening to spill, my eyes automatically clamp shut as I say, "Deep down, I know you're right, but it's still so hard to let go, particularly knowing they died doing something for me. I still feel responsible, so I want to live a life that honors all they did for me. I can't let them down."

"I promise, ultimately, they loved you and just wanted you to be as happy as possible. Right now, if you are completely honest with your-self, can you really say you are happy? Tell me the truth."

After taking a deep breath, my guilty admission escapes with a sigh as the air whooshes from my lungs: "No. If it weren't for my parents' dreams and the student loans, my law practice would involve helping charities, advocating for children, or some other form of public service. However, as irrational as it may sound, part of me thinks I would walk away from law altogether if given the chance to make a living creating food that makes people smile."

"See what I mean? You are not pursuing your own happiness, which I know would make your parents sad. Please start living your life before all the opportunities pass you by. I need to go now, but promise me you will think about filling out Athena's application today."

"Ok. I'll think about it. See you Saturday night." After hitting End on my cell, with my elbows on the table, I dip my chin and cover my closed eyes, taking a moment to calm my thoughts and reflect on my admission and Lowri's advice. It's obvious I'm torn, so the logical solution is to weigh the pros and cons of my options.

On the one hand, participating in Athena's competition would be a fantasy come true. But is it realistic? Winning the competition is a long shot for anyone, particularly a home cook competing against professionally trained chefs.

Is a mere chance at a dream enough with my massive, six-figure student loans to pay off? Keeping my current, well-paying, reasonably secure job means those loans will be paid off in a few more years. Even if my job drives me nuts most of the time, it's the practical option.

It's not like I could try the chef thing and come back if it doesn't work out. Watching others try to return after pursuing other career options has made it clear that big law firms don't give you a second chance. By leaving, you are stereotyped, albeit often unfairly, as not dedicated, not wanting it bad enough, or just not good enough. Young lawyers are easily replaceable with hundreds of other talented lawyers hovering in the wings ready to swoop in and take our places. Sure, after leaving my current job, I could probably find another, significantly lower paying job in law, but nothing remotely close to my current salary. Only a fool would walk away for an infinitesimal chance at a new career as a chef, and I'm not a fool. Therefore, the smart choice would be to get to work on the contract and let this fantasy go.

But on the other hand, Lowri is right. Happy is not an adjective for my current situation. My job is stressful and exhausting but safe. The thought of participating in Athena's competition conjures feelings of passion and fulfillment, lifting the weight of that stress. It would be like a beam of sunshine streaming through my morning window beckoning me to walk into a new, happy world.

That thought makes me ask myself, "Do I ever plan to live my life for *me*?" I've avoided thinking about my 30th birthday, which is in a couple of weeks, because it feels like a turning point. If now isn't the time to make tough decisions and changes, maybe it will soon be too late. Having taken the safer path for so long, maybe the fear of risk and change is holding me back more than the fear of disappointing my parents. Hmm.

With a new resolve, my hands move to the computer keyboard and start typing. Pulling up the rules on how to enter the competition, I vow to take a step for *me*. At least I can live in my fantasy a little longer before getting back to my real job. No harm can come from filling out the online application. As expected, the first set of blanks are for my first, middle, and last names, so I type Cassie Elizabeth Edwards. Wait a minute. Am I supposed to enter my full, legal name even though I never use it? Probably, so I change it to Cassandra Elizabeth Edwards. The next few questions are fairly predictable: address, date of birth, social security number, etc.

Then the application gets a little harder. They want a few pictures and a short video, along with some background on my cooking point of view. Good thing I posted a couple of simple videos on my friend's food blog. Hopefully, one of those will work. I doubt it really matters anyway. The Grand Athena is going to get thousands of applications, so they probably won't even watch my video. Besides, they are probably looking for a hunky male chef or a drop-dead gorgeous female chef. In my opinion, my dark blonde hair and blue-gray eyes would probably only hit the pretty or cute level. Also, Vegas tends to reward women with big chests and long legs, so those are probably the criteria for their female chefs too. If so, my 5-foot 3-inch, less curvy frame doesn't check those boxes either.

Two hours later, the application is finished. So much for the application not looking that hard. Now all that is left is to hit the "Submit" button. Is this a waste of time? Probably, but I just spent two hours on the application. It would be ridiculous to throw away that time and not submit it, right? Right. Mumbling, "Here goes nothing," I click "Submit." The application said that the four finalists will be announced in two weeks. It will be interesting to see whom they pick. Worst case, I have the thrill of being able to say I applied. That will make for a good story over drinks one day soon. For now, that contract still awaits, so it will be a long day and night of work, but at least for once in a long while, the smile on my face will make it a little easier.

CHAPTER FOUR

CASSIE

W hy won't my phone shut up? I'm having the best dream ever. I'm being worshipped by the most attentive, amazing guy I've ever known. He looks like a dark-haired version of Sean Cartwright. I don't want to wake up yet. What possessed me to set an alarm for an early workout? No! Just no! I grab my phone to hit snooze just in time to realize it isn't my alarm but a call from an unknown caller. Probably spam. These days everyone is trying to sell me solar panels for my rented apartment. Can't they figure out I don't have anywhere to put solar panels?

In my dazed state, I accidentally hit accept instead of decline and hear someone asking for Cassandra. Now I know it must be a marketing call. No one calls me Cassandra. I'm about to hit end when I hear the woman say, "This is Cynthia Andino from the Grand Athena. I am trying to reach Cassandra Edwards." Wow! I must have fallen back asleep and my dream is morphing into one about the cooking competition.

"Can you hear me? This is Cynthia from the Grand Athena calling about the Guest Chef Competition. Is this Cassandra Edwards?"

Coming out of my sleepy daze, I manage to say, "Yes, this is Cassie Edwards."

"Great. I have some exciting news for you Cassie."

Jolting upright, wide awake now, my mind races. Does this mean what I think it means? I can't believe I'm actually one of the finalists. "Really?!"

"Yes, I am pleased to inform you that you have been chosen as the alternate for the Guest Chef Competition."

Deep breath. Deflate slowly on the exhale. I knew it was too good to be true. So much for that great dream. Everyone that applied is probably an "alternate," and they want to sell us sweatshirts or other stuff to commemorate the event. "Um, thank you." Be polite. Don't let on how disappointed you are. "I'm sorry. I'm just waking up. Could you explain again who you are and what it means to be an alternate?"

"Of course. I am Cynthia Andino, the Director of Food and Beverage, or F&B for short, at the Grand Athena. We have completed our selection process for the Grand Athena's Guest Chef Competition. As the rules stated, four finalists were selected to compete for the title of guest chef. One alternate was also selected just in case something unexpected happens and one of the finalists is not able to compete. You were selected as that alternate. As the alternate, you have won an all-expenses paid trip to the Grand Athena to watch the competition and to be on hand just in case a finalist must be replaced. So, congratulations! Pack your bags and be ready to catch a plane to Las Vegas a week from today."

OMG! Watching the cooking competition in Las Vegas will be incredible. Tossing the covers off and swiveling to sit on the side of the bed, I ask "Are you kidding me?"

Calm and serious, Cynthia responds, "No. I'm not kidding."

As I pull up the calendar on my phone, I inquire, "How long would I need to be in Las Vegas?"

"The competition will take place over two weeks."

My smile reverses into a frown as it hits me that this is not merely a long weekend in Vegas. "Oh. I don't know if I can get that much time off work." I'm not thinking straight. I should've remembered the application indicated we would have to be available for two weeks.

"You said on your application that you were available to be in Las Vegas during the entire competition. Did we misunderstand?"

Standing up, I start pacing around my bedroom trying to think through possible solutions. After an awkward silence, speaking slowly to allow more time to think, I respond, "No. You didn't misunderstand." Pausing, and then continuing before Cynthia speaks, I say "Will I be busy all the time, or will there be down time when I could do remote work for my job?"

"You will be expected to be available full time throughout the competition. You may have a little free time each day, but we expect you to be available for all the events, tapings, prep sessions, and press conferences to help promote the competition. That is part of the deal. In exchange, you may get a little exposure from the videos, and you get an excitement-filled, two-week vacation in Las Vegas. All you need to do is say 'yes'."

Rubbing my eyes with my free hand and still hoping to make this work, I say, "I understand. I just need to check with my boss to see if I can get those two weeks off. With no real shot at participating in the competition, I need to make sure I have a job to come back to, you know?"

"Well, it's your choice, but we need an answer by 4 p.m. today. We had thousands of applicants, and most would jump at the chance to put this on their resume. If you don't want the alternate's slot, then we will give it to the next person on our list. Call me back at this number. If I don't hear from you by 4 p.m., then I'm sorry, but we will move on."

Speaking quickly, desperate for Cynthia to believe me, I say, "Please understand that I really, really want this. It's an amazing honor. I just need a little time to think this through and check in with work. I understand your deadline. Thanks so much."

"Ok. 4 p.m." The line goes dead.

After hugging myself and shrieking from the pinch that assured me this is all real, I ask the empty room, "What am I going to do?" Part of me is ready to jump on the plane. But I don't know of anyone at my level who has taken two full weeks off work. Hell, I don't know anyone at any level who has taken a week off without checking their email every day. If I don't go, will I always regret it? But if I can't get the time off, I would need to quit my job to go. How will I get another position? I can hear myself in an interview at a new firm trying to explain that I quit my old job to watch a cooking competition in Las Vegas for two weeks. That sounds flakey.

I need some caffeine and sugar to help get my brain going. From a calorie standpoint, I wish I liked coffee, but I don't, so hopefully there's a Coke left in the fridge.

After walking to my narrow, galley kitchen, I open the fridge with fingers crossed. Whew! There's one Coke left. Relief washes over me as I pop the top on the can and relish the burn of the first bubbles as they coat my throat. Now, Coke in hand, it's time to figure out what my options are.

I could take vacation time. But we only get three weeks off a year, which is for both vacation and sick leave. Unfortunately, one of those weeks disappeared when I had strep throat and another was eaten up with apartment moving and dental appointments for the removal of my wisdom teeth, so only seven days remain for a vacation. Even if they let me take those seven days off for the competition, what would I do for the second week, particularly when they might see me on social media at the competition in Vegas? What about one week of vacation followed by one week of unpaid leave? Would they go for that? They will probably laugh at me when I explain the reason for it. But if I don't explain, social media could bite me in the butt.

Of course, I could quit. Wait a minute. What has come over me? That's just silly. Why would I quit my job for one extra week of time off? I'm never this reckless. Then realization hits me. First, I genuinely want to watch the competition, even if it's just as an alternate. Second, this isn't the first time I've looked for an excuse to quit, so I must really be looking for an out from my job. Maybe a break is what I need to recharge and re-commit to my present career when I get back.

Before I lose my nerve, I'm typing an email to my boss. I type and erase several times before deciding to keep it simple with no real explanation as to why I'm taking the time off. That's what most of the guys on the team would do. They wouldn't overthink it. They wouldn't feel a need to explain or justify their decision. They would go for it and not look back. It's my turn to do that too.

> Dear Jackson,
>
> I need to take two weeks off work starting a week from today. Unfortunately, I will not be able to work remotely during that time. Given that I have only one week of vacation left, I will let HR know that the second week will be unpaid leave. I will complete my current assignments before I leave and confirm other team members can handle any new assignments during my absence.
>
> Thank you for your understanding.
>
> Best regards,
>
> Cassie

While it's out of character for me to tell Jackson what I'm doing rather than ask permission, I've watched the guys gain respect from this direct, no-nonsense approach. He sees them as assertive, decisive leaders, who go after what they want, so let's hope the same approach works for me too. However, subconscious gender bias lives on in the corporate sea, and navigating those waters can prove hazardous. My default has been to avoid risks, particularly after hearing Jackson chastise a couple of the women in our group for being too ambitious and overly aggressive. But the behavior of those talented women was indistinguishable from that of their male counterparts. Unfortunately, that reality means Jackson may consider my direct email to be presumptuous or something worse, rather than simply straightforward and to the point. Regardless, no going back now. If Jackson or the Firm doesn't like my plan, I guess I'll be looking for another job. So be it!

After pausing for a couple of deep breaths, second thoughts permeate my mind. Hopefully, I'm not messing up my life. No! Stop overthinking. Lowri's right. It's ok to pursue my passion even if that means dealing with the guilt and hurt from feeling I'll be letting my parents down. It's time to take at least baby steps toward fulfilling the dreams that first took root as a teenager at summer camp, even if it's only a one-time, culinary excursion to watch the competition at the Grand Athena. If I'm going to keep moving in a more positive direction, my new mantra has to become "Don't look back!" But subconsciously, I'm waiting for the shit to hit the fan. I'm expecting a furious email, or worse yet, a phone call from Jackson. Nonetheless, I'm proud of myself for taking a step in a new direction. I'm going to Las Vegas!

CHAPTER FIVE

EVAN

A ringing phone awakens me from a light sleep. Yawning, my hands explore the velvety-suede sofa in search of my cell phone. Then I realize it's not my cell ringing but rather the hotel room's phone, but where is it? Glancing around the room, my eyes finally spot the phone at one end of the credenza against the left wall of the suite's living room. After pushing off the sofa and taking a few quick strides, I rest the phone's receiver next to my ear. Barely delivering the standard "Hello," Sean, my best friend from college, declares, "Evan, why aren't we already in the bar having a drink?"

Rubbing my eyes awake and finger combing my nap-tousled hair, I respond, "Sean, glad you found me. I was handling a few emails before calling you, but let's meet for a drink." No need for him to know I fell asleep handling those emails. He would tease me mercilessly for dozing off midafternoon, but jetlag sucks no matter how much I fly. "You put me in the Grand Monarch Suite. That gave me a good laugh."

"Thought you would see the humor in it. You will never outlive that butterfly debacle."

"I know, don't remind me." My brother and sister will never let me forget that childhood blunder. Too bad they shared the story with Sean when we were in college, but I guess it was pretty funny.

"Well, sorry I couldn't meet you when you arrived. I've been putting out fires all day, and some are still burning. Let's meet at 7 for drinks in the Olympic Torch Bar. It's up the Grand Staircase next to the casino floor near the main theater and sports book. I'll have them reserve a table for us overlooking our water feature, the Aegean Sea."

According to my phone, it's 5 p.m. now, so that gives me plenty of time to shower and change. "Great. I'll find it. It'll be like old times."

"Sounds good. By the way, Evan, I want to discuss some business issues with you. Your advice would be appreciated. I'll explain in person."

"No problem. See you at 7. Ciao."

Before I head to the shower, my body demands some water to deal with the dehydration from the 14-hour flight. I walk to the bar fridge, thinking how surprised I am that Sean mentioned business on a call to meet for drinks, but manning the helm of the Grand Athena cannot be easy. As I down a bottle of water, realization hits that unlike me, he has found his path and place in this world. Unfortunately, he lost his father in the process, so it came at an unenviable price.

With my family's unusual background, it's not clear I will ever have a place or purpose of my own. The expectations are etched in ancient stone, but the work outlined for me, albeit important, could be done by anyone in our extended family. While, as required, I hide any discontent from the world, I crave being needed for *me*, for my college studies to matter and my life to have more meaning and impact. Who knew that being the middle child would make those goals so elusive? But in my family, it is just that way.

Perhaps spending the next month or so away from my family's expectations will allow me to carve a more meaningful future and reshape that ancient stone. Sean is one of the only people who truly understands my predicament, so this is the perfect place for me to think and strategize without being judged for questioning my situation, which honestly most outsiders would naively trade for in a heartbeat.

CHAPTER SIX

SEAN

Hovering over my desk waiting, hand outstretched, Emily prods me to hand over my edits on the contract I've been reviewing. With a bit of impatience, she nudges, "Mr. Cartwright, it's already 7, and you made me promise I wouldn't let you be late for your meeting with Mr. Catalinius. According to the latest text, he is already seated at the cocktail table I reserved overlooking the Aegean and has a drink in hand."

"Thanks, Emily. Get word to Evan that I am on my way and should be there in six minutes. Have a golf cart meet me in the Maze downstairs."

In her professional manner, Emily confirms, "Will do, Mr. Cartwright."

With a mildly frustrated head shake, I point out, "Emily, we have worked together eight months, or maybe longer, now. Would you please call me Sean? How many times must I remind you?" Emily is efficient, which is a critical trait for my executive assistant, but she can be overly formal when it's just the two of us, and while it shouldn't bother me what name she uses, it does. I am not my old-school father, who was a great guy and wildly successful, but rather stiff, businessman. My goal is to demonstrate I can be a strong, effective leader but still approachable. However, Emily's insistence on calling me Mr. Cartwright in one-on-one situations makes me question whether it's working.

Interrupting my thoughts, Emily says, "Yes, sir. I just texted security. The golf cart will be downstairs in one minute and drop you off at the stairs just below the Olympic Torch Bar."

Grabbing my suit jacket and sliding my arms into the sleeves, I hurry across the room to make my escape, saying "Great. Tell Evan's server to have my Macallan ready for me. I need a drink after today's crap."

"Will do, Mr. Cartwright. I mean, Sean."

Emily's attempt at my preferred moniker garners her a brief nod and upturn of my lips as I reach the flowing waterfall protruding from the back wall of my office. My palm placed on its right side causes the entire waterfall to move left a few feet revealing a hidden elevator. Turning to face my office, I straighten my tie and button my jacket as the elevator door closes. Descending rapidly, the elevator transports me to the Maze and my waiting golf cart.

Buried underneath the hotel and casino, the Maze repeatedly saves my butt because I'm always running late. The Maze's interconnected tunnels remind me of a small-scale subway system that never sleeps. As if the sun shines indoors, bright lights mimic around-the-clock daylight. And rather than trains, golf carts and fast-walking pedestrians race along the tunnels. With the color-coded, neon emblems and arrows painted on the walls and a phone app for backup, the Maze is fairly easy to navigate, providing efficient access to the various parts of the property. Thankfully for me, I can avoid the casino crowds and travel by golf cart between my office and almost anywhere on the property in under 10 minutes. And with the palm scanners only allowing approved personnel into the Maze, it is the most secure path to take around the property.

Once the golf cart is on its way, I reflect on Evan's text from the previous week. He wanted to know if we had a suite he could have for an extended visit, which was odd considering he usually has his whole life planned for months in advance and never does anything at the last minute. However, when I called to confirm, Evan's voice sounded stressed and maybe even a little depressed as he explained his situation. Even knowing about his work and family challenges, it still took me by surprise because traditionally my best friend is the calmer, lighter-hearted one of us. Hopefully, his time here will help him sort through his dilemmas. And, like he said, catching up will be great. We haven't had this much time together since college.

I shake my head, remembering our college days. Meeting Evan the first time at a post-game party our freshman year, I wouldn't have predicted our long-lasting friendship. Our team had scored on the last play of the game to beat our bitter rival, so one of my friends invited a bunch of people to celebrate at his off-campus house. The drinks were flowing, the crowd was chanting, music was blasting, and burgers charred on the grill.

When I went to grab a refill at the backyard bar, Evan stood nearby watching everyone as he sipped his drink with a rather bemused smirk on his face. Curious, I asked him if he wasn't into football. He retorted, "That wasn't football," to which I responded, "What the hell do you mean? That was football at its best." The conversation quickly devolved into a fierce debate as to the merits of "my" football versus his, which turned out to be soccer, because he grew up in Europe.

That was the first of many encounters on campus. Eventually, while still disagreeing on football and soccer, we found we had a lot in common. Not many people could relate to my having grown up in a penthouse apartment in a hotel and casino. While Evan's home was different, it was just as unusual, so he got it. Over that first year, we debated, teased, chastised, partied, and supported each other as if we were brothers by blood.

After hanging out so much our freshman year, we shared an apartment from our sophomore year through grad school. Along the way, we had quite a few adventures, though perhaps it would be more accurate to call many of them harmless misadventures. For example, I'll never forget the time we dyed all the swimming pools at the Athena green during Spring Break. It was St. Patrick's Day after all.

After quickly figuring out it was only harmless, swimming pool dye that would disappear in a few days, marketing decided it was a great idea and invited the guests to take a plunge.

But we weren't off the hook just yet because we were sloppy when we dumped the dye into the pool at 4 a.m., inebriated. Around noon, the head of security confronted us after finding the empty dye bottles and watching the surveillance video. Fortunately, in exchange for a promise to "stay out of trouble" and not dye the pools red at Christmas — guess he thought it would look too much like blood — looking amused, he walked away shaking his head and never mentioned it again. Now I realize we were not his biggest spring break problem.

When we finished our MBAs at the age of 24, our adventures became a tad more sophisticated, or at least we thought so. Evan and I took a year off and traveled around Europe. Memories of yachts, scantily clad women, nights drinking, and days sleeping until noon put a smile on my face. Thanks to our parents, money was not an issue.

I can't believe it has been nine years since I returned from that year in Europe. A lot has happened since then. Upon my return, I took my place beside my father at his Grand Athena. He was so proud of it and finally seemed proud of me when I joined him here. He kept saying that I needed to learn fast because before I knew it, the Grand Athena would be mine. Then two years ago, he collapsed on the casino floor from a heart attack. He never made it to the hospital. Suddenly, I owned and ran the most luxurious property on the Las Vegas Strip. That woke me up fast.

Fortunately, Dad taught me well, even though I didn't understand his methods at the time. When I first joined him at the Athena, he made me intern for one month in each of the departments. One month I was wearing a suit working in accounting and the next I was in coveralls working in maintenance. After that first year, I became Dad's sidekick and learned his job, but I had no idea how often I would look back on my first year for guidance in solving issues that arise now. Thanks to Dad's training, the Athena still runs smoothly most of the time. The hotel rooms are filled with happy guests, the casino is making tons of money, and we have a high percentage of long-term, dedicated employees. If it weren't for the food and beverage issues I am dealing with, I would say that things at the Athena couldn't be better. Hopefully, I can get this F&B mess worked out before anyone notices.

Evan will be the perfect sounding board because he studied business like me but will have an outsider's perspective on the problem. Plus, at 34, he is still one of the few people I trust. Not only is Evan like the brother I never had, but he also doesn't want or need my money. I can't say that about most of my other so-called friends.

After precisely six minutes, I am jolted out of my thoughts when we arrive at the stairs below the Olympic Torch Bar. I climb to the top and walk through the hidden panel behind a floor-to-ceiling mirror. Around the dimly lit room, flickering lights from the seashell candles softly illuminate faces at the cocktail tables. Indistinct murmurs and laughs compete with the music, creating a jovial atmosphere. As I cross toward the open-air balcony that overlooks the Aegean Sea, a slight evening breeze touches my face, reminding me that spring is still holding off the coming heat of summer.

Turning left, I spot Evan sitting at a table next to the balcony's glass wall, sipping a fancy-ass Boulevardier. They better have Macallan ready for me instead. He and some of his other European friends love Boulevardiers, perhaps because they all grew up in Europe, but they are not for me. I prefer to keep it simple: glass, ice, and Macallan — no complicated mixing and shaking required. On the other hand, Evan seems to enjoy the pomp and circumstance surrounding the preparation of his favorite drink. In some ways, that describes the differences in our upbringing. I was surrounded by money and excess set in a fast-paced world, so I was always in a hurry to grab my drink and move to the next pleasure. In contrast, Evan grew up in a more formal, elegant, and controlled environment where everything had to follow a strict protocol. When I would visit him at his family's place, "hurry up and wait" was a real thing, so waiting for a complicated drink to be prepared is in keeping with his style.

Slapping him on the back before sinking into the overstuffed, leather chair across from Evan, I say, "Hey man, it's great to see you. I don't think we've been in the same city since London last year."

With a sigh, Evan responds, "That's right. It's been too long."

Taking a satisfying sip of the Macallan that silently appears, I notice worrying dark circles under Evan's eyes. It looks like more than just jetlag. I had hoped my assessment of his stress on the phone was wrong, but now I don't think so. I apologize, "Sorry I was running late. Did you get my message?"

Glancing toward our nearby server with a slight smile and nod, Evan says, "Yes, I got your message from the server, but I finally had to send her away. Once she knew I was meeting you, she wouldn't take her eyes off me. Are all your employees that attentive to your friends?"

With a quick shoulder shrug, I say, "Hopefully, they are attentive to everyone, but especially my friends. While I'm sure my assistant, Emily, told them to take good care of you, maybe our server just likes the view. You seem to have that effect on women."

Waving off the comment, Evan jokes, "Look who's talking. By the way, the Athena is looking great. You've done a lot of updates since I was here last."

"We have. It's a never-ending battle to keep up with the competition," I say. This small talk is more superficial than usual for us. He is clearly avoiding the family issues he mentioned on the phone, but hoping I can ease into the topic, I add, "By the way, how's the family?"

Turning his swivel chair, Evan stares into the crowded room, avoiding my concerned gaze. After draining his glass, he says, "The family is fine. Maybe a little more dramatic than normal, though. I don't want to talk about them. As I mentioned, I needed a little time away. I remembered I had not been to the Athena since you took over, so it seemed like the perfect time for a visit."

"Understood. Your timing is perfect for me too. I could use your advice." Respecting his wishes, I drop the subject for now, but one way or another, I will help Evan destress while he is here.

Seeming relieved at the subject change, Evan turns back and asks, "How can I help?"

CHAPTER SEVEN

CASSIE

Panic is scrambled with my excitement because I'm leaving for Vegas the day after tomorrow, just three weeks after I hit submit on my application, and I'm not ready yet. The last few days flew by as I hustled to get all my assignments finished at work. Running through my checklist, I still need to finish my last work assignment, transfer my favorite recipes to my iPad, buy some travel-sized toiletries, and tackle the task of packing.

Packing for two weeks anywhere is hard, but two weeks at a cooking competition is especially daunting. Cynthia emailed a checklist for clothing, which includes cocktail clothes, clothes for the cooking competition, casual attire, bathing suits, and the list goes on, not to mention the shoes I'll need for all these outfits. But Cynthia's checklist is missing how many events of each type are scheduled for the two weeks, so who knows how many of each item they expect me to bring. Regardless, how am I going to fit all those clothes and shoes into my two small suitcases?

I reach for my phone, knowing it's time to seek Lowri's help. She's great at packing. After all, she traveled through Europe after college with one small suitcase and a backpack. Fortunately, Lowri answers on the second ring. A sigh of relief escapes me when I hear her friendly voice saying, "Hey Cassie, how's it going? Are you ready for your big adventure? You know they say 'What happens in Vegas, stays in Vegas,' so maybe you'll finally let go and hook up with a hot guy. Your dry spell needs to end."

"You're nuts. That's not going to happen. I'm not ready for anything serious."

"Who's talking serious? At least promise me that if you meet someone who interests you, don't immediately push them away like you have for the past few years. Give him a chance. Promise?"

Knowing that Lowri won't give up and I'm not going to meet anyone anyway, I have nothing to lose by agreeing. "Ok, I promise, but I'm not going to have the chance to meet anyone at the competition. Besides, I'm still pinching myself for reassurance I'm the alternate, and I'm frazzled over how to pack. Any chance you could come over tonight and help me figure out what to take?" My eyes are shut and fingers literally crossed as I wait for her response. Hopefully, she doesn't have big plans for tonight.

"Calm down. I can practically hear your heart racing through the phone. Of course, I'll be there right after work to help," Lowri reassures. "How about I bring the wine and you order pizza? We'll make it a packing party."

My shoulders drop several inches as the tension leaves. "Thank God. You're a lifesaver."

Lowri lets a soft giggle escape through the phone, saying, "You're so funny. Packing is the easy part. The hard part was convincing Jackson to let you leave work at the last minute for two weeks and still have a job when you get back. I'm not sure that would happen at my firm. I just survived the latest round of layoffs that they tried to disguise as performance-related terminations. We all knew they were actually cost-cutting measures."

Sighing, I say, "I know. It was surprising for Jackson to sign off on my leave without any fireworks."

"Based on your prior descriptions, it does seem out of character for him, but don't question it. Just count your blessings."

Frowning as I ponder why Jackson was so accommodating, I avoid further discussion of the topic, merely responding, "This whole experience is a lot to take in, but I desperately need your help packing. Left on my own, my suitcases will be full of shoes before I even start with the clothes."

Lowri responds, "Don't worry, you need three, maybe four, pairs of shoes. We will pick all your outfits to match those shoes. It's easy. I'll see you tonight."

"Great. See you then."

After talking with Lowri, I wonder again why workaholic Jackson was so quick to grant my unorthodox, last-minute request for leave. Grabbing my cell phone, I decide to reread his email:

Dear Ms. Edwards,

While a request such as yours would not typically be approved on such short notice, we understand that individuals, as well as businesses, experience unexpected obligations from time to time. Therefore, your two-week leave is approved. Please check in with HR at the end of your leave.

Best regards,

Jackson

When I first read Jackson's email, I was so relieved he had approved my leave that I didn't pay much attention to the actual wording. But as I stare at the email, on a second read, it sounds a little ominous. Why am I supposed to "check in with HR" when I return? Are they planning layoffs at our firm? If so, I just made it a lot easier for them to tell me not to bother coming back after my leave.

I try reassuring myself that I'm overthinking things again. Sometimes I wish I could turn off my mind's autopilot. Regardless, for sanity's sake, I need to work harder at adopting my mantra-goal of "Don't look back." I can't change this now, nor — if I'm honest with myself — do I want to. For the first time since college, I won't have any deadlines at work. Of course, that's only temporary. When I go back, assuming I still have a job, my calendar will be refilled quickly with a ridiculous number of projects and deadlines. But until then, I plan to enjoy this reprieve and the freedom that comes with it.

With the smile those thoughts produce, I plop down at my breakfast table, raise the lid on my work laptop, and concentrate on finishing my last assignment before I leave. With no new assignments on the horizon, I'll have time to take a long lunch break, which is a rare luxury, and transfer my recipes to my personal tablet. Cynthia insisted I bring my favorite recipes just in case a finalist drops out, and I need to step in to compete. While a likely waste of time, it will still be fun to have time to select and organize them.

During lunch, my pulse races as my recipe task turns into a daydream about the competition. I'm not even a real finalist, but my excitement level is through the roof. I better remember to set an alarm on my cell phone and leave it on the other side of my bedroom tomorrow night. Otherwise, missing my flight is a real possibility given my bad habit of sleeping through alarms or hitting snooze over and over again. I missed more than a few classes that way in college, and I can't let that happen this time.

CHAPTER EIGHT

SEAN

After savoring a slow sip of my Scotch, I ask, "Evan, have you heard about our Guest Chef Competition?"

"No."

Setting my Macallan on the cocktail napkin, I lean forward and whisper to avoid eavesdroppers. "Then I assume you also haven't heard that one of the judges for the competition was killed in a car crash about three weeks ago."

Having captured Evan's full attention, he leans forward with his elbows on the table. "No. That is terrible. What happened?"

"Well, the executive chef of our Trendz restaurant went back to Europe to help his family, so we decided to temporarily close the restaurant while we look for a new chef. After some brainstorming, we came up with the idea to invite both professional and amateur chefs to apply to compete for the title of guest chef for a month. The competition will air on Athena's Culinary Video Channel and include a lot of behind-the-scenes coverage, which should give the Athena some great press and buy us some additional time to find a permanent chef for Trendz. You see, our former executive chef was in charge of much more than just the one restaurant, so it's not trivial to replace him. Who knows, we may invite the guest chef to stay on."

Slowly stirring the fresh boulevardier that magically appeared, Evan says, "That all makes sense. Who was the judge that died?"

"Allison Bernard of Chez Bernard." Leaning back in the chair and turning my gaze to the calming water of the Aegean, I relive the call from Emily conveying the unexpected and tragic news that Allison was gone.

Evans pulls me back to the present. "I remember that place. It was one of your father's favorite restaurants. If I recall right, we went there the last time I was in town."

Nodding, I turn back to focus on Evan. "Yes, that's the place. The circumstances of Allison's death are troubling. We had invited the press and competition judges for an in-person press conference to pump up publicity for the event and make a last-minute push for applications from potential competitors. Unfortunately, Chef Bernard died in a tragic accident on her way home from that press conference." Cringing, I explain, "Apparently, she swerved off the road and smashed head-on into the side of a brick building."

Evan shakes his head as he clasps his glass in one hand and leans back. "Not only is it horrible that Chef Bernard died, but also it is not the type of press coverage you wanted for the competition."

After taking a fortifying sip of my Macallan, I swallow slowly and then respond, "No kidding, Evan. I liked her too. She was a friend. It was also a horrendously bad start to the competition. To make matters worse, the news reported that she mumbled something about champagne in her dying breath."

"Why does that make matters worse? Are they accusing the Athena of serving her too much champagne?"

Leaning toward the table and motioning for Evan to do the same, I explain, "According to the police, they didn't find any skid marks at the scene of the accident, so it looks like Allison never braked when she went off the road. The press have been reporting she was driving drunk after the champagne toast at our press conference, but I know she wasn't drunk. We only saw her have one glass of champagne, so I've been awaiting the toxicology results and final autopsy report."

Evan offers, "Maybe she fell asleep or had a heart attack?"

Shaking my head, I say, "No. This morning I got a call from Larry with the toxicology results. He is the Chief of Police and a friend of the Athena." Larry and I first met a few years ago when the Athena was dealing with a couple of guests who thought they could cheat the system. Since then, he has been helpful on a number of similar matters.

Evan asks, "What did the police chief say?"

Still not believing it possible, I share what Larry told me. "Apparently, Allison had enough prescription opioids in her system to knock out someone twice her size. With the alcohol, it was a deadly combination."

"Was she an addict?"

Firmly returning my glass to the table elicits a harder thud than intended, but I'm tired of the immediate, negative assumptions about Allison's character by the police, the press, and now even my best friend. "No way. She was a control freak and an exercise fanatic. I don't think she would purposefully take opioids. But when I asked around, Cameron said she heard Allison had a sore shoulder from a tennis tournament."

"Ok. Calm down, Sean. I am not judging Chef Bernard but merely want to understand what happened. By the way, who is Cameron?"

Evan probably doesn't remember, but for a short time, Allison was more than just a friend to me. Fairly quickly, we realized we shared a friendship more than anything else, so we parted amicably but remained close. When Emily called, it felt like a stab in the chest to hear Allison was dead, and the stabs keep coming when I hear the negative press reports about her. But taking a deep breath, I force myself to regain full control. "I know. I'm just tired of everyone assuming the worst about Allison. As for Cameron, she is the assistant to our Food and Beverage manager."

Opening his arms, palms up, Evan says, "Well, Cameron sounds like a reliable source, so you have your answer, Sean. Allison must have hurt her shoulder and accidentally taken too much of the prescription painkiller. She probably fell asleep at the wheel."

Head tilted down, eyes staring into what remains of the honey-colored liquid in my glass, I can't come to grips with that explanation, even though I know it's possible. "Maybe, Evan, but I'm not sure. In the past, she wouldn't even take an aspirin. She said it poisoned her system and would screw up her training. Besides, why would she drink the champagne if she was taking a drug like that?"

"I don't know. People change."

I'm not sure I agree with Evan, but I let it drop for now. Instead, I want to share more details about the call with Larry, so shrugging off the emotions for now, I continue, "Larry also gave me a heads up that they are going to interview some of the people from the press conference. Apparently, the police didn't find any drugs in Allison's car or in her home, which is strange if she was taking them for an injury. The police think she left her prescription bottle here or got the pills from someone at the press conference. If it wasn't for the other funny business around here, I might let it go."

"What other funny business, Sean?"

"Someone is messing with our food and beverage expenses, which impacts all the restaurants at the Athena."

"What? You've got to be kidding. Who would have the nerve to rip you off?"

"No, I'm not kidding, and I don't know who would have the nerve." After Chef Maurizio left, we decided to reorganize F&B to redistribute responsibilities in the future so the departure of a single chef doesn't have such a strong impact on the department. As part of analyzing our options, I wanted to review the most recent audit report, which had just been completed. The results were unexpected."

"What did you find?"

"I took over the Athena two years ago and everything looked normal in our audit the first year. However, the audit for the second year looks great for all departments except F&B, which is a big one. Digging deeper, I learned that about six months ago our F&B expenses started increasing significantly. During that time, we saw an increase of more than 20% relative to the previous year."

"Sean, that doesn't necessarily mean anything. Were revenue and profits up too?"

"That's exactly what I expected. But while expenses increased significantly, revenue didn't increase noticeably, and one month, revenue went down a little."

"Maybe the cost of food went up. For example, it is possible your chef thought it was important to buy even higher quality ingredients and more expensive wines, and then he didn't raise your prices to match the cost increases."

"You're probably right, but it bothers me that no one fixed the problem or brought it to my attention."

"What happened when you asked the department head about the increase in expenses?"

"Cynthia, our F&B manager, said it was a supply issue. Our prior chef for Trendz signed off on the ordering for all restaurants and catering at the Grand Athena. Cynthia said she asked him about it several times before he left. Apparently, he assured her that he had to change some vendors due to availability and quality issues. She said the new vendors didn't give us pricing as favorable as the prior vendors because we were a new customer. Cynthia said it should work itself out as the new vendors trust we'll be a long-term customer."

"Interesting. Could be plausible, I guess. But I would have thought new vendors might give you even larger discounts to get their foot into your gigantic door."

"I know. Something just doesn't seem right to me. With Chef Maurizio gone, it may be hard to get to the bottom of this, but Cynthia promised to follow up with him again."

"Is Cynthia good at her job? Do you have faith in her?"

"She is very good. She worked for my father before me. He had a lot of faith in her. He always told me to keep her happy because we're lucky to have her here. We'll see what else she can learn from Chef Maurizio, but in the meantime, I want to ask you for a favor."

"Ok. How can I help? Do you need me to call in some of my financial advisors to go over the books? I could also have my European contacts investigate your former chef."

"No. We've got the financial side covered, and I want more facts before I think about personally confronting Chef Maurizio. It is the competition that I need help with. When the competition was originally planned, I wanted to attend as many of its events and tapings as possible to make sure it runs smoothly and the Athena is shown in a positive light. That became even more important after Allison died shortly after leaving our press conference. But now I need time to focus on investigating and solving the F&B mystery, so I'm hoping you will cover for me at some of the competition events. We can explain that you are my old college friend, who is visiting and acting as my advisor for the competition. And don't worry — there are parties, drinks, and food. You'll love it."

Scrunching his face, Evan questions, "Won't they think it's weird that I am hanging around all the time? One of your staff members would be a more suitable choice."

I dismiss his doubts with a flick of my wrist, saying "No, they were expecting me to attend, but it's not unusual for me to send a replacement to events when I'm called away on more pressing matters. And, no, a staff member is not the right substitute for me. I already have plenty of staff members who will be there, but I'm looking for someone who will see the big picture and ensure the Athena's image is portrayed in the best light. This is even more personal to me after losing Allison. I need someone who is looking out for my best interests rather than merely being paid to be there. Besides, you are somewhat of a foodie yourself, so you will genuinely enjoy the competition. The bottom line is the competition starts in a few days, and I need your help. Are you on board?"

Evan gives in with a nod and relaxes back into the comfort of his chair. "Why not? It will take my mind off other, more serious issues for a few hours each day. But you understand, I am not willing to be on camera, right?"

Relieved that my best friend has agreed to help, I raise my glass in a salute. "I know and thank you. I will still attend the opening reception and final awards dinner and will handle any interviews, but your help will free up time for me to figure out the situation with the F&B department. I keep having this suspicion that someone is stealing from me, but I don't know how. And don't worry — no interviews or anything like that. Wear a baseball cap if you don't want to be recognized around the competition."

Evan laughs. "Fortunately, I am not recognized as often in the U.S. as I am in Europe, but a baseball cap? How very American. By the way, if I am going to do this, I need to know my way around the Athena better. Too much has changed since we roamed this place during college breaks. Can I get a behind-the-scenes tour before the competition starts? Is there someone who can show me around?"

Pulling out my cell phone to send the text, I say, "Great idea. I will have my assistant Emily set up a tour for you tomorrow. Also, given that you will be hanging out with people from my restaurant staff, you can give me your impressions as to whether any of them are ones I should be investigating. Right now, it's not clear whom I can trust. I just hope that either this is not a real problem or that the problem left with Chef Maurizio."

"Do you want to give me a quick overview of the key players? You mentioned Cynthia is head of F&B, but what should I know about the others?"

"You will also meet Cameron, whom I mentioned earlier. She is Cynthia's assistant. I'll hold off about the others for now. I don't want to bias your first impressions." Just as I finish my explanation, trumpets blare, brightly colored lights flash over the Aegean Sea, and the outdoor Olympic stage on the left side of the water lights up, capturing everyone's attention.

Evan gives me a look that conveys his amusement and slight annoyance at the interruption. Then a spotlight draws all eyes to the top of the outdoor staircase at the opening in the glass wall near where we are seated above the Aegean. Smoke wafts our way from the torches held by a man and woman, who are standing at the top of the stairs dressed in short, almost see-through, toga-like costumes.

Evan follows my lead, standing to lean against the glass wall, as the spotlight follows their descent down the staircase to the water level. They then run around a concrete path lined with torches circling the Aegean Sea. As the runners pass each torch, it lights up. The pair stop when they reach the base of the winding staircase encircling the cylindrical Olympic Tower at the end of the stage nearest us. As the Tower lights up with an orange glow, the pair begin their ascent up the winding staircase as the music beats in sync with their steps. When they reach the top, their torches light a ginormous concrete bowl, illuminating the night and signifying the start of the Grand Athena's Olympic Games. An intense, rapidly moving laser-light show draws our attention to the Olympic Stage. Spanning the area from the base of the Olympic Tower to the Strip, the stage quickly fills with "Olympians."

We watch bows and arrows fly, climbers ascend multi-story ropes, "stones" arc from throwers' hands into the Aegean, and a plethora of other reenactments of Olympic games that mesmerize the cheering crowd. After a few minutes, Evan turns toward me. "Sean, that's quite the production."

"It is. We added the stage and show the year before Dad died. You wouldn't believe how many people it takes to pull that off each evening at 8 p.m." My stomach growls, and I realize I haven't eaten anything since a light breakfast this morning. "I'm starving. If you don't have plans, let's grab dinner now that you've seen our show."

"Sounds good."

As we weave between the closely spaced tables to exit the bar, I ask, "Which restaurant would you like to try? Even our best Italian and French restaurants won't impress your European palate. So, how about steak and lobster at Athena's Prime Claw?"

"Probably not the best choice given that I haven't gone to a gym in the last few days, but who can pass up steak and lobster? Lead the way and tell me who came up with the new names for the places here. First, you have me meet you at the Olympic Torch Bar and now you are taking me to Prime Claw. A little corny, don't you think?"

As we walk past the cheering bettors watching the basketball games at the sports book on our right, I tell Evan, "Keep laughing all you want, but there is a month-long wait for a table at the Prime Claw unless you are a high roller or own the place. Be glad you went to college with the owner."

"Are you saying, I'm not a high roller?"

With a playful fist to his upper arm, I chuckle, "Never, but my sources tell me you haven't hit the high-stakes blackjack tables yet."

"True, but I will give you a shot at my wallet before I leave town."

I'm getting hungrier by the second, so I increase our pace as we pass by the clanging slot machines on our left. "You know I don't care about taking your money. What I do care about is getting some food. Who knows, maybe one of our gorgeous guests will also catch your attention. I know I could use a little distraction too."

With conviction, Evan confides, "Not on this trip. I am taking a break from women, but I can be your wingman."

Turning my head, I shout, "Stop right there," which brings us to an abrupt halt. Staring incredulously at Evan, I say, "Evan, you have never taken a break from women. Don't tell me — one finally broke your heart?"

Shaking off my hand, Evan dismisses my comment. "Of course not! You know better. I don't do serious. I like being a bachelor and have no plans to change that status any time soon. That's my brother's plan, not mine."

"Ok, but over a good bottle of wine, you can tell me why you are taking this so-called break." While we don't agree on cocktails, at least we can agree on a nice, full-bodied cabernet with our steaks. "Let's get going. Then I can show you The Omega, our rooftop nightclub."

CHAPTER NINE

CASSIE

I t turns out I didn't need multiple alarms or any of my other backup plans because I was so excited about my flight this morning that I woke up every hour thinking it was time to shower and head to the airport. Around 6 a.m., I gave up on sleep and started getting ready. The next thing I knew I was sitting on the plane flying to Las Vegas. Finally, my adventure begins.

Just as I finish rereading the instructions from Cynthia, I feel the jolt of the plane's wheels hitting the runway and bouncing a few times. Not the smoothest landing, but who cares? We're here. After the plane pulls up to the gate and the attendants open the door, I grab my carryon bag and get off the plane. Taking in the bright lights and chiming slot machines in the airport, I resist the urge to stop and try my luck. Instead, I follow the signs and take a long, steep escalator down to baggage claim. My mind is blown with all the enormous signs advertising shows with celebrity performers, magicians, beautiful showgirls, and even ripped male strippers from Australia! I wonder if I'll have time to see a show. Along the way, my mouth waters at the depictions of sizzling steaks, gigantic lobster tails, decadent desserts, and overflowing bottles of champagne. Other signs tempt with spectacular casinos where visitors can spin a wheel for a chance at a big win.

The only other time I was in Las Vegas was during college. Lowri, a couple of our other friends, and I came for a long weekend, but we stayed at one of the cheapest hotels on the Strip, soaked up the free drinks they passed out at the slot machines, and walked up and down the Strip until we had blisters from the spiked heels we thought we were supposed to wear. In reality, we didn't see much of the more opulent and extravagant parts of Las Vegas that I've heard about. Maybe this time will be different.

At the bottom of the escalator, the monitors show my bags will be coming out on carousel 5, which is ahead on my right. Walking in that direction, I see a guy in a black suit holding up an iPad with my name on it. That's when I remember the Grand Athena was sending someone to pick me up. Wow! Things are going to be different this time.

After I introduce myself, he tells me his name is Justin and helps me retrieve my bags from the turning carousel. Then Justin leads me out the side doors toward a limousine. Yes, a real stretch limousine with black paint so glossy I can see myself as if looking in a mirror. Justin opens the back door, and I slide across the plush, buttery, black leather seat into relative darkness. Once my eyes adjust from the bright sunlight to the dim, elegant interior, I take in the burled wood trim and side bars with cut crystal glasses and small bottles of champagne. Soft, but lively music spills from speakers surrounding me on all sides.

After taking his place behind the wheel, Justin tells me to help myself to the champagne, and we drive toward the Strip. Happily following his instructions, I pick up one of the bottles and grab a glass. Why not, right? I'm not working today. Actually, I'm not working for the next two weeks, which puts an even bigger smile on my face as I savor the first bubbles that pass my lips and tickle my throat.

Justin asks whether I want the fast route or the scenic route down the Strip. For once in my life, I'm not in a hurry to get to a meeting or late to meet my friends, so the scenic route it is. As we stop at the corner of the Strip, a fairytale castle on my left conjures images of Camelot and King Arthur. Shortly after turning right, we come to an abrupt stop. Midday traffic is bumper to bumper, but for once I don't mind. It gives me the chance to take in more of the fabulous sights. I see a giant lion on my right as we creep past an emerald-green hotel. Next, the Empire State Building appears on my left. I've longed for the chance to explore the restaurants in New York, so maybe I can at least sneak a visit to the Vegas version while I'm here. Then the Eiffel Tower beckons me to explore Paris. I can't wait to see all these places lit up at night. The options are overwhelming. Suddenly two weeks doesn't seem like long enough.

As we approach the Athena, Justin points out the Aegean Sea in front of the hotel where small sailboats sport royal blue sails as they zip across the enormous pond of water. Justin says the towers of the hotel are named after Greek Islands. The main rectangular building in front is called the Mykonos Tower, and a second building on the left is the Santorini Tower. The towers are breathtaking with bright white walls, lapis blue trim, and beautiful, fuchsia bougainvillea flowers draping over the balcony rails. Pointing to the right, he says the extremely tall, cylindrical tower, which has an exterior, circular staircase leading to the top, is called the Olympic Torch Tower. It's next to the Olympic Stage where performers reenact outdoor Olympic Games each evening.

As we sit at the stop light at the far end of the Athena, I ask Justin more questions about the Olympic Games. He says that each night toga-clad runners climb the tower and light a torch inside the gigantic concrete bowl on top. Wow. Climbing those stairs would be quite a workout. I'm not ready to apply for that job. Then we turn left following the curving road behind the Aegean Sea to the hidden hotel entrance.

After opening my door, Justin points me to the reception area. Walking into the lobby, I'm stunned by the bright and airy atmosphere. The electric blue and dazzling white decor make me think I stepped into a photo of the Greek islands. Bright fuchsia bougainvillea cascade from high ledges and pillars, and individual, white-washed reception desks dot the far side of the lobby. Huge concrete statues of Greek gods and goddesses stand behind each desk with an even larger statue of Athena standing in the center, reigning over the others. This place is truly spectacular.

After taking in as much as I can, I get in line to check in. A few minutes later, it's my turn. They ask for ID and a credit card, so I dig them out of my purse and hand them over. After some typing, the desk clerk gets on the phone, making me wonder if they lost my reservation.

Soon enough, the clerk is off the phone and telling me how happy they are that I have arrived. Then she asks if I want keyless access. If so, they need to scan my palm print. She explains it will save a lot of time during my stay, so why not? I put my hand on the pad and wait for the green light. I feel like I stepped into the future, but I guess the future is now at the Grand Athena. With the check-in process done, she tells me my bags will be taken to my room.

As she hands me a packet of materials to review, a well-dressed man appears and introduces himself as Christian Laurent, the head concierge. Christian welcomes me to the Guest Chef Competition and then offers to schedule a tour of the hotel and casino for me. I quickly take him up on the offer, so he asks me to follow him to a private lounge marked Concierge. As we walk inside to schedule the tour, Christian mentions there is a prep meeting tomorrow morning for the competition and that the opening reception is tomorrow night. Once the tour is scheduled, I realize I'm starving. I never had lunch. All I've had was that glass of champagne in the limo, so I need to drop off my carryon bag in my room and get some food.

As I leave the concierge lounge in search of the elevator to my room, I realize the lobby is an island surrounded by water. Behind the reception desks, a Greek village sits just beyond the water with shops, "outdoor" cafes, and abundant flowers. I do a double take because I'm not certain whether I'm indoors or outdoors. Small water taxis are transporting people between the lobby, the shops, the casino to my right, and what I assume are the Mykonos and Santorini towers with guest rooms. I even see several swimming pools in front of the shops. Walking bridges connect all the areas if you don't want to wait your turn for a water taxi. I've never seen anything like this. I'm going to have so much fun here.

When I reach my room, I take in the blend of comfort and modern elegance. Since I was an alternate, they told me I didn't get a suite, but they still gave me an ultra-deluxe room with an oversized king bed draped with a stunning turquoise, royal blue, and gold over-stuffed comforter and about a dozen decorative, seashell-shaped pillows piled high against a white-leather headboard that goes all the way to the ceiling. Running my hand across the satiny-soft, cotton sheets where the comforter is turned down, I can't even guess the thread count — it's so high. Sinking into the softness tonight will be divine.

There is a work area with a desk and a sitting area with a sofa and coffee table near the floor-to-ceiling glass doors that open onto a balcony overlooking the Aegean Sea and the Strip. It will be amazing when everything is lit up tonight. And don't get me started on the luxurious bathroom with stacks of extra-thick, fluffy towels next to a giant Jacuzzi tub on an elevated platform, providing a perfect view of the Strip while you soak. Needless to say, no complaints here.

An unexpected gift basket with fruit, nuts, and other snacks is sitting on the chrome and glass coffee table in front of the white leather sofa. Realizing the gift basket will suffice for lunch, I grab a snack to stave off my hunger so I can unpack and organize my clothes before my tour. After the tour, I'll still have plenty of time to look around because the prep meeting isn't until 10 a.m. tomorrow.

While munching on salted cashews and caramel corn laced with gourmet chocolate, I start unpacking, hoping I brought the right clothes. Despite the guidelines, I was still left to guess about a lot of things. It sounded like I needed everything from shorts to jeans to cocktail dresses. I assumed I would be doing a lot of standing and walking, so I brought sneakers, flats, and wedges. Of course, my cocktail dress screamed for high-heeled stilettos, so I brought them too— thus, the two suitcases and one carryon. If Lowri hadn't helped me, I would never have pared it down to four pairs of shoes and only two suitcases.

At 4:45 p.m., after unpacking, my phone alarm reminds me of my tour, so I hurry to the concierge lounge, where to my surprise Christian is waiting for me. "Hello, Ms. Edwards, it is good to see you again."

I'm smiling with excitement as I tell Christian, "Please call me Cassie."

"Of course, Cassie. Your tour guide was called away, so I am going to show you around the Grand Athena."

With a wave of my hand, I assure Christian that is not necessary. "You don't have to do that. I can reschedule for another time."

"No, I insist. It will be a pleasure to share our beautiful Athena with you. Follow me this way. We are going to start on the conference level, which is where your first meeting will be tomorrow morning. You must be excited to meet the finalists and host of our competition."

As we make our way to escalators near the back of the casino and head up to the conference level, I nod in agreement. "Absolutely. I keep pinching myself to make sure it's not a dream. This is a complete departure from my normal life in front of a computer pouring over contracts."

The escalator whisks us to a wide-open space filled with several comfortable sitting areas where small groups are congregating between meetings. Rather than the traditional dark wood you find in so many hotels, this conference area has an airy feel, as light from a wall of windows splashes against the other ash-paneled walls. As we walk across the space, my feet are cushioned by the island-inspired carpet with off-white, aqua, teal, and cobalt blue designs. It's a relaxing and happy space. I would sign up for a conference here in a heartbeat.

Christian points out, "Meeting rooms of various sizes are along the three sides of this area, and restrooms are down the corridor on our right. Your first meeting, however, will be in the large boardroom that is down the hall on our left. Let me show you the room, so you will know where to go tomorrow morning."

Enthusiastically, I admit, "I can't wait for tomorrow's meeting even though I don't know what to expect. I've seen cooking competitions on television, secretly dreaming of being part of one, but I've never been to one in person. Watching the chefs up close while they create masterpieces under the pressure of time and television cameras will be incredibly inspiring. I know I will spend the whole time thinking about what I would be creating if I were in their shoes. I can't wait!" Pausing, I realize Christian is staring at me with a big smile as we walk down the hall. I blush, saying, "Sorry, I let my excitement take over."

"You have nothing to apologize for. Your enthusiasm is contagious. You even have me smiling about it, and I don't know the first thing about cooking." Arriving at the boardroom, Christian continues, "You will need to be here at 10 a.m. tomorrow for the first competition prep meeting."

Looking inside, I see the side of a long conference table that stretches to my left with a large, wall-mounted television at the far end. Now, I just have to remember how to get back here tomorrow. "Great. Where is the next stop on the tour?"

"We are going to see the pool, so we need to go downstairs." Walking off the escalator, we turn left toward the back of the casino. When we reach a door that leads outside, Christian places his hand on a nearby scanner, and we exit onto a beautiful patio area overlooking multiple pools. Each pool has a small replica of a Greek ruin, such as the Parthenon or ancient columns with waterfalls. On the far side of the pools, I see cute little shops and people having food and drinks at small patio tables. The buildings sport the same blue and white theme to match their real Greek island counterparts. They are even draped with beautiful hot pink flowers that create a contrasting punch of vibrant color. That's when I realize we are in the area that I saw behind the lobby desk where I checked in. The water feature that creates the lobby island extends to the left side of the pool area and curves around in front of the shops and restaurants.

"Christian, this is amazing! How do you get to the shops on the other side of the pools?"

"You can either swim across, or there are walking bridges at the far left and far right of the pool area if you prefer to stay dry. From the lobby, you can also access the shops via the small water taxis."

"I could spend a week just hanging out here. I hope there will be time for relaxing by the pool while I'm here. A good book, some sun, and maybe a frozen drink would make an afternoon perfect."

"Cassie, I hope you have a little time to enjoy it while you are here, but I know they will keep you busy with the competition."

"Of course, my first priority is the competition, but as you probably know, I'm the alternate, so I doubt I'll have much of a role."

"Speaking of the competition, let me show you Trendz where the finalists will be preparing their food. It is on the other side of the casino overlooking the enormous pool of water out front that we call the Aegean Sea."

We go back inside and walk forever. This place is huge. On our way, Christian points out, "If you take a left here, the path leads you to the shopping area called Aphrodite's Way. It's like having the best shopping from Rodeo Drive, New York City, Milan, and Paris all in one place, along with some high-end restaurants and bars."

"That sounds fabulous. I can't wait to walk through and take a look, but it sounds a little too pricey for my wallet."

We keep walking and eventually reach the front area of the casino where I see the sign for Trendz. Guiding me up a wide marble staircase, Christian says, "Trendz and the Olympic Torch Bar are up the grand staircase, which gives them a beautiful view of the Aegean." As we enter Trendz, Christian explains, "This is where you will be spending a lot of time over the next two weeks."

I quickly see that it's a welcoming restaurant with dim lighting. Booths separated by privacy drapes line the walls, and tables for small groups fill the center of the space. A gorgeous bar area to the right of the entrance sports a three-story wine and liquor room behind clear glass. I can't even estimate how many bottles are in there. "Christian, how do they access the bottles that are at the top?"

"Oh, it is quite the show. The servers use the silk sashes you see tied up on the sides. They climb up the sashes like you may have seen in various acrobatic shows, grab the bottle, and slide down the sash."

"Wow. That would be fun to watch, particularly if the bottle is near the top."

"Well, that is part of the plan. The more expensive the bottle, the higher it is stored. The goal is to entice customers to purchase a more expensive bottle to see the server climb higher."

"Makes sense. That's a smart marketing idea."

"It seems to work. Follow me toward the back. I'll show you the kitchen. It is through those doors on the right."

Entering the kitchen, I'm surprised to see it's as big as the restaurant area. Amazing. There are multiple stations and every high-end commercial appliance you can imagine, including a walk-in refrigerator, walk-in freezer, multiple ovens, gas cooktops, salamander broilers, chillers, and two ice cream machines. With goose bumps covering my arms, I hug myself and take in the space. Eventually, Christian asks, "What do you think?"

As I stare at the fabulous kitchen, my eyes are a little watery as realization hits that my excitement about the competition will be tamed by the fact I'm only here to watch. When I notice the silence, I finally respond to Christian's question. "I'm stunned. It's incredible. I've dreamed of cooking in a kitchen like this."

Christian responds with a cheery, "Don't give up on your dreams, but for now, I should show you how to find your way back to your room."

Shaking off my momentary disappointment, my smile returns as I remind myself that I still would rather be here than at work.

CHAPTER TEN

CASSIE

Brimming with excitement, I woke up with plenty of time to spare and arrive at the prep meeting at 10 a.m. full of energy, which is a little surprising given that last night I couldn't resist trying out an Italian restaurant, exploring the hotel, watching people play craps, and then dancing at the Omega nightclub. Originally, I went to the nightclub so I could send a selfie to Lowri, planning to leave after snapping the photo, but then the crowd pushed me onto the dance floor, and I started having fun moving to the beat of the music. The next thing I knew it was almost 2 a.m., so I hurried back to my room to try to get some sleep. Just thinking about all I packed into one evening sounds exhausting, but with my adrenaline pumping from the freedom to explore without work deadlines looming, it was exhilarating.

I take in the boardroom as I enter, noting a long conference table for 12 and a buffet table loaded with coffee, tea, pastries, juice, and freshly sliced fruit. A few people are holding coffee cups and chatting with each other.

A woman wearing a charcoal gray business suit greets me. "Hello, I'm Cynthia Andino. You must be Cassie. We spoke on the phone a few weeks ago."

"That's right. It's great to meet you in person. I'm so excited to be here."

"Welcome to Athena's Guest Chef Competition. Please help yourself to the food and then find your seat. We are about to get started."

I quickly feel a little anxious and out of place because others in the room seem to know each other. A couple of people look vaguely familiar, but I can't place them. Walking up to a small group of strangers has never been easy for me, so instead I decide to get some hot tea and a pastry. That way, I'll have something to do and won't feel quite so awkward.

As I walk toward the food, I smile at a few of the others in the room. My smile is met with varying responses. Some smile back. Others seem to be sizing me up. They must be the finalists. They probably haven't figured out I'm just the spare.

I don't have long to think about it before Cynthia is telling everyone to take their seats. Clearly in charge, she sits at the head of the table farthest from the door, and everyone else fills up the two long sides of the table. Name cards have been placed on the conference table in front of the chairs, but I don't see my name on this side of the table. I wander to the other side of the table, looking for my name card. Not surprising, my seat is one of the farthest from Cynthia, signifying I'm the lowest person on this ladder, which I guess makes sense.

Soon we are all seated, and Cynthia starts the prep meeting. She quickly introduces Amy, the Competition Coordinator and host of the videos, who is sitting to Cynthia's left. Then we meet Sebastian, the Director/Producer, who is sitting to Cynthia's right. Wearing a faded blue T-shirt, torn jeans and a baseball cap, Sebastian is not trying to impress anyone with his attire. Next, Cynthia points out the lead videographer and the lead still photographer, but she doesn't mention their names.

Then Cynthia welcomes each of the finalists. This is the first time I learn who is competing. The finalists are Leon Boucher from Europe, Trenton James from New York City, Jayden Scott from Dallas, and Kai Kahale from Hawaii. Finally, Cynthia introduces me, the alternate from San Diego. I find myself sizing up the finalists as they had done to me earlier. Looking rather aloof, Leon has olive skin, large dark eyes, and an average build. Trenton is a rather large man with a perpetually gruff but confident expression. In contrast, Jayden is skinny with dull brown hair and a narrow face, and he can't seem to stop fidgeting. Kai seems the happiest of the group. He sports the perfect natural tan, an athletic build, straight black hair, and a welcoming smile. As I get to know them better, it will be interesting to see if my first impressions are right.

While I feel like I've spent too much time in meetings lately, this one feels different. Despite the competitive environment, an almost electric, energy permeates the air. I find myself listening to every word, excited to see what happens next.

Cynthia begins going over the competition rules starting with the basics from the packet of materials we received at check-in. Then she goes on to what she calls the Critical Rules. The first Critical Rule is no cell phones, no tablets, no laptops, no internet access, and no calls home from borrowed cell phones or land lines during the competition. They want our full attention on the competition with no outside influences or help. That's going to be tough.

Cynthia says we have ten minutes to text or email any family members, significant others, and emergency contacts. On an LED screen mounted on the wall behind her, an emergency phone number pops up. She instructs us to provide that number to our contacts for use only in case of an emergency. They can leave a message at that number, and the message will be relayed to us, provided it is truly an emergency. Everyone is furiously texting, except me. I don't have any immediate family to text. At the last second, I decide to text Lowri the emergency number just in case.

Cynthia instructs a quiet woman she calls Cameron to start collecting our electronic devices. Cameron reminds me of a shy librarian with her large glasses and hair pulled back into a bun. Apparently, she is Cynthia's assistant. As Cameron walks around collecting everyone's cell phones and tablets, Cynthia says violation of the device rule and internet policy will result in immediate disqualification. If we need access to our tablets for recipes we brought, they will arrange for us to view the recipes in a supervised manner. Who knew this was going to be such a strict environment?

When Cameron reaches me, I tell her that I'm not competing, so I'm not sure the rule applies to me. But Cynthia quickly speaks up and says the rule applies just in case I end up competing, and I'm glad I texted Lowri. Also, this confirms that Jackson won't be able to interrupt my break even if he tries. Now that's a relief and makes it worth losing my Internet access for two weeks.

Then Cynthia holds up a device that looks like a chunky black watch and explains they are giving each of us a communication device called a TekCuff that we must wear for the next two weeks.

The TekCuff fastens around the wrist like a watch and will keep us tied into the Grand Athena's communication system for the duration of the competition. Cynthia explains it offers text and audio messaging, alerts, alarms, a clock, and calendar functions. The cellphone and email functions have been disabled for the duration of the competition. However, when the competition is over, we will be able to keep our TekCuff and activate those features as well.

Next, Cynthia explains that Critical Rule #2 is that we are forbidden from interacting with the three judges outside of the competition events. Again, violation equals disqualification.

With those two Critical Rules covered, Cynthia moves on to the logistics for the competition. She explains that I won't be competing unless someone drops out or is disqualified. However, I will be required to attend all the meetings and events just in case I'm needed.

As Cynthia starts to go over the competition schedule, I hear footsteps. From my place at the table, I have the perfect view of the door, so looking up, my jaw drops when I see Sean Cartwright enter the room. He looks even taller and more handsome in person than he did on the videos I saw. But just as I start breathing again, a tall, dark-haired guy with an amazing tan and chiseled features follows Mr. Cartwright through the door. Our eyes lock for a second and his mouth curves upward, forming a hint of a smile before he turns his head toward Cynthia's end of the table. The as-yet-unidentified guy could be the one from my dream a few weeks ago. Well maybe not exactly, but this live version is even better, which is saying a lot. I swear my heart starts racing just remembering the dream Cynthia interrupted.

Murmurs from around the table fill the air, and heads all turn toward Mr. Cartwright and his dark-haired guest. Cynthia visibly stiffens and stops mid-sentence to acknowledge Mr. Cartwright. I'm surprised to see her rigid posture in his presence. In her position, she must interact with him all the time, but it seems his entrance put her on edge. Mr. Cartwright quickly tells Cynthia to ignore them, but she still takes a break in the agenda to make introductions. In response, Mr. Cartwright says hello to everyone and tells us to call him Sean.

Sean then introduces the gorgeous, dark-haired guy. "Everyone, this is Evan. He is a good friend of mine from college and will be attending some of the events during the competition in my place. We will be working with Cynthia, Amy, and Sebastian on filming locations, brand management, and issues related to promoting the Grand Athena. That means you will see both of us at various events throughout the competition. However, we will not play any role in judging or selecting the winner of the competition."

While Sean is talking, I can't take my eyes off Evan. Maybe it's the flecks of gold dotting his captivating brown eyes that have me mesmerized. Or it could be the way he runs his fingers through his wavy dark chocolate hair. When Sean finishes talking, Evan speaks up in a deep, sexy European accent that I can't quite place. "Hello everyone. It is a pleasure to meet you. I am looking forward to getting to know each of you during the competition." I'm certainly looking forward to getting to know him too. What am I thinking? He didn't mean it that way.

Evan continues, "Sean has shared the finalists' applications with me, so I know this will be a stellar competition. And as a true lover of food, I will enjoy the opportunity to sample your creations along the way."

OMG! Who is this guy? Is it hot in here? My palms are sweating and heart is racing. I've never had such an immediate physical reaction to a guy before. What's going on? His good looks and that deep European voice are drawing me to him like a magnet. I would love to run my hands through his dark, wavy hair and wrap my arms around his fit body. He looks like a tennis player. And those clothes look like they came from Paris despite their casual appearance. But it's his eyes that keep drawing me in with their gleam of mischief that tells me there is something fun behind that serious outward appearance. Just looking at him makes me feel like melting. It must be something in the Vegas air. I know I should stop staring at him, so finally I look down to regain my composure.

When I look up again, Sean is saying "We just wanted to say hello and welcome everyone, but we can't stay for the rest of this meeting. I look forward to the opportunity to chat with you at the opening reception tonight."

As they leave, Evan looks back over his shoulder and gives me a half wink. At least that's what I think just happened. But it could have been my overactive imagination hoping he did. He probably had some dust in his eye. There is no way I caught his attention. With his good looks, he probably dates models and movie stars.

The moment is broken when Cynthia picks up where she left off, going over the schedule for the competition. The opening reception is tonight. Then tomorrow the finalists will be giving demonstrations by the swimming pool during an event called "A Poolside Dip." Each of the finalists must prepare a dip that works well poolside.

Cynthia tells us that several food items are off limits because certain contestants, judges, and staff members have food allergies. Cynthia explains that only Cameron knows who is allergic to which items because they are treating all information related to health issues as confidential. Of course, those with the allergies are free to share the information if they choose. Cynthia then displays a slide on the large screen with the list of prohibited items:

- No bleu cheese
- No sesame seeds
- No peanuts

These are strictly off limits. Cynthia says to treat them as Critical Rule #3, and the finalists take notes.

Cynthia then tells everyone to write down the name of the dip they will make, along with the list of ingredients, and pass it to her. Cynthia collects the papers and looks up at me. "Cassie, where is yours? You need to turn one in, just in case." I feel like I have a new nickname, Just-in-Case Cassie, but I quickly think about which dips would work at room temperature and would hold up in the heat by the pool. Then it comes to me—I would make my favorite Salsa Verde. I write it down, along with the ingredients, and pass the paper down the table to Cynthia.

Next, Cynthia warns us about the judges' top three pet peeves: overcooked pasta, under-salted food, and sloppy food presentation.

Just before the meeting ends, we are told to arrive at the opening reception 30 minutes early for photos and short interviews, but we have all afternoon free. When we're dismissed, everyone disperses fairly quickly. Now I can enjoy a little free time. Should I hang out at the pool and read a book, explore the shops, or try my hand at black-jack? I'm not used to having so many fun options.

CHAPTER ELEVEN

SEAN

I t's been a long day searching for answers to the F&B issues, but
the opening reception for the competition starts in an hour, so I
need to head to my penthouse apartment in the Mykonos
Tower and change into a tux.

Walking to the elevator, I call Evan. He answers after a couple of
rings. "Evan, want to stop by my apartment for a quick drink before
we make our entrance at the reception?"

"Sure. Make sure your security knows I'm on my way. The last
time I was here, your father's security wasn't very welcoming when I
tried to meet you at his place. I do not relish the idea of being thrown
against a wall and handcuffed again."

"Are you still bent out of shape over that? It was hilarious. Besides,
he apologized. But don't worry, we have upgraded our systems. A
simple palm scan will clear you to my place."

"You're kidding, right?"

"No."

"Sean, I think I should worry that you have that information in
your computer system."

"Quit complaining. You willingly gave us that information when you checked in. You could have opted for an archaic key card instead or chosen to use the Athena App on your cell phone."

"I know, but the more I think about it, it is a little creepy for you to store biometric data for everyone. Aren't you worried about getting hacked?"

"Not really. We have the finest security system known. Besides, the guests love the technology. It's freeing not to carry around key cards and credits cards when you want to go to the gym or pool."

"Overall, I agree, but my data better be deleted when I leave."

"That's how it works. Now get your ass up here for that drink."

I spent most of my day talking with accountants. They just confirmed the extra expenditures are going to our new food and beverage suppliers. When the accountants told me the news, I was pissed. While I usually keep my temper in check, they heard an earful today because I have a very low tolerance when it comes to poor budgeting and wasting money. I want to know what the hell is going on.

Now that I have calmed down, I need to concentrate on figuring out this mess that just doesn't make sense. I've asked to accountants to dig deeper. I want to know whether we increased our quantities based on bad predictions and have a lot of waste. Maybe we purchased in bulk but significantly overestimated our needs. Or perhaps the wrong data was entered into our inventory and tracking system. When Evan gets here, I will tell him what I learned. He can keep his eyes open and, in the unlikely event he notices anything amiss, he can let me know. I am probably overreacting, but something is off, and I can't put my finger on it.

CHAPTER TWELVE

SEAN

After sharing the accountants' update with Evan, we make our way to Trendz for the opening reception. It seems only appropriate to start the competition in the restaurant where the winner will serve as guest chef.

Entering Trendz fashionably late, we halt just inside the entrance to survey the already buzzing festivities. A pleased smile lights up my face because our celebrity and high-roller guests have taken the reception seriously, showing up in force and dressing to impress. Adorned in lavish, cocktail dresses and tuxes, the jovial, champagne-sipping crowd drowns out the background music with their laughter and chatter. Bouncing light causes the thousands of carats of diamonds and colored jewels draped around their necks, wrists, and fingers to twinkle like sparklers in the dimly lit room. Hopefully, the press reports will match the excitement level of our guests and get this competition off to a strong start.

Turning toward Evan, I say, "Let's go. It's show time."

"I am right behind you."

Passing between the high-top tables, we weave through the crowd, repeatedly stopping to say hello to the various VIP guests, press, and staff.

A server presents us with flutes of champagne, which gives me a chance to search the crowd for Cynthia.

I tell Evan, "We barely saw the finalists this morning, so I want a chance to talk with them before the introductions."

Eyes fixed in the distance, Evan responds, "You already know quite a bit about them from their applications and the selection process, right?"

Shaking my head, I explain, "Only a few basics. I didn't watch their videos or even do a detailed read of their applications. I chose not to participate in the selection process because I didn't want my pick to have an automatic advantage. As a result, I don't know that much about them yet." But I'm not sure Evan is paying much attention to my response. His eyes seem fixed on an attractive woman across the room. Hmm.

Just as I'm about to give him a hard time about the quick end to his break from women, Evan says, "I must say I feel a little sorry for the alternate. Her name is Cassandra, right?"

Surprised at his comment, I say, "Yes, that's her name, but I think she goes by Cassie. Why do you feel sorry for her?"

Evan takes a sip of champagne. "It must be hard knowing you came so close to having a chance at the prize but didn't quite make it."

Waving off his concern, I say, "Well, she still received a free trip, a line on her resume, and will likely get some good press during all the events. By the way, I see the four finalists visiting with each other, but where is Cassie?"

Eyes still fixated on the women in blue, Evan uses his glass to point toward the four-foot ice sculpture of the goddess Athena. "Over by the ice sculpture. The one with the dark blonde hair and the blue dress."

Now, it makes sense. It's Cassie who is the target of his gaze. "Since you haven't taken your eyes off her, I assume you plan to personally express your sympathy for her situation."

The spell broken, Evan responds, "Of course not. I just thought she probably feels a little left out and alone — you know, like being the unnecessary spare."

"I bet you could give her some company later, but first let's find Cynthia. She can arrange a quick chat with each finalist and then I can make my speech." I also want to ask Cynthia what brand of champagne we're serving. It's ok, but not the quality I would have selected. Until the recent supplier issues, I had been so focused on the casino and hotel that I didn't give the F&B side enough attention. I had thought the team my father put in place was top notch and could be trusted, but now I'm not so sure. Cynthia is going to need to take tighter control of her department.

"How are things going so far?" I ask Cynthia as soon as we find her.

She extends her hand, waving dramatically across the room. "Just look! It's the event of the year. Everyone who is anyone is here, and as you can see, the room is brimming with excitement."

Cynthia is always a bit theatric, but she is bubbling over with her performance tonight. Maybe she has had a little too much of the champagne, which reminds me, I need to ask her about it. "Cynthia, what champagne are we serving tonight?"

I notice a quick twitch in her jaw, but her smile quickly returns as she summons a nearby server. She hands us all glasses from the tray, saying, "It's Veuve Clicquot. Don't you like it?"

I take a sip, and it's good. Huh. Maybe my taste buds were off earlier. "It's fine, thank you. How are the finalists doing?" As I look around to re-locate the finalists, I'm amused to notice Evan has found Cassie again and has his eyes glued to her back.

Returning to her ultra-upbeat persona, Cynthia shares, "I went over some last-minute logistics with them, so everything is set for the poolside demonstration tomorrow afternoon. We are calling it 'A Poolside Dip.'"

Getting into the spirit of the competition's marketing, I reply, "That's a catchy name for the event." In the background, Evan struggles to hold back a snicker and mutters something about another corny name. Ignoring him, I explain, "I'd like a chance to chat with the finalists before the toast."

"Ok. Let me round them up and meet you by the stage in ten

minutes. I'll introduce you to everyone. Then you can introduce them to the crowd and offer your toast."

"We also have one alternate, correct?"

"Yes, that is correct. She won't be participating in the competition. But do you want to meet her too?"

"Yes, Evan and I should meet them all. We want to congratulate them." It doesn't matter what Evan says, he clearly wants to meet the alternate, so I might as well accommodate his interest.

"Understood. I'll take care of it." And with a swirl of her chiffon skirt, Cynthia floats off in search of the finalists.

Evan and I spend the next ten minutes working our way toward the stage, shaking hands with more people than I can count along the way. When we arrive at the stairs at the side of the stage, Cynthia begins introducing the finalists. "Mr. Cartwright, this is our first finalist, Leon Boucher, who has joined us from France."

"It is a pleasure to meet you." A handshake is like the cover of a book. Maybe you shouldn't judge someone by it, but it certainly is an important first impression. Leon passes this test with a firm shake, indicating confidence and the ability to interact with others.

"Thank you, Mr. Cartwright. I am pleased to be here and hope this will be the beginning of a new career for me in the States."

Cynthia continues, "Mr. Cartwright, our next finalist is Trenton James from New York City."

Shaking his hand, Sean says, "Mr. James, welcome to Las Vegas. We are pleased to have you in the competition." Trenton offers a bone-crushing shake that lets me know he is either overcompensating or showing off. He will need a little refinement to fit in.

He responds with a husky-voiced, "Thank you."

Moving to the next finalist, Cynthia says, "Our next competitor is Jayden Scott from Dallas."

I reach out my hand as I say, "Welcome." After shaking Jayden's clammy palm, I force myself not to wipe my hand on my tux pants. That sweaty handshake tells me he's downright petrified to be here. Hopefully, he will pull it together quickly.

In a soft voice with a slight southern drawl, Jayden says, "I'm pleased to be here. I hope everyone will enjoy my new approach to Texas-influenced cuisine."

"I'm sure we will," I reassure. I just hope I don't need to shake his hand again.

Reaching the last finalist, Cynthia explains "Mr. Cartwright, Kai Kahale is our fourth finalist. He combines his French training with his Hawaiian heritage."

Sean smiles and says "Mr. Kahale, I look forward to sampling your creations. They sound fascinating." Kai offers a standard handshake that is welcome after Jayden's sweaty palm.

Turning to Evan's muse in blue, I say, "Cynthia, please introduce us to our alternate."

"Of course, Mr. Cartwright. This is Cassandra Edwards. She is an accomplished, self-trained home chef who took a break from her career in law to join us for this competition."

I hear Evan mutter "Intriguing," as he steps into the foreground. Since when does Evan mutter so much? It's the second time tonight.

Attempting to hide my amusement at Evan's reaction to the alternate, I say, "Ms. Edwards, we are very pleased to have you here. Thank you for joining us. We hope this will be a truly special experience for you and the finalists." I'm impressed as Ms. Edwards offers me a firm, confident handshake as she looked me squarely in the eyes.

"Thank you, Mr. Cartwright. I'm quite honored to be here. As a self-taught cook, I must say that I am in awe of this group of professional chefs who will be competing."

Cool and classy, Cassie makes a favorable first impression. Taking an opportunity to bring Evan into the conversation, I explain, "It is our pleasure to have you all here, and please, remember to call me Sean. I am sure you remember Evan from the meeting this morning. He has been my best friend since college, so I am thrilled he is here."

Evan offers "I am looking forward to learning more about your culinary talents. Thank you for letting me be a part of this event." Of course, I can't help but notice his gaze ends and lingers on Cassie, which she doesn't seem to mind. Her lips turn into a genuine smile as a slight blush tints her cheeks.

Regaining our attention, Cynthia asserts her corralling skills, saying, "It is time to move to the stage for the announcements and toast. Cassie, you can wait here."

Cassie responds, "No problem."

Evan quickly offers, "Ms. Edwards, I hope you do not mind keeping me company while Sean and the others go on stage for the toast."

Smiling, Cassie says, "It would be my pleasure."

As the finalists and I join the three judges on stage, a server rings handheld chimes to get everyone's attention. When the crowd quiets, I begin, "Welcome everyone. We are so excited you have joined us for the kick-off of our Guest Chef Competition. To begin, I would like to introduce our esteemed panel of judges, who are standing to my right. Please join me in welcoming Chef Gerard, Chef Holden, and Chef Indigo." When the applause dies, I continue, "They have been tasked with the difficult job of selecting the winner of the Guest Chef Competition. Now let me introduce our four finalists."

Motioning to each of the finalists in turn, I say, "To begin, I am pleased to introduce Chef Leon Boucher, who will bring his French influences to the competition. Next, Chef Trenton James, who hails from New York City, brings his flair for Italian cuisine. Our third finalist is Chef Jayden Scott, who promises us Texas-inspired creations. And finally, please welcome our fourth finalist, Chef Kai Kahale, whose upscale style is influenced by his love of both France and tropical islands. Please join me in congratulating these amazing finalists!" Holding up my glass as the applause dies out, I say, "Now, please raise your glass to toast these amazing chefs and join me in wishing them good luck in the competition. In just two weeks, one of these outstanding chefs will be named Athena's guest chef. In the Olympic tradition of the Grand Athena, let the games begin. Cheers!"

CHAPTER THIRTEEN

EVAN

After the toast, Cynthia ushers Cassandra and everyone from the stage out onto the balcony for photos overlooking the Aegean Sea. I follow to get some fresh air and take in the group I will be interacting with over the next couple of weeks.

When the photos are finished, everyone else heads back inside, but I notice Cassandra turn around to face the deep blue pool illuminated by glowing torches. Lingering behind, I find myself captivated by her wavy, honey-colored hair and petite body. She doesn't notice my quiet approach, so I gently tap her shoulder, pondering, "It's quite the spectacle, isn't it?"

As I move my hand from her shoulder to the balcony rail, she laughs and says, "That's an interesting choice of words for your best friend's hotel."

"I guess it is, but it always strikes me as rather comical to see neon versions of Italy, France, Greece, and New York City all within a few city blocks."

"I know what you mean, but somehow it's still mesmerizing and beautiful. It's like living in an amusement park where you're promised that all your dreams can come true, if only temporarily. Maybe everyone needs that feeling at times."

I turn away from the lights to stare at Cassandra. "I think you're more right than you know. By the way, Cassandra, are you holding up ok being the alternate?"

"You can call me Cassie. Everyone does."

I shake my head. "I am not everyone, so if you don't mind, I would like to call you Cassandra."

Looking amused, she replies, "It's strange, I've never liked the formality of being called Cassandra, but you make it sound so elegant. I think I would like you to call me Cassandra."

Smiling, I repeat my earlier question. "So how are you doing with the role of alternate? I noticed you tense up when they asked you to wait at the base of the stairs rather than join the finalists for the introductions."

"I don't know what you thought you saw, but I'm fine. It's an honor to be here. Besides, I have the easy part — no pressure. I'm just watching from the sidelines and taking it all in."

Leaning forward with my arms resting on the balcony rail, I lightly clap my hands. "Well done."

Raising her eyebrows in indignation, Cassie asks, "Are you mocking me? Did I say something wrong?"

I lean farther over the railing and let out a sigh. "No, but speaking from experience, your words sounded like a well-rehearsed answer crafted to cover up your real feelings. Don't get me wrong. I know it is an amazing opportunity to be one of the top five selected to be here, but I thought someone said you are in law. Are you a lawyer?"

Confused, Cassandra answers, "Yes, I'm a lawyer, but why does that matter?"

"Then that means you were probably a top student in school and probably are already successful at work. So, I would bet that you are not used to being the backup. My guess is that you are accustomed to being in on the action. Therefore, I suspect it is particularly hard for you to be part of all the fanfare but not able to experience the adrenaline rush of the competition itself."

"Wow. Everyone else just keeps congratulating me, so I keep saying how honored I am. And I am honored. You are the only person who noticed that I'm in a difficult situation. On one hand, it's very exciting to have any role in this competition, but on the other, I'm disappointed. I've even wondered if it would have been easier not to be here at all."

Turning toward her as she gazes over the water, I say, "I have been in situations where I am expected to play the backup role too, so I know it can be hard. But hopefully, before this is over you will find a way to make this experience worth it." As I finish, Cassandra turns and our eyes lock sending a bolt of electricity through me. I wonder if she feels it too because I notice her body start to shiver. Unsure, I ask, "Are you getting cold?"

Turning, she leans with her back to the balcony railing and looks down. "Not really. Just thinking, but we should probably go in. I'm sure Cynthia is looking for me by now."

Stepping closer, I place a hand on the railing on each side of Cassandra, causing her to look up. I stare into her eyes, and our lips are so close I can feel her warm breath. My eyes are asking permission. Then I feel her right hand warm my chest. At first I think she's going to push me away, but then her fingers gently wrap around the lapel of my tuxedo, holding me in place. That's all the encouragement I need. Pressing my lips firmly against hers as I move my left hand to the back of her head and lace my fingers through her hair, I pull her even closer. Then I gently run my tongue across the seam between her lips, silently asking her to open for me. She trembles and her lips part, inviting my tongue to explore further, so I deepen the kiss.

Too soon we hear Cynthia calling, and Cassandra pulls away like a teenager caught by her parents. Cassandra mutters, "Oh my God. We're not supposed to interact with the judges. I'm going to get sent home before the competition starts. How could I be so stupid?" Cassandra looks horrified, scared, and embarrassed all at the same time.

I whisper in her ear, "You didn't do anything wrong. I am not a judge. You are not going to be sent home. Take a deep breath and let's go back inside. Everything is fine." She nods slowly but doesn't look convinced. Her obvious regret bothers me, which is odd. I am not a bad guy, but it is not like me to give her reaction a second thought because there are plenty of other women who would be at my side with the snap of my fingers. But for some reason, my reaction to her is different, and I am not sure why yet. But whatever her allure is, I know I want more of Cassandra Edwards.

Placing my hand on the small of her back, I guide Cassandra through the French doors back into Trendz.

CHAPTER FOURTEEN

SEAN

Hoping for an uninterrupted chunk of time, I arrived at the office two hours earlier than my assistant Emily and buried my head in the piles of F&B financial documents that litter my normally uncluttered, walnut and chrome desk. Typically, I would review all these documents online, but trying to carefully follow the detailed numbers for the last 12 months necessitates paper copies, an orange highlighter, and a legal pad for my copious notes and questions.

Ring. Ring. Ring. Shit, it's my private line. Another interruption I can't ignore. First, security checked in when my image appeared on the security cams earlier than expected. Now this. So much for getting to my office early to work out the F&B problems. Hardly masking my annoyance, I answer, "Hello, this is Sean."

"Sean, it's Larry."

I run my fingers through my hair as I realize this day is not getting better. "Hi Larry. When the Chief of Police phones at this early hour, it's usually not a social call."

"We finally have more information on Chef Bernard's apparent accident."

"What did you learn?"

"After Cameron told us that Cynthia mentioned Chef Bernard was complaining about a sports injury, we checked with the chef's doctors, but none of them prescribed any opioids to Chef Bernard. The coroner also says the chef must have taken the pills before leaving the Athena for them to have had time to take effect."

"What does this mean?"

"Sean, someone at the event may have given her the pills, which she took willingly. However, another possible scenario is that someone spiked her drink at your reception. I'm not saying that's what happened, but we need to consider that possibility."

Shaking my head, I ask, "Why would someone do that? It doesn't make any sense."

"We don't know, but I promised to keep you posted, so don't shoot the messenger."

"Larry, let me know if you learn anything new. I just can't imagine anyone would have wanted to harm Allison."

"At this point, we haven't found any reason someone would target Ms. Bernard, so we also must consider she may not have been the real target. Can you think of any reason someone would want to sabotage the guest chef competition as a way to target you or the Grand Athena's reputation?"

Rubbing my temples, hoping to alleviate the building tension, I respond, "Nothing specific comes to mind."

"Let me know if you think of anything. In the meantime, watch your back. Talk later." The line goes silent.

Shit. In addition to having more F&B questions than when I started my deep-dive analysis this morning, Allison may have been drugged and died as a way to target me and the Athena. This day is not getting better.

CHAPTER FIFTEEN

CASSIE

At 10 a.m., we meet in the kitchen at Trendz to film the prep for the Poolside Dip event. This competition is starting to feel real. Staff scurry around, making last minute adjustments to the scene, the cameras are almost set to roll, hot lights illuminate the kitchen, and a contagious tension fills the air around the finalists. My shoulders tense as I watch Trenton repeatedly stretch his arms as if readying for a tough workout, Kai stare at his hands as if he is willing them to stop clenching and unclenching, and Jayden nervously rearrange the cooking utensils at his workstation. As I notice a few teardrop-shaped beads of sweat trickle down Jayden's forehead, I wonder if they are from the bright lights or nerves. Leon, who seems the calmest of the group, is even taking slow, deep breaths to ward off competition jitters.

After a few introductory remarks by Cynthia and Amy, the finalists are given a 10-minute warning before filming will start. I feel strange not helping while everyone is getting ready, so I walk over to one of the tables with supplies and dishes thinking I can straighten things up a little, but Amy pulls me back. She explains the finalists must do all the preparation themselves, and I need to stay in the background, so, after mumbling an apology, I find a place to stand behind the camera crew where I won't be in the way.

When the filming starts, a giant timer on the right wall is set to one hour. Before time runs out, the finalists must create one finished dip as well as prep ingredients to demo making the dip at the pool. It is quickly apparent that each of the finalists has a different style and personality when it comes to their cooking. For example, Trenton, calmer now, has organized his work area very neatly with each ingredient laid out separately, and he has started methodically prepping them one at a time. Jayden, on the other hand, is running back and forth to the pantry and haphazardly piling things on his station, not leaving much space to actually work. It's like he's never heard the term *mise en place*. Of course, while my goal is always to have an organized set-up with everything in its place, I don't always achieve it either. But Jayden is so disorganized, I wonder if he is used to having assistants do all the prep work.

When the timer expires, everyone stops working, and one by one the finalists roll carts with their food and tools for the demo into the refrigerator. During a quick wrap-up session, Amy announces that the demonstrations start at 2 p.m., but she wants us there by 1:15 p.m. to make sure everything is set up properly. She also wants to tape some interviews before the demos start. Until then, we have a break for lunch.

Looking at my TekCuff, I realize I have almost two hours for lunch. That gives me time to head to Athena's Crêpery, which supposedly serves savory crepes that rival those found in France. My mouth is already watering as I envision fresh spinach and mushrooms or ham and cheese filling a warm buckwheat crepe. Maybe they will even drizzle some béchamel sauce with a pinch of nutmeg over the filling. Now my stomach is growling. As I head out, Evan walks by and whispers, "See, everything is fine. You are still here. They did not send you home, so why don't you meet me for lunch? I'll send directions to your TekCuff." I'm about to decline, but he is gone.

I swear my temperature rises every time he gets close. I'd love to have lunch with him, but I need to keep a professional distance. He may not be a judge, but he is attending on behalf of Mr. Cartwright, so a repeat of last night would not be smart. Determined to follow my plan, I head toward the Crêpery. On my way, I feel the TekCuff vibrate, so I play the voice message, which says, "Take a water taxi to the Santorini Tower. Christian will be waiting to escort you to our lunch destination. He has been instructed to wait there until you arrive, so please don't keep him waiting too long. Ciao."

My whole body tenses when Evan's message essentially orders me to show up at the Santorini Tower. How dare he think he can tell me what to do? But as an image of his bemused face from earlier pops into my head, I'm surprised to realize my tension has evaporated because there is something sexy about Evan's insistent invitation. Should I follow his instructions? No, I have no desire to be bossed around, at least not outside the bedroom, and even then, only sometimes.

Why am I thinking about bedrooms? I need to focus on why I'm here. But why am I here? For an adventure. It's not like I'm competing. As they have made clear, I'm Just-in-Case Cassie, the spare who is "observing." Besides, if I don't show up, Evan makes it sound like Christian will be stuck waiting for me the rest of the day. He can't really mean that, can he?

At a minimum, I should relieve Christian of his duty, so I head to the water taxi. Before I know it, I'm approaching Christian whose face lights up with a smile when he sees me. Having second thoughts about lunch with Evan, I say, "Christian, it's so good to see you. Can you please give Evan a message for me?"

Shaking his head in disagreement as he turns to summon the elevator, Christian politely responds, "My instructions are to take you to him. Please follow me."

A little louder than intended, I quickly say, "Oh, no! I can't have lunch with him. I just wanted you to thank him for the invitation. Please give him my regrets."

Christian shakes his head again, accompanied by a shoulder shrug and upturned palms. "I'm sorry, but I can't do that. I am to stay here until you agree to have lunch with him."

While I was on the fence about whether to have lunch with Evan, this conversation is bringing out a stubborn streak in me. With animated arms, I firmly share my frustration with Christian. "That is ridiculous. I'm not going to be goaded into having lunch with Evan. As I said, I appreciate the invitation, but I can't join him for lunch. Please let him know."

Clearly, Christian is accustomed to dealing with frustrated guests because my reply doesn't seem to faze his determination. As if sharing a secret between friends, Christian calmly says, "Ms. Edwards, please follow me and give him your message in person. He is Mr. Cartwright's best friend, and I don't want to lose my job."

Squinting with confusion and incredulity, I matter-of-factly state, "If you would lose your job merely because I choose not to have lunch with Mr. Cartwright's best friend, that doesn't speak very well for either man!"

Calm no more, Christian rocks on his feet as he clarifies, "Oh, no! That is not what I meant. Mr. Cartwright is great to work for, and his friend is a very considerate person."

I fold my arms across my chest. "Then why are you worried about losing your job?"

"Please forgive my exaggeration. Mr. Cartwright expects me to take care of our VIP's requests. I merely meant to be persuasive, but I am screwing this up. Please just accompany me to the lunch destination. Of course, no one will force you to stay, but your host has gone to a lot of trouble, so I would hate to see his efforts go to waste."

Waving his explanation off, I say, "This whole thing is ridiculous, but I will tell Evan myself. This is not your fault. Take me to him."

"Thank you. Right this way." Christian places his palm over the hand scanner, and an elevator door opens. He stands to the side to hold the door while I enter. Without another word, we are transported to the penthouse level of the Santorini Tower. When the elevator stops, Christian gestures for me to exit, and soon I'm standing in the foyer of a magnificent, two-story suite overlooking the Las Vegas Strip. Christian says, "Welcome to the Grand Monarch

Suite. I believe lunch has been set up on the outdoor balcony. Please follow me."

With confident strides, I follow him ready to say my piece, but inside I'm the one with Monarch butterflies circling because every time I'm near Evan something about him draws me closer. As we walk onto the balcony, I'm overwhelmed at the fairytale-like setting. Fine white china with silver rims and intricately cut crystal glasses adorn a table-for-two with pale lilac linens with faint butterflies woven into the fabric. Soft yellow, white, and lavender roses fill the center of the table to complete the look of spring.

Evan stands on the balcony just past the table. God, he is handsome in his perfectly tailored, khaki linen pants and dark blue, collared shirt, having lost the tie from earlier and unfastened the top two buttons. His mischievously sparkling eyes are locked on mine and reel me in, causing me to question my decision to leave. How am I going to tell him I'm not planning to stay, when all I want to do is reenact the kiss from the reception balcony?

Why am I fighting this so hard? We are two adults. What is wrong with a nice lunch on the balcony of the most beautiful suite I've ever seen? What would be wrong with seeing where this goes? After all, I promised Lowri that if someone caught my eye, I would give him a chance.

But I know what's wrong. Since my parents died, I've put up walls to cope and protect myself. I've worked hard to become a strong, independent woman so I won't ever need to rely on someone else for a secure future.

None of my boyfriends have lasted very long because I push them away long before things might get serious. After losing my parents to a freak accident, the thought of losing someone else I care about is too much, so I don't let myself get that close to anyone.

But something is different with Evan. I'm trying to push him away before anything has really started. It must be this new adventure that has me on edge. I need to let loose, live a little, and quit overthinking everything. After all, it's just lunch with a new friend.

As we make our way across the large balcony, Christian says, "Sir, Ms. Edwards has arrived. Can I be of further service?"

"Nothing more at this time. Thank you very much."

After my internal battle with myself, I decided to stay for lunch but needing a safety escape, I call out, "Christian, can you be back here by 12:45 to show me the way to the pool for the demos?"

Christian says, "Of course, Ms. Edwards. Have a wonderful lunch. I will take my leave now."

Not knowing what to say, I start with "Evan, I didn't plan to stay for lunch. I came to deliver that message in person because Christian insisted he couldn't deliver the message for me."

"Why couldn't you stay? Are you afraid to be alone with me? Is that why you wanted Christian to come back at a set time?"

"It just doesn't seem appropriate," I blurt out. "I don't know who you are, and here I am in your hotel room. They took away all my electronic devices, so I can't even Google you. And I don't have any friends in Vegas to make sure I'm ok. This has horror movie written all over it. Besides, I'm here for the competition, so I need to focus on it."

Waving off my paranoia, Evan chuckles. "First, I think you just insulted me." Then, gently placing his hands on my upper arms and with a more serious tone, he continues, "But I have a little sister, so I know women need to be careful. I can assure you that you have nothing to fear. I will be on my best behavior during lunch, and you made sure that Christian will be back to check on you. Second, we have been through this before. I am not a judge. You are not a finalist. We are both adults and, based on our first chat last night, we enjoy each other's company. Let's have lunch and entertain each other with interesting conversation. A chef such as yourself would never want to waste amazing food, right?"

"When you put it that way, I feel rather silly. You're right. It would be sad for good food to go to waste."

"Good, let's have a seat. You will be even happier to know that the suite's private chef, Eduardo, is in the kitchen preparing to serve us lunch, so as much as I would like it to be otherwise, we are not alone."

Just then Eduardo appears with two plates and explains, "I am pleased to serve you a salad composed of spring greens tossed with a light lemon vinaigrette and adorned with a rainbow of radish discs, asparagus tips, multicolor carrots curls, thinly sliced avocado wedges, fresh strawberries, and edible flowers. Please enjoy."

"Evan, this looks like a work of colorful spring art."

"It does. While we enjoy our salads, tell me a little more about yourself. All I know is that you work hard at your law firm and you love cooking. What else should I know about you?"

I quickly finish my first bite of the scrumptious salad and smile at Evan. "I'm not sure there is a lot more to tell. I love to read. My favorite vacation would be sitting by the beach with a frozen, fruity drink and a good book. I hate to admit it, but I love to watch detective shows on television. I also look forward to the opportunity to travel more. I've always dreamed of taking time off to sample the actual food and wine of Europe rather than just the American versions. What about you?"

After wiping his mouth with the linen napkin, Evan says, "I'm not that interesting."

Setting my fork on the china plate with a soft clink, I place my folded arms on the edge of the table and fix my full attention on Evan. "Come on. Turnabout is fair play."

"What do you mean?"

With a quick shoulder shrug, I explain, "I mean that I shared things about me. You have to do the same. It's only fair."

Leaning back, Evan contemplates my question more seriously. "Ok. Let's see. I also love travel and beaches. When visiting Sean here, I am known to enjoy a few games of blackjack. I work in the family business. My father is about to retire, so I will take on more responsibilities soon; that is the main reason I am spending some time here for a break. My brother is also getting married soon, so that will expand our family. That's all I can think of now."

Just as I am about to follow up to ask about the family business, Eduardo clears our plates and presents a beautiful second course consisting of a filet of trout topped with finely crushed pecans and lemon butter served with a small side of roasted broccolini with red pepper flakes. As Eduardo quietly pours glasses of an oaked Chardonnay, I remark "Evan, this lunch is lovely. Thank you for sharing it with me." Taking a bite, an "Mmmm" escapes my lips, followed by "This is delicious. I love the hint of spice. It wakes up the taste buds without overpowering them."

Evan looks amused as he raises his glass for a sip of wine. "I am glad a chef such as yourself approves."

"Don't be funny," I say laughing. "You know I'm not technically a chef. Besides, while I suspect the real chefs in the competition are snobbier than I am, even they would approve of Eduardo's excellent meal."

"Given you made the top five for this competition, I would think you are a real chef too. Are there any foods you don't like?"

"I'm not a professional chef, and I don't think being the alternate in this competition magically elevated my status. As for food likes and dislikes, I know even amateur chefs like me are supposed to be willing to try anything, but I can't stand mayonnaise. Also, I don't want to eat raw fish, so no sushi for me. What about you?"

"My parents have always expected me to be polite and eat any and everything put before me. But if given the choice, I would never eat eggplant or Brussels sprouts. And to be honest, I am not a fan of mayonnaise either."

"Really? I always thought I was the only person in the world who doesn't like mayo. Now I don't feel so alone."

"You are definitely not alone."

"Did you say your father is retiring soon?"

Before answering, he leans forward and runs his thumb over my bottom lip, making me quiver from the touch. "I didn't want to risk the butter dripping onto your shirt," he says, but his husky voice and eyes dipping to the V-neck of my shirt belie his words. I think he just wanted an excuse to touch me. Evan continues, "Yes, my father is planning to retire very soon."

With lips still warm from Evan's touch, I try to focus on our conversation, which is hard to do while staring into his inviting and captivating eyes. "What does he plan to do when he retires?"

"My mother and father plan to spend more time traveling and doing charity work, I think."

"That sounds nice. You mentioned that your brother is getting married, and you also mentioned a sister. Do you have any other siblings?"

With a headshake, Evan wipes his mouth with his napkin. "No, just my older brother Alex and younger sister Briana. What about you?"

"Just me."

"That's interesting."

"I don't know if it's interesting. It seems normal to me. Are you and your siblings throwing a retirement party for your father?"

"There will be a party of sorts. Given my brother's upcoming wedding, we will have a lot of events scheduled around the same time."

Having finished my trout, I lean forward, resting my arms on the table. "You must be looking forward to being with your family for all the festivities."

"It will be rather overwhelming, but hopefully all the events will go off as planned." Placing his hand on my arm, Evan says, "You know what, I have an idea. You said you wanted to travel and sample European food and wine. You should accompany me to the retirement and wedding events. They will be a lot more fun if you are with me."

My heart stutters at the thought of knowing Evan well enough to meet his family. But we just met, so I know he's kidding around. Keeping it light, I smile and point out, "While that sounds like fun, we barely know each other. There must be someone you are closer to that would make more sense to take to such personal events."

While gazing directly into my eyes, Evan reaches for my hand and intertwines our fingers. Pulling my hand to his lips, he gives it a soft kiss and caresses it with his thumb, making me tremble as electricity charges through me. "If you are asking whether I am in a relationship, the answer is no. In fact, I cannot think of anyone I would rather take with me. In case it is not clear, I am very attracted to you, and I strongly suspect the feeling is mutual."

Without thinking, I nod.

Squeezing my hand, Evan continues, "But it's not just the physical attraction that draws me to you. You make me smile. Even though I am facing some extremely stressful business choices, talking to you over lunch has relaxed me for the first time in quite a while. Call me selfish, but I suspect you would keep me smiling and sane even during the upcoming wedding festivities, which I'm sure you know tend to bring out stress in families. In return, I will show you my beautiful island and its treasures while we get to know each other better. What do you say?"

I'm taken aback because he seems so serious, but I wasn't sure I was ready for lunch today much less a trip to Europe with him. However, I can't deny the sparks flying between us. Buying time to collect myself, I say, "I'm flattered, but you haven't even told me where the events will take place."

"At my home, which is on an island just south of France and Italy. You will love it."

"It sounds like a dream trip, but I need to go back to work after the competition is over. I don't think I'll be able to take more time off for quite a while."

Evan gently places my hand back on the table, releasing it to take a sip of his wine. Suddenly, I miss the warmth of his hand enveloping mine. Setting his glass back on the table, he says, "Don't say no just yet. I bet we can think of a way to work out the logistics."

I'm sure Evan is not truly serious about his spur-of-the-moment invitation, so I simply respond, "I doubt it, but it does sound like fun." Just then Eduardo reappears with small servings of raspberry sorbet served with a shot glass of limoncello to pour on top. It is the perfect light dessert with just enough kick from the alcohol to make me wish I could take that trip with Evan. I guess it is good I'm not actually competing after wine and limoncello for lunch!

Standing up and reaching for me, Evan says, "Cassandra, let's move over to the sofa in the lounge area and watch the people traipsing along the Strip below. We still have a little time before Christian returns to save you."

I let Evan take my hand and guide me to the sofa. As we sit down, I say, "Evan, I'm sorry about that. I shouldn't have insulted you. I just don't ..."

"Cassandra, I am just teasing you," Evan interrupts. "You have nothing to apologize for. You were smart to ask Christian to check up on you." He places his arm around my shoulder and pulls me closer. "But that isn't going to stop me from wanting to taste those luscious lips of yours again."

Staring into his eyes, I realize I have no plans to stop him as his mouth moves closer to mine. Then his warm soft lips meet mine, and it's as though a jolt of electricity shoots through me. It's even more powerful than the prior kiss.

The next thing I know our tongues are dancing with each other, and Evan's hand is running up and down my arm. Without thinking, I wrap my arms around his neck, holding on for dear life as our kiss intensifies. His teeth lightly nip my lower lip as his hand slides under me to gently pull me onto his lap. My eyes are closed, wishing this would never end.

My left arm leaves his neck and starts roaming over his hard chest as he moves his mouth to nip at my right ear. I shudder as it tickles and turns me on at the same time. As I tilt my head back to let Evan taste my neck, I hear footsteps and quickly scoot off Evan's lap. While I'm trying to catch my breath, I hear Christian say, "Pardon me, but it is 12:45 and time for me to escort the two of you to the pool for the demonstrations."

"Christian, you are quite prompt," Evan says. "I *usually* admire that. Please escort Ms. Edwards to the pool, but I need to handle of a couple of things first. I will meet you there shortly. Cassandra, let me walk you to the door."

"I am ready to kill the next person that interrupts us," Evan whispers into my ear.

I laugh. "I think they are just protecting me from myself."

As we near the door, Evan says "Thank you for joining me for lunch."

"It was lovely. Thank you." As I head out with Christian, I can't quit smiling.

Christian comments, "It seems like you enjoyed lunch, not that it is any of my business."

Smiling, I agree, "Yes, lunch was nice." Did I just say that? Really? I just called the best date in recent memory "nice." Had I been of a mind to share my true thoughts, I would have said lunch was amazing, delicious, exhilarating, pulse pounding, and fucking great, but those thoughts are best kept to myself. As the elevator descends, I hope there will be more "nice" lunches in the near future.

CHAPTER SIXTEEN

CASSIE

For a sun and beach lover, walking into the pool area is like walking into heaven on earth. After a few steps, I take a minute to absorb my vibrant, sunny surroundings filled with swimsuit-clad partiers and upbeat music blasting above the hum of poolside conversations. The crystal blue pools are glimmering like diamonds as the sunlight bounces off the water's surface. The iconic Greek ruins I noticed from the lobby are even more spectacular up close, emerging from the pools' depths as if they're floating on water. From my college art history course, I recognize that the rectangular pattern of columns in the far pool forms a replica of the Parthenon, and the columns atop a curved, marble arch in the pool to my right must be the Arch of Hadrian. Other random columns topped with ornate scroll-shaped designs rise out of the near pool, but I'm not sure what ruin they are meant to depict. Thinking back to my course, I recall that columns with scroll-shaped designs are called Ionic style, which makes me giggle because when we were studying them, they reminded me of upside-down palmier cookies with their connected, double spirals. Of course, a lot of things remind me of cookies and food in general. Some of the columns even have waterfalls flowing from their precipices, drenching couples, who are embracing in the pools below.

Watching the happy couples kiss makes me wish Christian hadn't interrupted the toe-tingling kisses with Evan. But I felt like a teenager whose parents came home early when Cynthia almost caught us last night and again when Christian walked in on us today even though Evan already explained I have no reason to worry because he's not a judge. It's more likely, me once again trying to protect myself from getting close to anyone. But why am I pushing him away so soon after we met. Am I scared that I'm already too attracted?

As a server in a blue and white, filmy mini-dress carrying a tray of frozen drinks with bright blue straws brushes by me, I realize I've been standing here getting lost in my self-analysis for way too long. This is not the place to be distracted by such serious thoughts. Instead, I should let the party vibe envelope me and enjoy a beautiful afternoon at the pool. As my eyes linger on the white lounge chairs that look like comfy beds, I wish I could stretch out on one. Maybe even better, I could sample a frozen, fruity concoction in one of the private cabanas lining the sides of the pool area.

But those thoughts quickly vanish when the music suddenly disappears, and my attention is drawn to Amy as she announces the Poolside Dip demos will be starting at 2 p.m. The music obscured the film crew's shouts of instructions as they moved equipment into place to set up for filming. It appears the finalists all arrived extra early and are already working at the tables placed beneath each of four, small pergolas draped with gauzy white fabric. Given the pressure they are under, the finalists are clearly motivated to make sure they use every second to prepare. As I work my way through the small crowd of a couple of dozen curious onlookers, I move closer to the tables and take in the aromas of sautéing garlic and fresh minced herbs — not the usual poolside scents but nonetheless welcome.

I'm thinking how much fun it would be to stand under one of the pergolas chopping cilantro and squeezing limes to demo my dip when I sense someone approaching me from behind and feel a tingling sensation run through my body. Before I can turn around, Evan whispers in my ear "See, aren't you glad you didn't skip lunch with me? You still had plenty of time to make it to the demo on time."

An involuntary shiver runs down my neck, and I turn. "Stop that."

"Stop what?" he asks, a reserved grin on his face and a twinkle in his eyes. I just pointed out the facts. You had nothing to worry about from our moment on the balcony last night or our lovely lunch today."

"You know what I mean. The whispering in my ear."

"I only whispered so no one would hear that you had been concerned."

"Oh." Then, without another word, he turns and, with hands casually deposited in his pockets, saunters toward the finalists and crew. I think I may regret having told him to stop anything.

Soon Sebastian, Amy, and one of the camera guys approach because Amy wants to interview me, which triggers a mix of emotions. As strange as it sounds, the idea of being on camera is more exhilarating than frightening, and the idea of sharing my thoughts on the cooking event is a dream come true. As the camera guy moves into place, I quickly smooth down my hair and check that my required competition attire of black cotton pants and a tucked-in, button-up blouse is in place. A few jitters still bubble to the surface because I don't want to blow my chance to shine given that my backseat role will not provide me many opportunities like this one. "Don't mess up" starts competing with the mantra of "Seize the moment." Maybe my initial confidence and excitement aren't as powerful as the fear of failure.

My thoughts are interrupted when the cameras start rolling and Amy introduces me. "Everyone, meet Cassie. She was selected as the alternate chef for the competition. Cassie, are you excited to watch the demonstration?"

"Absolutely. I'm also excited to have a chance to taste the finalists' dips."

"What is your favorite dip for a poolside event?"

"I love Roasted Pineapple Tomatillo Salsa because it can be served at room temperature and would hold up well under this warm, poolside sun."

91

"Cassie, that sounds delicious. What goes into your tomatillo salsa?"

I'm having fun and any nerves are subsiding quickly as we talk. "It's easy. You combine roasted tomatillos, jalapenos, onion, and pineapple with fresh cilantro, fresh lime juice, and a little salt. You can also add some roasted garlic if you like."

"I'll try that sometime. It sounds like you are ready to step in quickly if one of the finalists bows out."

"Oh, that won't be necessary. They are all here and ready to compete. I'm just enjoying getting to watch and learn from these masters."

Sebastian yells, "Cut," and Amy turns to me. "Great job. You're a natural. Thanks, Cassie. Enjoy the demo."

Sighing in relief that it went well, I respond, "I will. Thanks for including me in the interviews." Then they move on to interview the finalists.

After the interviews are complete, it's time for the demonstrations to begin. Amy reminds everyone that each finalist will be given 10 minutes to show how to make their dip. Then we all get to taste.

After drawing for presentation order, the crew shouts instructions and scurries to move the cameras and lights in front of Trenton's table for the first demo. Clipboard and pen in hand, Cynthia checks off items on her list while Amy touches up her makeup in preparation for hosting the demo. Ready and waiting with his chin up, lips pressed into a straight line, arms crossed, and chef's knife in hand, Trenton exudes a serious, no-nonsense attitude.

When the filming starts, I'm torn between watching the live demo and watching it on the almost life-sized screens set up on raised platforms throughout the pool area. Amy's white-toothed smile and vivacious energy fills the screen, welcoming everyone to the demo as she introduces Trenton and his roasted tomato, kale, and garlic dip. As the camera moves from Amy to Trenton, I can't help but feel a pang of envy, wishing it was me in front of the camera. But that was not meant to be.

Over the chop-chop sounds of Trenton's knife rapidly hitting the cutting board, Trenton's commanding and noticeably gruff voice explodes from the speakers around the pool as he explains how to mince the garlic and chop the kale for his dip. Good thing he isn't auditioning for a television show because his brusque manner is not very approachable. He sounds like he is bossing around his kitchen staff rather than teaching a novice audience.

With a swift turn of the wrist, Trenton swirls a couple of table-spoons of olive oil into a pan that sits atop a portable burner. Soon we hear a soft sizzle as the garlic hits the oil. Just as the aroma hits my nose, Trenton explains it's time to add the kale. Then with a flourish, Trenton sprinkles crushed red pepper flakes from high above the pan, dotting the green kale with the red and yellow flakes as he shares that a little spice activates the taste buds and enhances the other flavors.

Not lacking in confidence, Trenton plows through the rest of the presentation, adding tomatoes that he roasted earlier. Once the dip is finished, Trenton plunges a pita chip into the tomato and kale mixture. The dip-covered chip quickly disappears between his thick mustache and beard as his dark eyes pierce the camera. He concludes by kissing his fingertips and declaring the dip "pure perfection."

Trenton may not be the friendliest chef, but based on the demo, he has a good skill set and his dip looks and sounds delicious. I can't wait to give it a taste and verify the flavors are truly as perfect as Trenton proclaimed. I should also ask him why he chose pita chips instead of toasted French baguette slices, which would have been my first choice.

Jayden is up next. After about 15 minutes for setup, the cameras roll, and Jayden explains he is making Texas Fondue. The contrast between Trenton and Jayden is dramatic, both in confidence and physical appearance. While Trenton bellowed his instructions, Jayden is talking so softly that Amy keeps interjecting comments intended to encourage him to speak up. And the lilt at the end of his sentences makes it sound like he's asking questions rather than instructing. As far as looks go, while Trenton is an imposing figure with a hair-covered face, Jayden has a sparse, scraggly mustache and a thin frame that is swallowed by his chef's jacket.

As Jayden steps through his demo, I'm confused by his choice of dip. At first, I assume that Texas Fondue is a creative name for an upscale version of a warm, Texas cheese dip, but I'm wrong. He's making a Southern sausage gravy served with toasted biscuit and cornbread cubes for dipping. I'm sure it's going to taste great, but who knew gravy could be called a dip? Regardless it's an unusual choice for poolside, particularly on such a hot day.

When the dip is finished, I feel sorry for Jayden because, as he dips his cornbread into the gravy, his chef's hat blows off his head and floats away in the pool. Looking like he is about to chase down the hat, Amy reaches for his arm and pulls his attention back to the camera to conclude the segment. For his sake, I'm glad this isn't a competition round.

As the demos continue, I'm learning that filming shows is not the day of glamour I'd always thought it would be. Each "informal" 10-minute segment is taking at least 30 minutes to an hour given all the time for moving cameras, setting up microphones, and making sure the chefs are ready to go. When I asked one of the photographers standing near me if this was normal, he told me this was much faster than normal. Apparently, they often spend all day on a 30-minute segment. Interesting. And not only does it take a long time, but conditions are also more challenging than I had realized. We are at a hot pool in direct sunlight but dressed like we are in an indoor, air-conditioned space, so the chefs are battling sweat, while trying to remember to smile. All being professionals, the chefs do a great job of dealing with the conditions.

By 3:20, Kai brings a calm, self-assured tone as he starts his demonstration of his Papaya Tapenade. If I didn't know he was a chef, his laid-back attitude, nicely tanned skin, and fit physique might have led me to think he was a surfer ready to use his muscular arms to paddle out in search of the next wave. But as he explains the steps for his recipe, I find myself immediately connecting with him and trusting his knowledge as a chef. His never-faltering smile and easygoing personality invite me to join his journey as he conveys his genuine desire to share his work with the audience. He's also creating some interesting flavor combinations. I never would have thought to combine minced olives with finely chopped papaya, red pepper flakes, and minced garlic. But he makes it sound delicious and new, particularly when he explains that he likes to serve it with taro chips, purple potato chips, and sweet potato chips for a tropical-meets-French fusion.

As Kai points out, his dip is great for a poolside party because it can be served at room temperature. If you ask me, Kai just nailed the presentation with his friendly personality, intriguing combo of flavors, and theme-appropriate dip. I will definitely be in line to taste it.

Finally, it's Leon's turn. Looking fresh and prepared despite the high temperatures and having to go last, Leon prepares his white bean dip. He explains it has a smoother texture than hummus and can be made using canned cannellini beans, so the dip doesn't take long to make. Based on the crowd's reaction, I'm not the only one who finds Leon knowledgeable, and his French accent is a little sexy.

With quiet enthusiasm, Leon explains that all the ingredients go into the food processor and a few pulses will transform the beans, olive oil, crushed garlic, salt, a dash or two of hot sauce, fresh rosemary, and parmesan cheese into a creamy dip. After a quick taste, Leon adds a dash more salt as he explains the dip can be served warm or at room temperature. It sounds perfect for a poolside party. I've never liked the consistency of hummus because it's grainy, so Leon's dip would be a great substitute. I should ask him if he has ever tried adding a squeeze of lemon too.

The crew is still filming as they wait for Leon to taste the final version of the dip, but it looks like he forgot that part. Being a seasoned host, Amy steps in and asks Leon what he recommends for scooping up the delicious bean dip, which reminds Leon to taste it for the camera. While moving a pre-made bowl of the dip into the center of the table, Leon keeps his eyes on Amy and picks up the conversation, explaining that any type of chip will work, but he is using tortilla chips today. That's an interesting choice. Given the dip reminded me of hummus, I'd expected him to use pita chips. But that's a good tip. I need to remember to think outside the box and not always go with the traditional choices. After all, this is a great chance for me to learn from some professional chefs, and that's one way I can elevate my cooking to match theirs.

Leon grabs a tortilla chip and loads it with the bean dip. Then he stuffs the whole chip into his mouth. Within seconds, he gets a strange look on his face. Oh no, he can't talk with such a full mouth. That's another tip for me. If they ever ask me to taste something on camera, I better take a tiny bite, so I can immediately comment on the flavors.

I keep watching, but it's making me uncomfortable to see him struggling with his overstuffed mouth. While I wait for Leon to regain his ability to speak, I glance around the pool area to see what else is going on. Evan is standing a couple of feet behind me watching everything. As our eyes lock, I hear a commotion in the direction of Leon's table. Quickly turning back, I see Leon clutch his throat, stumble backwards, and fall into the pool with a hard thud as his head collides with the nearest concrete column and then slides slowly down, leaving a trail of bright red blood on the column as his limp body disappears under the water's surface. Screams ring out around the pools as my hands instantly cover my open mouth, and I add my barely audible "OMG!" to the chaotic chorus.

A lifeguard on my left abandons his perch and jumps into the pool with an elongated flotation device in tow. Staring at the water, I'm worried that no one has pulled Leon's head up yet. The lifeguard needs to hurry. It seems like everything is moving in slow motion, and I feel so helpless with so many people between me and the pool. Why didn't someone from the crew jump in to help him? They are closer than the lifeguard.

It seems like an eternity but is probably less than a minute or two when the lifeguard carries Leon's lifeless body out of the pool and lays him on the deck. After checking for a pulse and leaning down to listen for signs of breathing, the lifeguard starts CPR as another lifeguard quickly joins him to help. A pool of blood forms under Leon's head, a sign he hit his head hard as he fell. The second lifeguard tries to control the bleeding by applying pressure with a towel, but there is still a lot of blood. Next thing I know, EMTs are rolling a gurney through the pool area and taking over. They stabilize Leon's neck, load him on the gurney, and rush him out.

That's when I realize silent tears are running down my cheeks as a warm hand rests on my back. Evan whispers in my ear, "I want to hug you and pull you against my shoulder to protect you from this bloody mess, but I know you would protest." I keep quiet, but he is wrong. Even though I should protest, I want him to wrap his strong arms around me right now.

The pool party has quickly turned somber. The music is gone. The big screens are black. The only sounds are hushed whispers and the noise from camera equipment and lights being disassembled and moved. As I watch in a daze, the hotel's pool staff announce the pool is temporarily closed and encourage the crowd to disperse. This is the bloodiest accident I've ever seen, and it wasn't clear whether Leon was breathing when they wheeled him away. The EMT was still doing chest compressions until just before they left. The thought that Leon might not be alive makes my body shake, causing me to draw my arms across my torso in a steadying hug.

Sean quietly enters the pool area accompanied by several employees dressed in security uniforms. He walks purposefully toward Cynthia and Amy, and after conferring, Cynthia announces that everyone involved in the competition should move to the largest cabana on the side of the pool. They will meet with us shortly.

CHAPTER SEVENTEEN

CASSIE

As if in a trance, we start making our way to the cabana. Security personnel have stationed themselves by the demo tables where Leon fell into the pool. They are turning guests away who get too close or try to get back into the pool. I guess they must be worried about the blood. How will they get it cleaned? Do they have to empty the pool? And why are my germophobe tendencies surfacing when I should be worrying about Leon? His enthusiasm was infectious, and his food today was spot on. It would be a shame for one of the leading finalists to be knocked out by such a freak accident. But would that mean I get to compete? Am I a horrible person for even thinking about that now? This is just awful.

Sean enters the cabana and stops in front of the assembled group. Cynthia and Amy follow closely and take a position nearby. Amy is staring at her shoes, using her index fingers to wipe her eyes as tears and mascara run down her cheeks. Given she was standing within a foot or two of Leon when he fell into the pool, she's clearly shaken and distraught. Cynthia, who is at least 20 years her senior, takes on a motherly role with an arm around Amy's shoulder, pulling her close. But Cynthia's wrinkled brow gives away her underlying concern.

Running his hand through his hair, Sean looks worried as well, but he stands tall and in control as he raises his other hand to silence the groups side conversations. Addressing the crowd, Sean says, "Everyone, let me have your attention for a few minutes." An eerie quiet descends over the group. "Leon is being transported to the nearest trauma center. I know you are all as concerned about him as I am, but unfortunately, it may be several hours before we receive an update on his condition, so I ask for your patience during that time."

Everyone starts throwing questions at Sean about whether Leon is going to be ok and what is going to happen with the competition. Holding up his hand for silence, Sean continues, "Right now, that is all we know. We all hope and assume that Leon will get his head stitched up and be back here very soon, but we don't have any more details at this time. Therefore, we are going to put the competition on hold for a day. Please be sure to always wear your TekCuff devices so we can keep you updated. However, if you don't get a message before then, everyone should plan to meet in the Zeus conference room at 3 p.m. tomorrow."

I'm shaking as though an arctic blast filled the cabana. I can't help trembling as my mind keeps replaying Leon falling backward and hitting his head on the column while clutching his throat. But how can I be shaking when I know it's over 100 degrees poolside?

Then, a strange, tingly warmth fills me as Evan discreetly places his hand on the small of my back. I'm coming to like him showing up this way. His breath tickles my ear as he whispers, "You may not be just an alternate much longer. That looked like a nasty head injury."

I feel like a heel that the thought already crossed my mind. Deep down though, it seems wrong to hope for a chance to compete at Leon's expense. I never thought they would actually need an alternate. Or if they did, I thought it would be because of some less traumatic reason, like someone coming down with the flu or landing another job before the competition started. "Evan, what a terrible thing to say. As much as I would like to compete, I want Leon to be ok."

"Of course, you want him to be ok. We all do. I was just stating a fact, nothing more. Meet me at the Grand Monarch Suite in an hour. We can have a drink and talk."

"I'm not sure I want to be alone with the image of Leon's head hitting the column on auto replay in my head, but I'm not sure I'd be very good company either."

"There is no reason for you to be alone after this. Don't worry about entertaining me."

"How do I get access to your floor?"

"I will ask Christian to escort you. He will come by your room in an hour."

"Thank you." The next hour is going to be a long one.

CHAPTER EIGHTEEN

CASSIE

I'd hoped getting away from the scene of the accident would have a calming effect, but after reaching my room, my mind still won't stop spinning. I can't get rid of the gruesome picture of Leon leaving the trail of blood as he slipped under the water. Hopefully, Leon will be ok.

But what if Leon can't return to the competition? How would I feel about competing? I feel guilty even thinking that I may get to compete because that would mean Leon isn't doing well. I decide to take a hot shower and clear my head while I wait for Christian to show up.

Soon after dressing, Christian arrives to take me to Evan's suite. I assume someone in Christian's position must be kept informed about important issues involving the Athena, so I barely have my door open before I'm asking, "Christian, have you heard any news about Leon?"

Christian responds, "Hello, Ms. Edwards. No, I haven't heard any updates about Mr. Boucher."

I explain, "I was hoping you would know something. He was bleeding so badly, and I tend to be a worrier." Without further conversation, we soon walk to Evan's suite, where I say goodbye to Christian as Evan answers the door.

"Hello, Cassandra. Please come in. You look refreshed. Are you holding up ok?"

"I'm feeling better after a hot shower and a little time, but I'm still shaken. Have you heard how Leon is doing? Christian didn't seem to know anything."

Pulling me into a hug, Evan says, "Not yet, but I'm sure he is in good hands at the hospital."

"I'm sure you're right, but it seemed like he was under water for a long time."

In a reassuring, matter-of-fact tone, Evan says, "I don't think he was under water that long and head cuts bleed a lot, so I am sure he will be fine. However, I doubt we will get an update until morning, so we will have to wait patiently until then."

With his arm around my shoulders, we walk to the sofa, as I explain, "I know, but today's events created a lot of uncertainty in the competition and dredged up bad memories of another accident. I'm trying not to freak out."

"Well, I ordered some snacks, and we can sip some wine and relax. How does that sound?"

"Perfect. Maybe you can tell me a little more about where you are from. I may want to add it to my list of places to visit."

Evan turns on some music and opens a bottle of wine. After he hands me a glass, he joins me on the sofa in front of floor-to-ceiling windows overlooking the Strip, and we talk about his homeland. Evan explains, "We have beautiful, soft, white sand beaches with warm, crystal-clear, turquoise water. A few beach resorts are popular tourist destinations, but we have private coves that are my favorite hide-aways. Some are only accessible by boat."

Resting an elbow on the back of the sofa, I turn toward Evan and say, "You make the beaches sound perfect. I love to curl my toes into warm sand. What does the rest of the island look like?"

"We have lush green rolling hills surrounding the towns and villages, which are filled with Mediterranean-style buildings and homes. It is quite beautiful. You would also probably love our food, which is best described as a unique blend of Italian and French coastal cuisine."

After hearing his description, I say, "Ok. I'm sold. I'm adding it to my list, but I just realized I don't think you told me the name of the island."

As Evan starts to answer, his phone rings. He has a brief conversation, and after concluding it, he returns to the sofa and puts his arm around my shoulder, pulling me close. "Sorry about that. My brother had a quick question for me."

I snuggle against his warm chest comforted from the craziness of the day. But I need to be careful because it's not only comfort I'm feeling. And while it's hard for me to let someone get emotionally close after losing my parents, I've also never been one for a casual hookup. Given that Evan and I aren't even from the same country, that's all this could be. Regardless of what my head is warning, there is an electricity flowing between us that I've never felt with anyone else. Just then, he bends his head and starts nibbling on my earlobe and peppering warm kisses along the side of my neck. This man is going to drive me wild.

Not wanting to lead him on, I need to move away, but before I do, he takes my wine glass and sets it on the coffee table in front of us. Then he places both hands on my face and pulls me toward him. Our lips collide as if there's a magnetic force pulling us together. Soon our tongues are exploring with fervor. I know there was a reason I thought I should put a stop to this, but I can't remember what it was.

My right hand starts caressing the taut peaks and valleys of his chest as his left hand makes its way down my arm and across my body. That's when I realize my thin shirt and lace bra are doing little to hide my excitement. Evan notices too and rolls my nipple between his fingers as I moan with pleasure. Then he reaches down and massages the bare skin of my inner thigh as our lips stay locked and move in unison.

Evan's hand moves up my leg and rests where my thigh joins the rest of my body. He pulls his lips away and looks into my eyes as though asking permission to take the next step. But that brief break brings me back to my senses.

Catching my breath, I say, "Evan, you are amazing and I like you a lot , but this is moving too fast for me. This may be Vegas, but I'm not a one-night-stand type of person—not even a two-night-stand person. I'm sorry if I gave you the wrong impression."

Evan takes a deep breath. "You didn't give that impression, but it doesn't mean I don't want you. We can slow things down if you prefer. Let's take some food out onto the balcony and enjoy the fresh air."

"Evan, I probably should leave. I don't want to lead you on, nor do I want to make choices I will regret tomorrow."

"Please don't leave. Let's keep each other company and talk like we planned." Smiling, Evan continues, "I promise to be a gentleman even if I would prefer not to be. I will walk you back to your room at the end of the evening. Deal?"

Relief washes over me that Evan is showing respect for my boundaries and still wants to spend time with me. I don't want to be alone right now and trusting Evan's word, I say, "Deal. Thanks for understanding."

Evan leans forward and kisses my forehead. Then he declares, "Let's go. I am starving."

Like toggling a light switch, Evan's open lust for me morphs into a genuine and immediate desire for food. I appreciate his understanding, but I know I've put off a tough decision because the electricity and sexual tension between us will likely resurface soon.

CHAPTER NINETEEN

SEAN

I look up from my desk to see a flustered Emily closing my office door. That's strange. Emily is always composed and never closes my door, I think before asking, "Emily, what's wrong?"

"Mr. umm Sean, I just got a call from the front desk. There is a police detective there who insists that he must talk with you immediately about Mr. Boucher's death. He says he will not take no for an answer. It is urgent. I didn't even know Mr. Boucher died!"

"Emily, take a deep breath. Then tell me, did the front desk check the detective's ID?"

Taking my advice, Emily lets out a deep breath. "Yes, they gave me the information from his ID, and I wrote it down. His name is Geoff Fielder, with a G for Geoff. He is with the Las Vegas Police Department's homicide division."

"Ok. First, call security and have them send up two officers to stand guard at my door just in case this Detective Fielder isn't who he says he is. Remember the guy who showed up with forged credentials from Scotland Yard last year and insisted he had to inspect our vault?"

"Who could forget him? He was dressed up like Sherlock Holmes!"

"Not all imposters are easily identifiable as fakes, so we can't be too careful. After you speak with security, go downstairs and check his ID yourself. If it checks out, then bring him to my office, so I can find out what is going on."

"Yes, sir."

After Emily leaves, I call the Police Chief to check up on this Geoff Fielder. You can't be too careful in my position. Hearing his voice, I say, "Larry, this is Sean Cartwright at the Athena. How are you doing today?"

"Sean, I'm doing fine. Do you need our help today?"

"You tell me."

"What do you mean?"

"Well, there is a Geoff Fielder downstairs who claims to be from your homicide division. Do you have a Detective Fielder on your force?"

"Yes, he is one of our fastest rising stars. But I don't know why he is at your place today. I thought they already finished their interviews related to the Chef Bernard incident."

"Apparently, he is insisting on meeting with me about an accident that took place here yesterday. One of the chefs in our Guest Chef Competition choked on some food, fell backward into the pool, and hit his head. Unfortunately, I learned late yesterday that he didn't survive the head injury, but why would that lead to a visit from homicide? Lots of people witnessed the accident. It was even videotaped as part of the competition."

"Well, that type of accident doesn't usually make it to my desk. My best guess is the coroner found something out of the ordinary during the autopsy."

"Hmm. I sent my assistant down to double check his ID and bring him up. I just wanted to make sure he was legit. We get a lot of crazy people pretending to have various reasons for getting access to my office. The last one was dressed in full regalia, entourage in tow, claiming he was the Pope here to bless me."

"Don't I know you get the crazy ones?! Well, Geoff is about 38 and around 5-foot-10 with short, medium brown hair. He also speaks with a slight Southern accent from his days in Louisiana."

"Thanks Larry. And know, we will cooperate with your department if there are any issues."

"Thanks, Sean. We know we can count on you. Hopefully, this is a simple follow-up to tie up some loose ends."

As I hang up, I hear three firm knocks on my door. "Come in."

"Mr. Cartwright, the security office said you needed protection this morning."

I motion for the security officers to enter. "Yes, we have someone claiming to be a police detective on the way up. Given the abundance of fake IDs, I am being cautious and upping my security, but I have reason to believe this person is legit. However, please remain by my door while he is here. If you hear anything out of the ordinary, don't knock. Just walk in."

"Yes, sir."

A lighter knock on my door signifies that Emily is back. "Enter."

"Mr. Cartwright, Detective Fielder is here to see you. Everything appears to be in order."

"Thank you, Emily." Standing, I greet the detective and direct him to a guest chair. "Detective Fielder, what brings you here?"

"I assume you know that a Mr. Leon Boucher died here yesterday."

"Not exactly. My understanding is that he died at the hospital, not at the Athena."

"Were you present at the event with Mr. Boucher?"

"No, I did not attend the event. When I was notified that an ambulance had been called in conjunction with the competition, I went to the pool. At that point, emergency personnel were loading Mr. Boucher onto a gurney and taking him to the hospital."

"What do you know about the incident?"

"My understanding is that Mr. Boucher choked on some food that he had prepared for a poolside demonstration. In his struggle to clear his throat, he tripped and fell into the pool, hitting his head. I was informed that he later died at the trauma center."

"Not exactly. I am told that Mr. Boucher was participating in a competition. Is that correct?"

"What was the cause of death if not the choking or head injury?"

"We will get to that, but first, please answer my question. Was the event part of a competition?"

Leaning forward on my elbows, I raise my voice saying, "I don't appreciate your attitude. We are mourning the loss of Mr. Boucher, and if his death wasn't an accident, I have the right to know what happened. But yes, we are holding a competition to select a guest chef for our Trendz restaurant, and Mr. Boucher was participating in one of the events."

"Mr. Cartwright, this is an ongoing police investigation. We are not required to share our findings with you. My understanding is that this is the second death associated with the competition, correct?"

Pounding my open palm on the desk, I let the detective know that he is not in charge of this meeting, and I will not tolerate disrespect in my own office. How dare he not only twist the facts but also act like I have no right to know what happened to Mr. Boucher? My temper rises as I exclaim, "I will be speaking with Larry about your complete disrespect shown in the wake of a death here. And you are incorrect. There has been no other death during the competition. If are insinuating that the death of my friend Allison Bernard is related to the competition, you are way off base. She died in a tragic car accident. It is true that she was scheduled to be a judge in the competition, but as far as I know, her death had nothing to do with the competition."

Bristling, Detective Fielder counters, "First, feel free to contact the Chief. I am just doing my job. As for Ms. Bernard's death, we have not closed that investigation. In fact, we understand that her accident was caused by a combination of alcohol and opioids that she apparently consumed at a press conference here at the Athena."

"Mr. Fielder, I don't see why you think that is related to the competition. However, we have been, and will continue to, cooperate with the investigation to the extent we have any information. Now, why is it you think Mr. Boucher died from a cause other than the head injury he sustained when he fell?"

"It's Detective Fielder. The autopsy revealed a different cause of death. We now need to determine whether it was an accident or murder."

Taken aback at the direction this conversation is going, I question, "Murder? You've got to be kidding. If we are going to help you with your investigation, you need to tell me what happened."

"Can I trust you to keep what I share with you confidential?"

"Of course."

"Mr. Boucher was highly allergic to sesame seeds. According to the autopsy, he consumed hummus during the demonstration."

Squinting in confusion, I ask, "What does that have to do with being allergic to sesame seeds?"

"One of the main ingredients in hummus is tahini. Tahini is sesame seed paste."

"Sounds like a horribly unfortunate accident," I say, relaxing slightly.

Detective Fielder shakes his head. "We have reason to suspect otherwise. Mr. Boucher wore a medical-alert dog tag indicating his allergy, so he knew to be very careful. Further, he was a chef, so he would have known that hummus contains a form of sesame seeds."

Leaning back in my chair, I steeple my hands under my chin. "I see. What do you need from us?"

"We would like to find the containers from the demonstration yesterday. We would also like to interview everyone who was around when the food was prepared and those who were at the demo."

"Understood. We are scheduled to have a meeting with most of those people this afternoon to give them an update on the plans for the competition. Why don't you join me there?"

"I will. In the meantime, we need access to the leftovers from the demonstration and any videotapes you have."

"The videotapes are easy. However, I can't promise that the food from yesterday is still around. We had no reason to suspect any issues, so it was likely cleaned up and discarded. Cynthia Andino is our F&B manager. She can show you around. Then we can arrange a meeting with the head of our security so you can see the videos. However, you may also want to meet with Amy. She is running and hosting the competition. They filmed the prep session and poolside cooking demonstration, so the camera crew should have quite a bit of video."

"Thank you."

"My assistant Emily will set it all up." I quickly pick up the phone and give Emily the instructions. Then, I continue, "Now, about the interviews, first, I will be sitting in on them."

"That would be highly irregular."

"I don't care. This is my hotel, and I want to get to the bottom of this quickly. These people are much more likely to cooperate if I ask them to, and I also will be able to provide background information on some of them."

"Well, maybe that isn't a bad idea."

"Second, my best friend is here and has been attending all the events to cover for me when I cannot participate. He will likely have some helpful information and observations as well. Therefore, I would suggest when you are ready to interview people, you talk with him."

"I have no problem with that."

There is a knock on the door. "Come in."

"Mr. Cartwright, I have everything arranged. Should I escort Detective Fielder to the prep kitchen in Trendz now? Cynthia will meet us there."

"Yes, please. Then see that he gets to the security office in time to watch the videos before we meet with the competition group this afternoon."

"Of course, Mr. Cartwright."

CHAPTER TWENTY

SEAN

Pacing back and forth across my office, I digest the news and decide to call Evan. He picks up after a couple of rings, and I blurt out, "Evan, we need to talk. Leon Boucher died yesterday."

"That is terrible news."

I rub my chin and sigh. "It gets worse. They think he was murdered."

"You must be kidding," Evan says with astonishment.

I wish I were kidding, but this is real and whether I like it or not two people connected with the chef competition are now dead. "Can you come by my office now?"

"Sure. See you in 15 minutes."

"Thanks."

Pocketing my cell phone, I keep pacing. F&B expenses have been skyrocketing despite my recent efforts to determine the reason, and the spending limits I put in place this month are only stop gap, protective measures. This competition was supposed to be a great marketing event to bring positive attention to Athena's outstanding culinary options. Instead, we lost Chef Bernard before the contest even started. Now we have lost a well-known European chef to sesame seeds of all things! These catastrophes seem unrelated, but I am starting to wonder if they are more than coincidences. My father always said follow the money. Is it possible that both deaths are related to the rising food and wine costs?

Evan walks in and, without preamble, asks, "So what killed him?"

"Hummus."

Eyebrows raised and head shaking in incredulity, Evan asks, "Hummus? How do you die from hummus?"

Thankful for a gigantic office that allows room to pace, I continue with slow strides, hands in pockets, as I explain, "Apparently, he was allergic to sesame seeds. Hummus contains tahini, which is made from sesame seeds."

As the situation sinks in, Evan leans against the front of my desk, ankles crossed. With a shake of his head, he says, "Wow. That is unfortunate."

"What do you remember from the prep and demonstration?" I ask as I turn to face Evan.

Evan stares at the ceiling in thought. "Well, Leon was making a white bean dip. I remember thinking it looked like hummus. Other than that, I don't remember many details."

"Did anyone assist him in prepping the food?"

With hesitation, Evan replies, "Definitely not. Cassandra asked if she could pitch in and help the finalists, but Amy said that was forbidden."

"So, Cassie didn't go near the food the finalists were preparing?"

Evan squints in confusion. "No, that's what I just explained. She stood by and watched."

"Did she have any opportunity to switch out his prepared bean dip for hummus?" I ask as I lower myself into one of the guest chairs in front of Evan.

As if offended, he stares down at me and says, "I don't think so. Don't tell me you think she killed him."

"She had the best motive of all."

"That is absolutely ludicrous," he argues protectively. "She was not anywhere near him. The other finalists were in much closer proximity both when the food was prepped and at the demonstration."

"Calm down. I'm just stating the facts. The police are going to watch the security videos and the video footage from the pool in 30 minutes. Let's join them and see for ourselves."

Evan responds with a clipped, "Fine."

"There's another problem. They want to interview you."

He waves his hand, indicating I've misjudged the situation. "Why is that a problem? Besides, I didn't see anything."

"Your true identity is going to come out. Even if you give them your alias, they will figure out who you are."

"You know very well that it is not an alias. It is just a shortened version of my real name that I use when I want to travel under the radar, which is usually fairly easy in the States. After all, not many people pay much attention to our small island nation. I don't even think the press noticed me at the opening reception."

He's right. People in the U.S. don't typically recognize him on the street, which is why he wanted to spend some time here. Unfortunately, that anonymity is threatened by the fact Leon died under suspicious circumstances. "You have done a good job staying out of the U.S. press. However, now that the police are conducting a murder investigation, they will check everyone's background. In my opinion, you would be wise to tell them who you really are if you want any hope of them being discreet."

Turning to sit in the guest chair next to me, Evan doesn't look happy as he responds, "Shit. Can we trust them to keep my identity secret?"

I glance at him. "Maybe. If it were the Chief of Police, it would be no problem. However, the detective they assigned to the case is a new guy out to prove his worth. Based on my meeting with him, he is rather arrogant and likes to throw around his power, at least verbally."

"So much for some quiet time away," he says with a shake of his head. "My family will not be happy if the press ties me to a murder investigation. At a minimum, let's see if we can keep my name out of police reports that are available to the press."

"I'll see what I can do. We can talk with him privately before the interviews. I already told him that I plan to be present when he interviews everyone." I walk toward my office door and grab my suit jacket from the hook, as I say, "Evan, I feel terrible about getting you into this mess, but let's go meet Detective Fielder in the security office to watch the videos.

CHAPTER TWENTY-ONE

SEAN

Each time I enter the back of the small auditorium that serves as Athena's security central, it strikes me that we have created an ultra-modern, steroid-enhanced version of NASA's control room. Lights are low for easy viewing of the curved floor-to-ceiling displays covering the front wall. Those displays provide eyes on the entire Athena hotel, casino, and grounds. Terraced rows of charcoal-gray tables line the room in front of the wall displays, each containing numerous computer workstations that are operated by black-suited security agents. Supervisors roam the area via the middle and side aisles of stairs leading from the back of the room down to the front displays. Their footsteps are suppressed by the thick, black carpet, so with everyone focused on their work, the quiet of the room is only broken by necessary whispers and keystrokes.

Panning the room, I locate Detective Fielder and gesture to show Evan where we are headed. Reaching the bank of workstations, I whisper, "Detective Fielder, I see you found our security headquarters."

Respecting the room's quiet, he whispers, "Yes, sir. They are setting up the videos for me to review. They have collected the security tapes and the footage shot by the camera crew for the competition."

"Great. Let me introduce my best friend from college, Evan Catalinius. He has been kind enough to attend the competition events on my behalf when I was tied up with other duties."

"Good afternoon Mr. Catalinius. I will want to talk with you about the events that led up to Mr. Boucher's death. However, it is not appropriate for you to be here now."

"Detective Fielder, Evan is staying. This is my hotel and casino. I say who is allowed where and when. Those are my terms if you want to see the videos now. Otherwise, leave and don't come back without a court order. We are all trying to figure out what happened, and I want the people I trust here, particularly when he was at the events in question. Because he was present, he may notice things that seem out of place whereas you and I would discount them as unimportant."

Gritting his teeth, but acquiescing, Detective Fielder says, "Fine. Play the videos of the food prep session. I want to see anything that shows Mr. Boucher, the food he was prepping, or anyone who came near it."

Standing shoulder to shoulder, eyes glued to the monitors, we watch as the videos play, but we don't see anyone come near Leon's station while he is prepping his food. He leaves it a couple of times to get equipment and ingredients, but we don't see anything unusual. As the video continues, we see Leon filling a serving bowl with his finished dip as well as bowls with ingredients to demo his dip at the pool.

Detective Fielder taps the security agent on the shoulder, indicating he should stop the video. The detective asks him to rewind and replay the part where Leon is placing his containers on a rolling cart. But everything looks normal to me. Then Leon rolls the cart into the walk-in refrigerator.

Rubbing my tired eyes, which are dry from staring so intently at the monitors, I say, "Please stop the video. Detective, did you see anything amiss?"

"No. I wanted to see what containers he used, so we can verify the same containers show up in the poolside video."

"I see. Please restart the video." Looking for any small thing out of place, we see that soon after Leon exits the refrigerator, the other three finalists, one by one, wheel their carts into the refrigerator. Hmm. Were any of the other finalists in the fridge long enough to tamper with his food? I don't think so, but it wouldn't take long to make a switch if someone planned ahead.

"Detective Fielder, are they sure he consumed hummus or was tahini added to his pre-prepared bean dip?"

"Good question. I will ask the coroner to clarify that point. We need to know whether someone altered his food soon after he prepared it or substituted a new bowl of dip at the pool. That information will tell us when the tampering took place and who had the opportunity to do it. It certainly doesn't look like he accidentally put any tahini in the dip while he was preparing it."

"No, Detective, it doesn't. But we should check the poolside videos as well."

"Yes, I would like to see those next. But first, how do I find out who had access to the walk-in refrigerator between the time of the prep and the poolside demonstration?"

My feet are already tired from standing in one place for so long, so I try to shift my weight without drawing attention. After all, I am supposed to be the monument of strength and endurance at the Athena, as my father was. But even though we are watching uneventful portions of the video at double speed, this is taking longer than I had hoped. I assumed with all our cameras, our security team would have already identified the culprit before I arrived, but I was wrong.

Knowing we need to continue, I say, "We can watch all the videos of the kitchen. We can also check with Cynthia to see who was working the event and who brought the carts to the pool. Then there is also the video of the poolside demonstrations. Unfortunately, there would have been a few opportunities for someone to add an ingredient or make a substitution, but I assume they would have been caught on video."

"I agree, Mr. Cartwright. It is unfortunate that the scene was not secured after Mr. Boucher consumed the dip."

Annoyed at the Detective's insinuation that the Athena's procedure was improper, I bark, "Detective, you know very well we had no way of knowing this was anything other than an accidental fall. And we did immediately station security officers at the location of the accident. I'm also told you retrieved some of the unwashed dishes from the Trendz kitchen."

"We did," Detective Fielder says, backing off, "but anyone you recognize who comes near Mr. Boucher's food. Also, please make sure to look for anyone who appears out of place or unexpected."

"We will." The video starts playing. Then catching something unexpected, I scrunch my eyes and command, "Stop the video and go back about 15 seconds. Can we watch it in slow motion?"

As the video replays, Evan asks, "Sean, what did you notice?"

"It's strange; the guy who walked by the table is one of my friends. He used to be one of our biggest food suppliers, but during my recent review, I noticed we haven't been using his company anymore. What would he be doing at the pool?"

"Mr. Cartwright, what is his name?" Detective Fielder asks.

"Wes."

"Why did you stop using him as a supplier?"

"I don't know. I have been trying to get to the bottom of some recent changes, but our head chef, who oversaw the suppliers, no longer works here. He made the changes. I'm trying to collect more info before reaching out to him to fill in some gaps."

"Would a disgruntled supplier want to sabotage your event?"

"I can't imagine that. I've known him for years. Besides, how would he know about Leon's food allergy?"

"Good point, but it is still strange that he was there. We will want to talk with him. Who knew about the food allergy?"

"I'm not sure. My understanding is that anyone involved in the competition who may be tasting food was asked to submit a list of allergies. Then the finalists were told they could not under any circumstances cook with those items during the competition."

"So, everyone was told who was allergic to which items?"

"I doubt that. While many people choose to openly share their allergies, others only share on a need-to-know basis. Therefore, out of respect for privacy, we treat allergies provided on questionnaires as health-related information, and the law requires us to protect health info as confidential. Because of this policy, I would expect that the list of allergies was provided without matching them to specific individuals, but we can check with Cynthia. She would have overseen that aspect of the competition."

"Ok. Can we see a wider-angle view so you can point out the other people you recognize?"

"Sure. As you can see, each finalist has his own table. Amy is the one in the blue top and white shorts. She is overseeing the competition and is the on-camera host. Cynthia is the one in the suit with the clipboard. She is our F&B manager. Evan is standing near Cassie, who is the alternate. If the competition proceeds, she will replace Leon."

"I see. So, Cassie had the most to gain by Leon's demise."

"Maybe. Maybe not. She is a home-trained chef. All the other finalists are professional chefs. So even if she competes, we don't know how well she will stand up against the pros. That means the other chefs may have had more to gain by getting rid of a well-respected competitor, such as Leon."

"Interesting. Why did you include a home-trained chef in such a high-end competition?"

"Optics mostly. The goal of the competition was to get widespread attention, so we invited everyone, including home cooks, to apply. We liked the idea that we were giving everyone a chance to chase their dream. That's what Las Vegas is about. Everyone has a chance to change their life here. In this case, one home cook made it to the top 5, which was a little surprising and is quite an accomplishment. Even though she didn't make it into the final 4, we are including her in some of the interviews and events, which is good press for us and gives her some publicity as well."

"Got it. So, she was the token 'real person.' But as an alternate, you didn't risk her actually winning, right?"

"That is harsh and was not the intent. I left the selection of the finalists and alternate to Cynthia, Amy, and Sebastian, who is the director and producer. You can ask them how they selected these individuals. I played no part in the actual selection process."

"Mr. Catalinius, were you involved in selecting the competitors?"

"No. I wasn't even aware of the competition until I arrived for an extended vacation and to visit Sean. When I arrived, Sean asked if I would attend a few events in his place. It sounded like fun, and I looked forward to sampling the food created by these top chefs."

"You seemed rather cozy with the alternate in that video."

"Not really. Given that she is not actually competing, we have found ourselves watching the events together. So, we have chatted a couple of times."

"Detective, it is almost time to meet with the finalists and others involved in the competition to inform them of Chef Boucher's death and give them an update on the plans for the competition. I still can't fathom that any of the finalists would kill someone just to be the guest chef at one of our restaurants for a month. But if you want to interview them, they will all be assembled in a few minutes.

"Mr. Cartwright, we all know people have killed for much less, so yes, I want to interview them. I also want to interview the alternate."

CHAPTER TWENTY-TWO

CASSIE

When I arrive at the back of the Zeus ballroom, it's set up with a podium at the front and rows of chairs facing forward. It reminds me of generic setups for conference presentations, but we all know that isn't why we're here. Cynthia and Amy stand near the front with their heads tilted toward each other and hands shielding their mouths, not wanting others to eavesdrop.

Scanning the rest of the assembled crowd, my eyes find frowning faces and wrinkled brows, and I overhear opinions as to the likely fate of the competition and whether Leon will return. Even the crew is conjecturing as to whether the competition will be cancelled, which would cut their filming assignment short. The uncertainty makes the tension in the room palpable.

I find the finalists collected in a corner and join their conversation. The stress has put them in a talkative mood. Their concerns are deeper than those of the staff and crew because the finalists have a lot more riding on the competition. As each one shares their situation, I listen with empathy. Trenton explains he needs to move west because his ex-wife moved his young children to California. If he can't find a new job, he will seldom see his kids. Jayden lets it slip that he lost his job in Dallas due to creative differences with the restaurant's owners.

Maybe the owners weren't impressed with gravy as a dip, but I keep my thoughts to myself. Then Kai laments he is tired of being pigeon-holed and wants a venue that will allow him greater freedom to fuse his French and island cuisines and thinks Las Vegas is the perfect place. They also share that Leon mentioned wanting to move to the U.S. permanently, but he has to find a job here before he can get a visa. Plus, they are all counting on the publicity from the televised competition and possible future shows on the FFT channel to boost their careers.

When almost everyone has arrived, Cynthia tells us to take a seat. There are no empty chairs next to the finalists, so I look for one else-where. Finding an empty spot next to some of the camera crew, I take a seat and ask my new neighbors whether they have heard any news. They haven't. I share that I don't have any news either. Then we spec-ulate as to whether management will delay the competition until Leon can return.

Behind me, someone is muttering that this competition is jinxed and is being cancelled. I hope not. I'm not ready to go home, much less go back to work. Aside from Leon's accident, this has been the beginning of a wonderful adventure and a welcome break from Jackson and his fake deadlines. I've watched talented chefs create interesting dishes. I've had a glimpse of a behind-the-scenes, profes-sional cooking competition. And I pinch myself as I realize I want more time with Evan, even if it can't be anything serious.

Having run out of small talk, I shift nervously in my seat as my brain runs at full speed. Will the competition continue? Is Leon out for the duration? Am I going to compete in Leon's place? Will they move forward with the other three finalists given that one event already has been completed? It was just a demo though, so it may not count. Do I even want to compete given the circumstances? Is this competition truly jinxed?

My blood pressure is rising with each passing minute. Then the room goes quiet. I turn to see Sean and Evan, wearing suits fit for a New York runway, and another man in a noticeably less expensive blue suit walking into the room. Sean signals for Cynthia and Amy to remain at the back, which seems strange, given that they have always stood alongside Sean at prior events.

As the men walk toward the podium, I expect Evan to look for me. Instead, as he glances around, he doesn't stop to smile or even acknowledge me. That's weird. Maybe he's being professional, or maybe he's upset I didn't let things go further last night. Now that I think about it, Evan was a little distant after I slowed things down last night. At the time, I thought he was being respectful, but now I wonder if it isn't something more.

Heads slowly follow the men's long trek across the room, and as we wait for someone to say something, it becomes eerily quiet. A coldness runs through me as I have a premonition that bad news is coming. Then, in his deep, authoritative voice Sean says, "First, thank you for your patience as we waited for more information about Mr. Boucher's condition. It is with great sadness that I must report that he did not make it. I am certain you are all just as upset about Leon's death as I am. Therefore, out of respect for Mr. Boucher, we are going to wait another day to determine how to proceed with the competition. I would like to thank you for your patience as we work through this difficult situation and determine the best plan moving forward. In addition, the police are required to investigate incidents such as this, so they want an opportunity to talk with everyone to understand how Mr. Boucher fell into the pool."

In a cacophony of voices, questions are hurled at Mr. Cartwright. He simply holds up one hand and says, "Please hold your questions for now. Let me first introduce Detective Fielder. He can explain more. Detective, please take the mic."

"Hello, everyone. My name is Detective Fielder. I am handling the investigation of the death of Leon Boucher. We want to understand the events that led up to Mr. Boucher's choking and falling into the pool. Therefore, we would like to have short chats with everyone to determine what you noticed. This is standard procedure. I would like to thank you all in advance for your cooperation. We don't expect to take much of anyone's time and hope to have this case closed quickly."

Murmuring fills the room. Some seem appalled they are expected to talk with the police, while others seem outright scared. Maybe they have watched too many police interrogations on television. My reaction is different though. Detective Fielder's comments don't make sense to me. Something is off. Standard procedure? No way. Determine the events that led to choking? Is the detective kidding? Leon put a large, dip-covered chip in his mouth, and it blocked his airway. What needs to be investigated? People choke all the time. Fortunately, they don't do it near a concrete column in a swimming pool, but there's nothing mysterious or sinister about choking and hitting your head when you fall.

The detective regains everyone's attention, saying, "Please let us do our investigation. Since everyone is already assembled, we will proceed with the interviews. Mr. Cartwright, where will we be doing the interviews?"

"We will divide the interviews between the conference room next door and an office so interviews can proceed in parallel. Also, just so everyone knows, no one is being singled out. My best friend gets to go first. Even he must talk with the detective."

Nervous laughter cuts a little of the tension in the room as Sean continues, "Emily or another staff member will direct you to the right place when it's your turn. In the meantime, I will have snacks and drinks sent in to keep you from starving. Thank you for your help."

CHAPTER TWENTY-THREE

SEAN

irecting the detective toward the conference room exit, I say, "Detective, let's head to my office. We can conduct the interviews of the key people there. I assume you have officers who can interview the crew in the conference room next door."

"Isn't there somewhere closer than your office that would work?"

"Not that would work for me. In addition, my office gives us greater privacy, which I prefer. We can take a shortcut through the Maze."

"What's the Maze?"

"It's our underground tunnel system for quickly getting around this place."

"Convenient."

We use the nearest Maze entrance and are in my office within 10 minutes. I note that Emily has already read my mind and added an extra guest chair beside my usual two to accommodate the interviewees. She's the best assistant I have ever had. After motioning for Evan and Detective Fielder to have a seat in front of my desk, I sink into my plush, high-back leather desk chair, which will be much more palatable than sitting on a conference room chair for the rest of the afternoon.

Not wanting to waste time, I say, "Detective, I assume you are ready to interview Evan, but before you start, we wish to share some additional information with you. You undoubtedly will figure it out anyway, but we would rather be up front with you to avoid you thinking there were nefarious reasons for keeping something from you." Gesturing toward Evan with an extended hand, I explain, "When you met Evan earlier, he was introduced as Evan Catalinius, which is technically accurate. However, he is more formally known as Garret Evan Louis Francesco, Prince of Catalinius."

Doing a double take, Detective Fielder asks, "Did you say prince?"

With a cross between amusement and mild annoyance, Evan interjects, "He did. But Sean's introductions usually also include that I am merely the spare prince. For short, when the press is being kind, they usually refer to me as Prince Garret. However, I am trying to take some private time away from my public life, so I would greatly appreciate it if you keep my name and my title out of the press. That is why I am traveling under one of my middle names, Evan."

"I understand. As long as it doesn't impact the investigation, I will honor your request for now. How do I address you? Is it Your Highness?"

"If we were going with titles, it would technically be Your Royal Highness. However, for now, please call me Evan or Mr. Catalinius."

"Ok. My apologies, but I don't think I know where Catalinius is."

"That is why I usually can fly under the radar in the States. Not many people are familiar with Catalinius. It is a small island country off the coast of Italy and France."

"I assume you are exercising diplomatic immunity in this matter. Is that correct?"

"Detective, I have no need for any sort of immunity. I had nothing to do with this incident, and I am happy to share with you anything I saw in case it is helpful. Sean is my best friend, and I want this cleared up for him as soon as possible. I just want my name kept out of your reports and the press. I do not want to embarrass my parents, who are the king and queen, or my country by having our name connected with a murder investigation in Las Vegas."

"So, where are your bodyguards?" the detective asks with raised eyebrows.

Evan's jaw clenches. "I didn't bring any. As the spare heir, I don't typically face many threats, particularly not in the U.S. Besides, Sean has great security here. Now, let's get on with this. What questions do you have for me?"

Detective Fielder, opens his pocket-sized, spiral notepad and asks, "Who had access to the food Mr. Boucher ate during the demonstration?"

"That is hard to say. I guess anyone with access to Trendz could have gone into the kitchen after everyone left. There were also a number of people at the pool, including staff, crew, other finalists, and hotel guests, who could have had access," Evan says, looking markedly more relaxed now that the real questions are underway.

"Who had the most to gain by his death?"

"I didn't know the man, so I do not have any way of knowing if he had enemies. I would assume the other finalists would have seen him as a threat though."

"What about the alternate? What is her name?"

"Her name is Cassandra Edwards. Some people refer to her as Cassie."

Detective Fielder inquires, "Wouldn't she have even more to gain than the other finalists?"

"Detective, I highly doubt Cassandra had anything to do with this. She stood on the sidelines. I don't think she went near the food."

"Mr. Catalinius, the perpetrator is usually the person who has most to gain. Wouldn't that be the alternate because she doesn't have a chance at the prize unless someone is knocked out of the competition? Given those facts, why are you so certain she wasn't involved?"

"I have spent some time chatting with her and getting to know her while we watched the filming. She seems to be a respectable woman," Evan says in a clipped tone, his protectiveness showing itself again.

"Did you see any suspicious activity at any point during the preparation of the food or at the pool during the demonstrations?"

"No. But I wasn't looking for anything. This was supposed to be a fun event."

"If you were here to get away from everything for a while, why were you attending the competition events where you risked being recognized?"

"Sean asked for me to attend some events to allow him time to deal with a pressing matter. My assumption was that I could stay in the background without much risk of being identified. However, being identified as a witness who was interviewed as part of a murder investigation is more of a problem for me."

Detective Fielder jots notes before saying, "Mr. Catalinius, thank you for your cooperation. Do you plan to remain in Las Vegas?"

"I haven't decided yet. I was planning to stay at least another two weeks. Maybe a month."

"If that plan changes, please let me know in case I have any more questions for you. And, if you remember anything else, please let me know. I have left my contact information with Mr. Cartwright's assistant."

"I will."

Turning toward me, Detective Fielder says, "Mr. Cartwright, I have a quick question for you before we move to the next interview. What was the pressing matter that required your attention?"

"Detective, I don't want to go into the details of unrelated hotel and casino business."

"Mr. Cartwright, let me be the judge of whether it is unrelated. What was the pressing matter?" he says more firmly.

"We have had some issues with unexplained increases in food and beverage costs over the last few months. I am trying to track down why. I was also hoping Evan might see something that would help explain the situation while he was casually hanging around the competition."

Turning back to Evan, Detective Fielder inquires, "Mr. Catalinius, did you see anything that explains this issue?"

"Not yet. The competition had barely started when Mr. Boucher died."

"Thank you. Let's bring Ms. Edwards in next. Mr. Cartwright, can you have her brought up?"

"Yes." Putting the phone on speaker, Sean asks, "Emily can you bring up Cassie Edwards?"

"Of course, Mr. Cartwright."

"Emily, please bring her through the Maze," Evan instructs.

"Mr. Cartwright will need to approve that option."

"Sean, show her some respect," Evan implores. "There is no need to parade her through the main areas when we know how upset she was yesterday. After the news of Leon's death, she is bound to be even more distraught. Besides, a distraught woman walking through the Athena is not good for business." Detective Fielder's face jerks up from his notepad when he hears the request, but he remains silent and goes back to making notes.

"I'm not sure she will be that distraught, but fine. Emily, please bring Cassie up via the Maze. Do the same for all the finalists when it's their turn."

Evan looks pissed at my disregard for Cassie's mental state, and to contain his emotions, he is gripping the arms of his chair and gritting his teeth in a scowl. If not for the detective's presence, I think he might be ready to take a swing at me. This is a new look on Evan, and one that has me concerned because I'm leaning in Detective Fielder's direction. If someone did tamper with Chef Boucher's food, Cassie has the most to gain. Evan needs to open his mind and stop thinking with his lower extremity before it is too late.

CHAPTER TWENTY-FOUR

CASSIE

While waiting my turn to be interviewed, I should grab a snack, but I'm too nervous. I can't fathom the police would go to this much trouble to investigate a choking accident. There must be something more to it. I can't figure out what it could be though. How could it have been anything more sinister? Regardless, I didn't have anything to do with Leon's death, but the idea of being interviewed by the police is still intimidating.

I almost jump out of my seat when Emily surprises me from behind with a tap on my shoulder, saying, "Cassie, it's your turn."

While it felt like I was waiting forever, I realize I'm the first person she has come to get. Oh no! What does that mean? Trying to mask my anxiety, I smile and say, "Ok. Where do I go?" Inside, I'm barely holding off a panic attack. It's my nature to worry because in the past good things, such as being selected as the alternate for this competition, have sometimes come at a very high price. I'm still dealing with the fact that one of the best weekends of my college life, law school graduation, was destroyed by the horrifying call that both of my parents had been killed. The hardest part about today is that I sense something is wrong, but I have no idea what it could be, so I don't know how to prepare for the blow I fear is coming.

Emily softly replies, "Just follow me."

I get up, knees weak, and follow her out the door and toward the end of the hall, but it's a dead end. "Emily, where are we going? I thought the interviews were in a nearby conference room."

"Some are, but some are in Sean's office, which is further away. We are going to take the shortcut through the Maze."

"What's the Maze?"

"A series of underground tunnels. You'll see. You just have to know where the hidden entrances are and have the authorization to use them."

"It hadn't occurred to me there are underground tunnels, but that makes sense. It reminds me of the secret passages described in novels about old castles." We walk to the end of the hall, and Emily places her hand against the palm of the man in a large painting. The wall pops inward and we walk through. The hidden door closes almost instantly, and we walk down a staircase to a waiting golf cart. Next thing I know we are out of the golf cart, riding an elevator that opens into Sean's office.

Emily leaves me there, saying, "While many people may know or suspect that the Athena has an underground tunnel system, we do our best to keep the locations of the hidden entrances a secret for security reasons. The nondisclosure agreement you signed prevents you from discussing the Maze even with others involved in the competition."

I nod in acknowledgment, but if the Maze is such a secret, why did they let me see it? Are they bringing everyone up to Sean's office this way? Well, I soon get my answer. Evan walks up to me with an outwardly calm but concerned expression. It looks like his hands are balled into fists inside his pockets. Is that as a reminder not to pull me into an embrace? I hope that's it. In a soft voice, he asks, "Are you ok?"

Whispering back, I say, "I'm not doing great. This whole thing is horrible and confusing. I can't believe Leon is dead, and it makes no sense why they are investigating a choking accident."

"I know. Hang in there. Detective Fielder is going to ask you a few questions." Turning and extending his right arm, Evan gestures to the guest chairs by Sean's desk. "Come have a seat."

I've never seen an office this big or with so many things vying for my attention. If circumstances were different, I would enjoy a closer look at the photos of celebrities on the wall to my left, what looks like a Miró painting behind Sean's desk, and the view provided by the forty or so feet of floor-to-ceiling windows on my right, showcasing the Strip. Even the furniture is unique and modern, and I wonder if the woven tangle of white acrylic and chrome piece across from the sofa by the windows is a table, a chair, or an art sculpture.

Barely having had time to perch on the edge of my seat, which is sandwiched between Evan and Detective Fielder, I'm caught off guard when the detective says, "Your friend Evan insisted they bring you up through the Maze. Am I to assume you two are close?"

Common sense tells me to answer the questions without further reaction, so after taking a deep breath, I respond, "Detective, I met Evan through this competition. Because I am the alternate, I've mostly been standing on the sidelines at the events. Evan has been doing the same, so we have had a few opportunities to chat while we watched. He has been kind to me."

"I see. Just how kind has he been?"

With a tilt of my head and eyes squinted in confusion, I say, "I don't understand your question, and based on your tone, I believe I should be offended."

Coming to the rescue, Evan sits up straight and barks, "Detective, you are way out of line. We understood these interviews to be about Leon Boucher's death, not whether I am nice to someone. It is my practice to treat all people well."

Not backing down, Detective Fielder admonishes, "I am letting you and Mr. Cartwright sit in on these interviews against my better judgment, so either stay quiet or leave."

Holding up his hand to silence the detective, Sean states, "Detective, we are cooperating with you, but we expect you to be respectful to our employees and guests. I agree with Evan, you are out of line here. Either investigate the incident, or you are the one who can leave."

"I am investigating. If your best friend is having an affair with a participant in the competition, then that is highly relevant."

Now I'm mad rather than nervous. My personal life is none of his business. Indignant, I interrupt the debate between Sean, Evan, and the detective, saying, "I am not having an affair with Evan. Now do you have any other questions for me?"

Moving on, Detective Fielder instructs, "Please explain to me what you know about the food Mr. Boucher prepared and tasted at the demonstration."

Scooting back into the chair, I tell him everything I know. He takes notes and then asks, "Did you assist Mr. Boucher in preparing his food?"

"No. I offered to assist anyone who needed help, but Amy, who is the host of the competition, said the finalists were not allowed to receive any help. So, I just stood around and watched."

"Why did you offer to help?"

I shrug. "I felt silly watching everyone work so hard while I did nothing. It made me feel rather useless. Besides, I love to cook, so I always offer to help when in a kitchen."

"So, you didn't like being left out?"

Boy, he likes to twist words. Shaking my head, I clarify, "That's not what I meant. I was willing to pitch in. Nothing more."

"Did you see anyone tamper with any food?"

My body stiffens as I wonder if that is the real reason the detective is here. "No, of course not. Why would someone tamper with the food?"

Detective Fielder stops taking notes and locks eyes with me. "Ms. Edwards, what food was Mr. Boucher allergic to?"

"I had no idea he had any food allergies."

In disbelief, the detective questions, "Really? How can that be? All the participants were told to avoid certain foods because of allergies, correct?"

Nodding, I reply, "That's correct. We were given a list of foods that either contestants, judges, or staff were allergic to. However, we were not told who was allergic to which ones."

The detective drops his gaze to this notepad. "What were those foods?"

Hmm. I know I wrote them down, but I'm not sure I remember all of them. After thinking a minute, I say, "Let's see, I wasn't participating so I didn't try to commit the list to memory, but I seem to remember we were told to avoid bleu cheese, sesame seeds, and peanuts."

Following up, the detective says, "So you're telling me that you didn't know who was allergic to any of those foods, correct?"

"That's not what I said. I said that I didn't know Leon had any of those allergies. I did know at least one person who was allergic to bleu cheese."

Snapping his head up, the detective's interest is peaked. "And how did you know that and not know about Mr. Boucher's allergy."

I hadn't meant to be obtuse, so I clarify. "Simple. I'm allergic to bleu cheese. But I don't know if anyone else is also allergic to it."

Annoyed at my benign explanation, Detective Fielder asks, "Do you know why Mr. Boucher chose to make white bean dip instead of something else?"

"Not really."

"Did you hear him say that white bean dip is a good substitute for people who can't eat hummus?"

"No, I don't recall hearing him say that, but that would be true." Then a light bulb goes off in my head. Pointing a finger at the detective, I exclaim, "Wait a minute. Sesame seeds were on the list of prohibited ingredients, so he wouldn't have been allowed to make hummus in the competition. Maybe that's why he made bean dip instead."

Eyes focused on my face, the detective asks, "Why would not being allowed to use sesame seeds preclude him from making hummus?"

Shrugging, I explain, "Tahini is in hummus. It's made from sesame seeds."

"How do you know that?"

"From my cooking experience. It's commonly known. I would expect all the finalists know it."

"We'll see."

"Leon was the one allergic to sesame seeds, wasn't he?" Now the questions are starting to make more sense. They must think someone sabotaged his dip. Did they replace it with hummus and essentially poison him?

"Who, other than you, would want him out of the competition?"

Me? That's absurd. Did I make myself look like a suspect by knowing that tahini is made from sesame seeds? And to make matters worse, I'm sure I was acting nervous when I arrived, which probably made me look guilty. That's how it is in the movies. The police always suspect anyone who acts nervous. My mind is running at full speed, amping up my nerves again, but I need to defend myself, so I interlace my fingers on my lap to steady my hands and answer, "First, I did not want him out of the competition. Second, he seemed like a nice guy, so I have no reason to think anyone else wanted him out either."

"Come now, you were disappointed to be the alternate rather than a finalist, weren't you?"

"Given that I'm self-trained, it is remarkable that I was selected as the alternate at all. Sure, it would have been great to compete, but I would never knowingly cause harm to anyone. Further, I never touched any of the food involved. If someone did taint his food as you have been implying, it wasn't me."

"Then why did we find your fingerprints on the container of hummus?"

I gasp as I jump to my feet in utter disbelief. "What? That's impossible," I shout. I look toward Evan and almost miss the fleeting look of shock that is instantly replaced by a stoic expression. Sean's face has also turned stone cold. They can't seriously think I did this, can they?

Sinking back into the chair, reality hits that I'm at the top of their suspect list.

CHAPTER TWENTY-FIVE

SEAN

I thought Detective Fielder would never leave. Thank God, he had other police officers interview the bulk of the witnesses in parallel and then give us quick summaries of those interviews before leaving. Otherwise, we would have been here all night.

With drinks in hand, Evan and I are both quiet, staring into space as we think through what we now know about Leon's death. Based on the interviews we participated in and the officers' summaries of the others, the staff, crew, and finalists characterized Leon as calm, friendly, and focused on moving to the States. He wore a medical alert bracelet, so he was aware of his allergy. He prepped his own food, so he had no reason to think it was hummus instead of bean dip, making an accident less likely. While we still don't know for certain if this was an accident or a murder, it is looking more and more like someone helped Leon check out. I turn to look at Evan, thinking the worst part is that the fingerprint evidence indicates his new "friend" Cassie likely killed Leon.

Evan breaks the silence. "Sean, quit looking at me with that 'I told you so' expression. I know you are thinking Cassandra is guilty, but I don't think so. I am not typically that wrong about someone, and her background check was clean. I didn't ask for the details of her life, but my security guys back home said there were no red flags. Not even any yellow caution flags. Besides, she was genuinely upset last night."

Surprised, I say, "Wait a minute. What background check?"

"After we learned Leon was dead, I had Cassandra checked out as a precaution. The report came back squeaky clean."

"You slept with her!"

"No. But even if I had, we wouldn't be discussing it now."

"Why not?"

"We trade stories about casual flings. She's becoming a friend."

"Friend? Right! You aren't getting off that easy, but for now you need to open your eyes to the bigger issue. With one of the chefs out of the competition, she gets to compete for the prize. And her finger-prints were on the bowl of dip that killed Chef Boucher. If they hadn't also found other unidentified fingerprints on that bowl, she would be under arrest now."

"I know, but she could have accidentally touched that bowl even before the dip was put in it. Everyone was walking around the kitchen and watching the chefs set up. Remember, even though she wants to be a chef, she is trained as a lawyer. If she were going to kill Leon on purpose, she is too smart to leave fingerprints on the bowl."

"Maybe she thought she wiped off any fingerprints and missed one."

"I doubt it. I can't help feeling something is very wrong here. I have spent my whole life on alert for people trying to trick me or pull something over on me. I don't get that vibe from Cassandra. I'm never this wrong."

I'm starting to wonder if Evan is glossing over his feelings for Cassie. "Are you really that into her? You usually would walk away from trouble rather than defend it."

Leaning forward, elbows on his knees, Evan says, "You know that I don't do serious. It has been helpful to have someone I enjoy spending time with to distract me a little each day, particularly given that I am sorting through heavier, personal issues right now. I also don't want to see her life ruined, but that is all this is."

I'm not sure I'm buying that Evan's interest in Cassie is merely fleeting, but he's right, I've never seen him do serious. As I walk back to the bar for a refill, I say, "Right. Let's go over the various interviews and see where that leads us. Cynthia seems to think if it wasn't Cassie, it had to be one of the finalists trying to get rid of a key competitor. She argued they are the only ones with anything to gain."

"That is a real possibility. But other than the finalists, the other main player here is the host, Amy. But didn't you think Amy seemed genuinely shaken? I don't think she was faking it, and I am not sure what her motive would have been."

Returning to my chair, I say, "Evan, I agree. Amy seemed upset. Of course, she is used to being on camera and may be a good actor."

"Maybe. Also, I would guess most of these people are not used to being interviewed by a homicide detective, so that probably upset them as well. As for the finalists, I thought all three were either upset, pissed off, or both. In fact, they seemed more focused on whether the competition would continue than the fact that Chef Boucher was dead."

"I noticed that and found it unsettling. They were a somewhat selfish group, but they have a lot to gain if the competition goes forward. That could also mean at least one of them was capable of helping Mr. Boucher out of the competition."

"I must say I was impressed with how professional Cynthia was. She seemed to be holding it together."

"Yes. My father hired her two or three years before he died. She has always had a professional, albeit at times dramatic, approach."

"Sean, I have an idea. Did you consider that maybe the assailant didn't intend to kill Mr. Boucher but rather wanted to make him sick enough to drop out?"

"That's an interesting angle. If that is the case, then the killer could be anyone we interviewed. The killer could have been genuinely upset that Leon actually died rather than just becoming ill. Hopefully, the police will find something in the rest of the video footage. I'm still wondering when the hummus was switched for the bean dip. Did you notice if any of the finalists lingered in the fridge when they took their cart in?"

"No. Too bad there isn't a camera inside the refrigerator. Though, come to think of it, maybe it was an accident after all."

"What do you mean, Evan?"

"Well, what if Leon planned to demonstrate the bean dip is a good substitute for hummus. What if he was planning a taste test to allow people to compare his bean dip with hummus? Perhaps he just accidentally grabbed the wrong container to taste."

"Interesting. I don't remember seeing him prepare hummus on the prep video, though."

"He could have used pre-made hummus and grabbed it from the fridge when he rolled his cart in."

"True. We should check the video of the cart at the pool. But there is another problem. He knew sesame seeds were on the 'do not use' list. Using that ingredient would have disqualified him."

"Maybe he didn't understand it that way. He didn't use the ingredient in his recipe. He would have been using the hummus for comparison."

"You're sounding like a lawyer. Do you think he would take that chance? I still think we would have disqualified him, but it is possible he didn't see it that way."

"So, what is next, Sean?"

"Most importantly, you need to stay away from Cassie."

Grimacing, Evan responds, "That doesn't seem right."

Staring directly at Evan to ensure I have his attention, I emphatically state, "I will not have you endangering yourself while at the Athena by consorting with a murder suspect. If something happens to you, I don't want to call your mother, the queen, to explain."

Turning away, Evan agrees, "I will be careful. I must admit that I do not know what to think about Cassandra right now, but my gut is still telling me that she was not involved."

With a laugh to lighten the mood, I conjecture, "That's probably just your cock talking."

"Ha ha. Don't worry. I said I will be careful, but if Leon's death was not an accident, then his death, Chef Bernard's death, and your increased expenses may be linked together."

"But we don't have any evidence tying them together."

"No real evidence, but there are too many bad things happening to keep writing them off as unrelated. You need to get to the bottom of the unexplained food expenses fast."

Acknowledging that the coincidences are adding up too fast, I respond, "I agree. This situation is incredibly frustrating, and, in the unlikely event the deaths are related, it's a dangerous situation. At least the police are investigating now and will hopefully resolve the two deaths quickly. Police involvement should also dissuade any saboteur or murderer from further action because they are likely to be caught quickly. As for the unexplained F&B increases, tomorrow the finance guys are giving me a detailed summary of invoices for each F&B supplier for the past year. Let's hope that is enough information for me to identify the problem or at least figure out a pattern that would explain the expenses."

My plan sounds ok to me, but I have a nagging feeling it isn't enough. To make matters worse, it hit me that if the deaths are related to the F&B issues, then it's highly unlikely Cassie or one of the finalists are to blame. They weren't selected until well after those problems arose. That would make Evan happy, but it would mean the culprit is an Athena employee or vendor. With that thought in mind, I ask myself, "Other than Evan, whom can I trust?"

CHAPTER TWENTY-SIX

SEAN

I tossed and turned last night with concerns about the F&B issues and deaths looming in my dreams. Finally, giving up on any hope of restful sleep, I showered, dressed, and was in my office by 7 this morning to pore over more financial data. At 9 a.m., I took a break to call Detective Fielder, asking for a meeting to discuss whether or not to cancel the competition. He's on his way to my office now, so I texted Evan to let him know.

Evan doesn't need to be here, but I want his opinion. As royalty, he and his family also balance security concerns and public relations issues regularly, so he will add another, experienced opinion to the mix, which will be useful. Besides, we have a tough decision to make about Cassie, and Evan will kill me if I don't let him weigh in on that issue. While the presence of her fingerprints on the bowl is far from conclusive, it's the only physical evidence and the best lead the police have so far. That makes her the number one suspect, so we must decide whether to allow her to compete in Leon's place. Between the bad publicity if she is arrested and the responsibility to keep everyone safe, it's not an easy decision. While it's not Evan's call, out of respect for our more than decade-long friendship, the least I can do is include him in the discussion.

"Emily, both Evan and Detective Fielder will be here in a few minutes. Can you have some coffee sent in?" I call out to my assistant.

"Yes, sir. Do you also want some fruit or pastries?"

"Some fruit would be great. Also, please figure out when I can get to the gym today and block off an hour." A workout will help me clear my head.

"Will do. Anything else?"

"That's it. Thanks."

Evan and the refreshments have barely arrived when we hear a brief knock on the door, and Emily shows Detective Fielder in.

Evan and I are seated on my leather sofa, so I invite Detective Fielder to sit on the white sculpture-like chair across from us. Lacking patience, I immediately ask, "Detective, have you figured out what happened?" I ask impatiently as soon as he is seated.

He pulls out his ever-present notebook and calmly responds, "Not yet, but we are making progress. However, we need some additional fingerprint samples."

Confused, I respond, "I thought you already had the fingerprint results."

"Not all of them. Ms. Edwards turned up quickly because she was fingerprinted when she became a lawyer. As I mentioned yesterday, we have at least one more set of prints that we haven't been able to identify yet. We would like to take prints from everyone we inter-viewed yesterday to see if we find a match.

"Ok. Emily should be able to help coordinate the process. What else are you doing?"

"We are running checks on everyone and having our video experts analyze all the footage more carefully. It will take some time to get through it. We also wondered if you would be willing to ask your guests to share any video they may have taken during the demonstra-tion at the pool."

"Detective, we can't let the guests think this is an unsafe environ-ment, so the answer is no."

"We had hoped for your cooperation, but we can go around you on this one, if necessary."

"We are cooperating, but there are limits. We will not invade the privacy of our guests and ask to look at their cell phones. You can find another way. As you indicated, you already have more video than you can analyze."

"Mr. Cartwright, I suspect we will be revisiting this topic, but we can leave it for now. What have you decided to do about the competition?"

Needing an infusion of caffeine, I pick up my coffee mug from the table before explaining, "We haven't decided. That's why I asked for this meeting. I would prefer to proceed with the competition, but I want your input about Cassie. Technically, she should be stepping in to compete now. However, if you are about to arrest her, then that would cause another problem with the competition."

"Ms. Edwards is a person of interest, but we are not ready to make an arrest. However, while we finish the investigation, we need to keep everyone who has been involved in the competition in Las Vegas. Therefore, proceeding with the competition may be the best way to do that."

"Are you convinced Mr. Boucher was murdered?" I ask.

"We don't have a better explanation, so more likely than not, we are looking at a homicide."

"Do you think he may have been planning to let the guests compare the bean dip with hummus? It's likely we stock pre-prepared hummus in the walk-in fridge, so he could have grabbed it and put it on his cart when he was in the fridge. Evan suggested that maybe he just tasted the wrong dip."

"That's an interesting thought, but we didn't see two serving bowls or a pre-prepared container of hummus in the videos."

Evan glares at me. He looks like he didn't sleep well either last night. I wonder if he went against my advice and spent it with Cassie. Then I respond, "I see. If we are going to proceed with the competition, let's turn back to the toughest decision. What should we do about Cassie?"

Before Detective Fielder can respond, Evan moves to the edge of the sofa and adamantly argues, "This should not be a tough decision.

Cassandra should replace Leon as per the rules. Not only would it be entirely unfair to exclude her from the opportunity to compete, but it would also unjustifiably cause irreparable harm to her reputation when the police are not even sure Leon's death was anything more than an accident. We all know that everyone is speculating about Leon's death, and if Cassandra doesn't compete, everyone will assume it's because she is the prime suspect. That accusation and the associated gossip will follow her forever. As they say, you cannot un-ring that bell."

Attempting to calm Evan, Detective Fielder responds, "I agree the competition should proceed according to the rules. If that means Ms. Edwards competes, then that is the way you should proceed. With your permission, we will have undercover officers on hand during the competition to keep an eye on things and ensure everyone's safety. Continuing with the competition will keep the competitors and crew here, and it may force the guilty party to show his or her hand."

"Ok, as long as you feel comfortable that we can keep everyone safe. I will call a meeting of the crew, staff, and finalists for tomorrow morning to restart the competition. Can you have your people in place by then?"

"Yes, but I want to make sure that no one outside this room knows that we have undercover officers here."

"Ok. I will only tell Emily and Cynthia." I stare directly at Evan as I make my statement to make sure he receives the unspoken message that he cannot share this information with Cassie.

Detective Fielder responds, "No. I mean absolutely no one other than you and Mr. Catalinius. There is no reason anyone else needs to know. We can assign them real jobs in the kitchen, and they will do the actual work for that job. I can't risk another leak. I'm already concerned that the allergic reaction and fingerprint was may have leaked to the press."

Before I can respond, Evan is on his feet, livid. "What do you mean the info about Cassandra's fingerprint was leaked to the press? Are you trying to ruin her career?"

Detective Fielder responds, "Please calm down. I said it *may* have been leaked. One of the officers told me a reporter from the local newspaper was lurking in the police station when the fingerprint analysis came back from the lab. He feared the reporter may have overheard the discussion before they realized who was present. We have asked the newspaper not to print any details about the matter at this time."

But Evan isn't mollified. He responds, "Asking the newspaper is not the same as ensuring that they do not print such speculation. You need to make sure this story does not show up in print."

"Mr. Catalinius, we do not have the level of control over the press that some other countries do, but we have taken the steps we are allowed to take. Now, Mr. Cartwright, what do we need to do to get our undercover officers in place here?"

"If you want them to have the proper security badges and access, then we need to at least tell Emily. She will need to work around some systems to make that happen. What jobs do you want them to do?"

"You can tell Emily," Detective Fielder relents, "since she hasn't been involved in any of the events. But let me make it crystal clear, no one else can know, no exceptions. As for their jobs, which jobs would be the easiest to have them do where new faces wouldn't be questioned?"

"We could have one of them on security. It would be easy to explain increasing security. The other one could be on clean up duty in the kitchen during prep sessions. I think they could easily fade into the background that way."

"That works."

"Ok. Coordinate with Emily. I will fill her in and make it clear that she cannot share this info with anyone."

"Great. Make sure she understands that someone's life may depend on her discretion."

"I will. However, I am concerned we are effectively setting our finalists up as bait for a potential killer."

CHAPTER TWENTY-SEVEN

CASSIE

As I walk into the competition meeting, the aroma of freshly baked bread and coffee draw my eyes to a table filled with at least three types of mini-quiches, brioche rolls, fresh fruit, coffee, and tea. I would normally be filling a plate with samples of each, but I don't think I can eat now. I don't even think I could keep down my usual hot tea, so I pass on the breakfast offerings and head to my spot at the conference table.

My stomach is churning from nerves and, to be honest, outright fear. In the hallway, Trenton told Kai, "I overheard Cynthia telling Amy the police found Cassie's fingerprints on the bowl," so I guess they all have heard the rumor that I'm the prime suspect. Leaning forward with my hands covering my face, I try to hold it together. It's funny, I thought my job was stressful, but this is a whole new level of stress. Never in my wildest dreams would I have thought I'd be a murder suspect. God, I hope the law firm doesn't get wind of this fiasco. If they do, I won't have a job to go home to.

When Sean and Evan enter the boardroom, I move my hands away from my eyes and hazard a glance at Evan. With tousled hair, he is smoldering in a dark blue blazer, cream-colored polo shirt, and khakis, but the dark circles under his eyes give away that he is tired, just like me. I haven't spoken to him since the interview with Detective Fielder. I'd hoped Evan might reach out to me, but he hasn't. He must think I'm guilty too. Or at least, he doesn't want to be associated with a murder suspect, innocent or not, and I can't blame him.

I hear Sean whisper to Cynthia and Amy that he's going to handle the meeting. Then he starts with, "Thank you all for meeting us here this morning. We appreciate the patience you have shown over the last two days while we worked through the procedures and logistics in light of Chef Boucher's tragic death. After careful consideration, we have made the decision to proceed with the Guest Chef Competition. Round 1 will take place this afternoon."

Questions start flying from the attendees. "Does that mean the investigation is over?" "Was it an accident?" "Has the murderer been arrested?" "What is the new competition schedule?"

A different question is running through my head: "Does this mean they believe I'm innocent?" But I don't say anything.

In his characteristic signal for silence, Sean holds up his hand and says, "While I am not going to take individual questions. I will go over some of the logistics, so please let me continue."

The room quiets. "First, the investigation is ongoing. The police have not yet made a final determination about the accident, but they hope to have the case closed quickly. Therefore, we have decided to proceed with Rounds 1, 2, and 3 of the competition as planned. Each round will feature one of the three traditional courses of a meal. That means Round 1 is appetizers, Round 2 is entrées, and Round 3 is desserts. However, we will not be doing any more demos given the delays in moving forward. That said, there will still be interviews and photo shoots around the property that you will be asked to participate in. I am also pleased to announce that Cassie Edwards will be competing as the fourth finalist. Given that none of the actual competition rounds had started, we have determined she is allowed to compete."

My head shoots up in reaction. Did Sean just say I am competing? Hopefully, that means I'm no longer a suspect. But before I can bask in that positive thought, Trenton's brusque voice interrupts as he blurts out, "Why are you letting a killer compete?"

Sean responds, "No one here has been accused of anything, so I do not want to hear another comment of that nature. As far as we know, Mr. Boucher's death was just a very tragic accident. I expect each person in this room to treat everyone else with respect and courtesy. Deviation from that expectation is grounds for dismissal or disqualification."

Trenton's question simultaneously pisses me off and makes me feel like an outcast. How can I stay here? I'm conflicted, and my mind begins racing, a numb fog overtaking me. I can't believe the competition is going forward, and I'm supposed to compete after everything that has happened.

Trembling as if an ice-cold breeze blew by, I crave the touch of the only person in the room who could provide solace. I want to snuggle against Evan's warm body for a comforting hug and feel his strong hand against my back pulling me close, even if just one more time. But that doesn't seem likely, and even if the rules allowed, I don't have family to call for a pep talk. I could call Lowri, but I don't want to pull her into my realm of problems. She has already seen me through enough tough times since I lost my parents.

Sean continues, "As originally planned, the competition will conclude with what we are calling the Final Dinner in Athena's Wine Cave where the winner will be announced. Now we will adjourn until 2 p.m. at which time you will all meet in the kitchen at Trendz for Round 1." Then he and Evan leave the room.

I close my eyes to gather my thoughts, but I can hear others gathering their belongings followed by their soft footsteps on the carpet as they gradually leave the room. A few whisper not-so-kind words as they leave. I hear "murderer," "she doesn't stand a chance," and "she should leave the competition to the pros." But I don't even bother to open my eyes. I don't want to know who uttered those words.

Soon the room is quiet, but I don't think my legs are stable enough to walk. Maybe if I sit here until everyone leaves, no one will notice.

Then I can make my way back to my room where I can figure out what to do next.

When I think everyone is gone, I open my eyes and put my hands on the table to push myself up. That's when I see Evan standing in the corner across the table from me with his hands in his pockets. His tired eyes are focused on me as if he's trying to see into my soul. "Evan, I saw you leave. What are you doing here?"

"I returned after the others left. We need to talk."

"About what?"

"What do you think? This mess."

"Oh. Ok."

Still leaning in the corner, Evan asks, "First, how are you holding up?"

Elbows propped on the table allowing my fingertips to massage my temples, I respond, "Not well. Everyone seems to think I'm either a murderer or unqualified to be here. While the latter may be true, I'm not a murderer! However, I have no clue how to prove I'm innocent. I probably should have already hired a lawyer, but I was afraid that would make me look even guiltier. Even though my specialty is corporate law, I thought I knew enough to get through a basic interview with the police. Now I'm not so sure that background is enough because despite what Sean said about it being an accident, if the case is still open, I suspect my innocence is still in question."

Hands remaining in his pockets, Evan approaches the table, stopping directly across from me. "Your instincts are right, and because of that, Sean is telling me to stay far away from you. However, my gut is not sure Sean is right, which means part of me wants to find a way to help you."

A tear escapes and trickles down my right cheek. "How can you help me? Besides, I can't imagine it's good for your family's business to associate with a murder suspect." As I wait for Evan to respond, he looks everywhere, except at me. He must be rethinking his desire to help me. Then he strides to the corner of the room and quickly returns, placing a cube-shaped box of tissues in front of me. Grabbing a tissue, I wipe away my tears and share a closed-lip smile in response to his thoughtfulness, as I watch him roll out the chair directly across from me.

Leaning forward, forearms on the table and fingers interlaced, Evan stares directly at me with a gaze so serious I'm almost scared to hear what comes next. Returning the intense gaze, I analyze Evan's face as he says, "You have no idea how right you are about my family and its business. But I stand by my friends when they need my help. And I would like to think that we have become at least friends."

His statement of support means a lot, and I'm relieved he thinks we are still friends. I hope we are more than just friends, maybe he does too. But even if our short time together has been a true romantic connection, I don't want to be the cause of friction with his family, so I graciously explain, "Evan, thank you so much for saying that, but you need to protect your family and its reputation. I didn't do anything wrong, and I have to figure out how to prove that I wasn't involved. Don't they have security tapes that would show if someone tampered with Leon's food?"

Leaning back in his chair, Evan shakes his head. "They haven't found anything on the tapes yet, but they are still going through them."

This whole mess is so confusing. "How did my fingerprints get on the serving bowl? Do you remember seeing me touch his bowl? Do you think someone is setting me up? You won't believe what is running through my head." My rate of speech accelerates as I explain, "I started wondering if maybe this is like a movie plot. Maybe someone used tape to transfer my fingerprints onto the bowl. My mind just keeps running through all these outlandish possibilities because I know I didn't kill him. If I don't clear my name, this is going to follow me for the rest of my life, even if I avoid prison." I take a deep breath, needing air after my rant.

In a soft, calming voice, Evan says, "Slow down. I don't know how your fingerprints got onto the bowl. I don't remember seeing you touch anything the chefs were using, but we can go over everything we both remember from the prep session and the poolside demo. However, right now you need to get in the mindset for preparing your

Round 1 appetizer. The competition starts in a few hours. Afterward, we can discuss whether there is anything we can do to help the police get to the bottom of this mess. Let's meet in my suite at 8 p.m."

"You mean you still want to help me? You believe me? What about upsetting your family?" I'm overwhelmed with gratitude and emotion. As I attempt to dry the remaining tears with more tissues, Evan comes up behind me. His strong hands clasp my upper arms, and he gently helps me to my feet, quickly turns me toward him, and pulls me into his chest.

With his right hand tight against my back and his left cradling my head, Evan whispers, "I am probably being too trusting, but yes, I believe you. Let me worry about my family. If all goes well, your name will be cleared without them ever hearing about the events here. Now start focusing on the competition. Keep your eyes and ears open this afternoon. And be careful. If Leon was killed, then you may be in danger too."

Snapping my head back to look Evan in the eye, I gasp, "I hadn't thought of that." Someone could be trying to eliminate more of the finalists, not just Leon. And now I'm one of them.

CHAPTER TWENTY-EIGHT

CASSIE

After talking with Evan, I know it's time for me to take action. I wouldn't have survived college and my job if I weren't tough, and it's time to toughen up again and take control. I have a once-in-a-lifetime opportunity to compete against the best. That's what I'm going to do. I'll also take Evan's advice to listen and learn. Maybe someone will say something that clues me in to what is really going on around here. Then after Round 1, I'll meet Evan to plan our next steps. With renewed hope and a sense of empowerment, I head to the kitchen in Trendz.

When we are all assembled, one of the crew has us draw casino chips Vegas style to determine which station we will use. I draw the $100 chip and get to pick first, which allows me to select the station closest to the pantry and walk-in fridge. Even though the other finalists must walk between my prep table and stove to get supplies, it will be fewer steps for me, and time is going to be critical. As a bonus, they tell me I get to keep the chip! Trenton draws the $25 chip, which allows him to pick second. Drawing the $5 chip, Kai picks third, and Jayden is left with the $1 chip, so he walks to the remaining station.

After we are settled at our stations, the cameras start rolling as Amy goes over the rules saying, "Welcome to the prep session for Round 1 of the Grand Athena's Guest Chef Competition. You will each have 60 minutes to create an appetizer that reflects something special about you. Remember, Trendz is a fun, upscale but unpretentious restaurant, which means, as in the past, its chef has wide latitude to express their style. For example, a prior chef once offered a sampler that paired three high-end wines with three versions of short-rib sliders on the same menu as his famous Wagyu filet mignon served with a balsamic glaze. So, relax and let us learn something about who you are — not who you think we want you to be. That means your appetizer doesn't need to be fancy — just delicious, eye catching, and personal.

We have installed a timer on the wall. Be careful not to lose track of time. I will count you down to the start: 5...4...3...2...Wait! I forgot to tell you about the twist. You must use the dip you made for the demo in some way in your appetizer. Cassie, you must use the dip you wrote down at the first meeting. What was it?"

You've got to be kidding. "Tomatillo Pineapple Salsa Verde."

Holding up the slip of paper, Amy confirms "That's right! Ok, everyone get ready. 5...4...3...2...1...COOK!

The other three finalists brush by me as they run behind me in a mad rush to the pantry and fridge. Rather than be trampled, I let them pass before following to grab tomatillos, onions, and jalapenos to roast for the dip. First lesson: when Amy says COOK, run for the pantry. The clock is ticking, so don't waste time.

As I fill a large bowl with the ingredients from the pantry, I rack my brain for the best way to incorporate the Tomatillo Pineapple Salsa Verde into the lobster and avocado bruschetta that I plan to garnish with thinly sliced strawberries or maybe radishes and cilantro leaves. I could completely puree the dip and drizzle it on top, but that doesn't seem very creative. Hmm. I will figure something out, but I need to get these ingredients prepped and under the broiler quickly because roasting them will take 21 minutes. It's going to be tight to get everything done in an hour. As much as I hate the idea of wasting time on multiple trips to the fridge and pantry, I'll go back for the lobster tails and the other ingredients later.

A cacophony of pans clanging on cooktops, oven doors opening, and knives chopping fills the kitchen as the aroma of sautéing garlic from Trenton's station competes with the smell of Jayden's food frying in a vat of oil.

As we cook, Amy goes from station to station asking questions. With a camera hoisted on his right shoulder, one of the crew follows her to capture the exchanges. It's hard to concentrate while also wanting to listen to what the other finalists are saying. Over the kitchen noises, I hear Trenton explain he is serving his roasted tomato and kale dip on miniature, bake-fried cheese ravioli. I admit that sounds good. Kai tells Amy he is using his papaya tapenade as a relish on pork sliders. Who wouldn't like those? The competition is definitely stiff.

As I finish prepping my salsa ingredients and get them under the broiler, I wonder what Jayden is going to do with his dip. He called it Texas Fondue, but it was actually just sausage gravy. It will be interesting to see how he fits that into an appetizer. Then I hear him say he's making mini chicken tenders served on bamboo toothpicks with a drizzle of the fondue. Amy said our appetizers don't have to be fancy, and there is nothing wrong with comfort food, but it sounds simple for a competition like this one. I guess he is limited in what works with the gravy. Regardless, I'm relieved that my appetizer will fit in and won't be the simplest one.

Amy comes to my station as I'm closing the oven door. "Cassie, what are you making for your appetizer?"

"I'm making Lobster and Avocado Bruschetta."

"That sounds good. Tell us more."

"Well, I'm spreading a thin layer of avocado butter on toasted baguette slices. Then I'll top them with bite-sized pieces of lobster and garnish with cilantro leaves and a slice of strawberry or radish."

"I can't wait to taste them. How are you incorporating your dip?"

Fortunately, as I was prepping the dip ingredients, I figured it out. "I'm mixing my Tomatillo Pineapple Salsa Verde with the avocado butter, which will enhance the flavor of the avocado and complement the lobster." I may put a few drops of the salsa on top of the lobster too. I haven't decided yet.

"Cassie, I'm sure it will be delicious. I will let you keep working. Don't forget to keep your eye on the clock!"

Speaking to all the finalists, Amy says "Ok, everyone, work fast. You have only 45 minutes left on the clock. We can't wait to see your finished appetizers."

Confirming with the wall clock that 15 minutes have already passed, I run to the fridge to grab the lobster tails. Having forgotten to grab a bowl to carry everything, I try to balance the lobster tails in my arms as I grab butter, avocados, lemon, lime, cilantro, strawberries, and radishes from the pantry. If I can keep from dropping everything, avoiding another run to the pantry for ingredients will save me a couple of minutes, which is critical because time is flying by.

Barely making it back to my station with my armload of ingredients pressed against my chest, I bend forward to let everything gently fall from my arms. Then I rush to my oven and turn the tomatillos and other veggies. I'll need to turn them again in seven more minutes. I'll use that time to prepare the lobster in a little butter and lemon. While it cools, I can prepare the avocados, strawberries, and radishes. That will leave just enough time to toast the baguette slices. Shit! I forgot to grab a baguette from the pantry! Running back, I grab one and hurry back to my station.

When I smell something burning, I panic, thinking it's my tomatillos. I check them and sigh in relief. They are browning with a few charred bits, which will be perfect. However, someone else screams "Fuck!" Looking around, I'm surprised to see it came from Jayden, who is always quiet and introverted. Then I see what has him so upset. He is pulling small, black lumps of coal from the deep fryer that were supposed to be his fried chicken bites. Hopefully, he will have time to fry another batch.

When Amy announces we have 15 minutes left, I'm already hustling to mash the avocados and before adding a squeeze of lime juice to keep them from turning brown. Thankfully, they are ripe and easy to mash.

Each time I check the wall clock, I expect that only another minute or two will have passed, but it seems like every time I look another 5 or 10 minutes have elapsed. That means I better quicken my pace to get the dip ready, so I throw the tomatillos and other dip ingredients into the food processor and pulse it a few times. After a quick taste, I add a little more salt and then mix a little of the dip with the smashed avocados. I run back to the pantry, dodging a camera guy who is trying to follow me, to find plates and a squeeze bottle for the salsa to make decorating the plates easier. Returning to my station, the clock indicates I have only five minutes to assemble everything and make it look good.

When the bell rings, we all stop and walk back from our stations, hands held high to indicate we are done. Smiling broadly, I high-five Kai, who is at the station next to me. That was a wild, exciting adrenaline rush! I did it! I actually completed a competition round, and my appetizers look great! A dream come true.

I haven't felt this alive in a long time. I've also never known 60 minutes to fly by so fast. I barely got the last cilantro leaf and dot of salsa in place when Amy called time. But now that it's over, I realize just how hot the kitchen has become with the cooktops, ovens, and intense lights for the cameras. I'm dripping with sweat, and with random wisps of hair escaping my ponytail, I probably look like a mess, but I wouldn't change a second of this experience!

Once the cameras stop rolling, Amy explains "Judging will start in 15 minutes, so stay close by. When the judging starts, the cameras will be rolling again both here in the kitchen and in the judging room. You will each be meeting with the judges individually, so as the printed rules state, I want to remind you that you will not know what they think about the other chefs' appetizers. Unlike many other competitions, there are no eliminations. You will all be cooking in all three rounds, but you will not know any results until The Final Dinner. We want to keep the information about how everyone is doing a secret until the very end to build suspense, so the results will be a complete surprise to everyone. As the rules state, you can be disqualified if you violate this rule. Do you understand?"

We all nod. At least I don't have to worry about being eliminated.

Amy continues, "Don't go near your station or anyone else's station. Feel free to grab something to drink while you wait for the judging to start. There are cold water bottles and stools have been set up where you can all wait. Any questions?"

Silence. Crashing after the intensity of the cooking round, we are too tired to ask anything at this point.

As I grab a bottle of water, I wonder how well my appetizer will compare to the others, but I'm determined to hold my head high and be an active participant in this competition. The other finalists are at the table chatting with each other, so I join the group and wish them good luck. At first, I mainly listen because I'm not sure what their reaction to me will be. But Kai pulls me into the conversation, asking if I've tried any fruits other than pineapple in my salsa. He thinks mango or papaya might work well. Trenton is still cold toward me, but he remains reasonably civil. At least the common bond of the Round 1 experience seems to be making my presence tolerable to them.

Slightly reassured, I ask them what they know about the judges. This is the first time we are interacting with them, so I'm nervous but also excited. Other than what I've seen on TV competitions, I don't know what to expect. I follow most of the cooking shows on the FFT channel and a few other chefs who have famous cookbooks, but I don't know much about these judges. They all have successful restaurants, so I'm kicking myself for not having a broader knowledge about well-known chefs in general. After this competition, I will pay more attention.

However, the other finalists seem to know more about the judges than I do and are quick to share. I think they want to scare me, but information is power, so I absorb it all.

Apparently, Judge Gerard is super picky about presentation. Even one stray drop of sauce annoys him. Judge Holden loves salt and wants everything over-salted. That's not good for me because I tend to go on the lighter side when it comes to salt. The third judge, Judge Indigo, replaced Chef Bernard when she died in the car crash. They say he hates cilantro. These preferences may not bode well for me. I probably under-salted my food, and there's cilantro in the salsa. Oh well. I can't change that now.

One of the crew members taps me on the shoulder and says "It's your turn. Follow me to the judging area."

Before we leave the kitchen, the crew member instructs, "When you go in, the camera will already be running, so walk in slowly and stop on the big red X. Amy will welcome you. The judges will taste your appetizer. Then they may ask you a few questions and will give you feedback. Got it?"

"Got it."

Pushing the door open, he wishes me, "Good luck."

Letting out a deep breath, I say, "Thanks," and walk in.

While we cooked, they transformed the restaurant into a set for filming. It's dark, except for carefully focused spotlights, illuminating the three solemn judges, who are seated behind a long table on an elevated platform. They look ready to attack anything that offends them in the least, so I better prepare myself to smile through the worst!

The table is draped with a black cloth that skims the floor, and a mirror-like silver dome placed in front of each judge. Cameras and crew are positioned along my path to the judges. In autopilot, I halt abruptly when my sneakers land on the illuminated X. Taking another deep breath and clasping my hands in front of me to avoid fidgeting, I smile and try to soak in the moment. I can't believe I'm really standing here.

When I notice Sean and Evan standing off to the side, my smile widens. It hadn't occurred to me they would be here, but it makes sense. Evan returns my smile, but Sean's face is neutral at best.

After Amy welcomes me, the judges ask where I'm from. "San Diego." Why did I start cooking? "My grandparents encouraged me and sent me to a culinary summer camp in high school. After that, I was hooked." What does the competition mean to me, and what will I do with the money if I win? "It's a chance of a lifetime for me as a home cook to compete against these professional chefs. The money would allow me to pay off student loans and pursue a career that is more in line with my dreams rather than what others have expected of me. It's a chance to start fresh and leave behind some baggage." I'm not sure why I shared the part about others' expectations and my baggage. I rarely even admit those things to myself. But I tell myself to keep smiling — no regrets.

As the judges taste my appetizer, I cross my fingers that the toasted baguette slices didn't get soggy during the wait.

The judges point out things they like and things that could be improved. Fortunately, Judge Gerard doesn't criticize my presentation, which for him is the same as having complimented it. However, he would have preferred one larger piece of lobster rather than the multiple, small bites I used. I expected Judge Holden to want more salt, but she wants "a lot, lot more salt." At least she likes the way I incorporated the dip.

Judge Indigo looks at my cilantro-laced appetizer, then at me, then back to the appetizer. This roller coaster goes downhill fast when he starts with "I absolutely despise cilantro. Never have liked it. Never will." Not good.

Remember to keep smiling. I can handle this. Although it was difficult, I worked hard to learn how to accept criticism and learn from it in my regular job. I need to use what I learned to control my emotions here. I can't argue with the judges. That never looks good. And I don't want to start crying, so I grit my teeth behind my smile and try to breathe evenly. For extra measure, I push a fingernail into the palm of my hand, which usually staves off tears.

After a dramatic pause, Judge Indigo, with a huff, says, "However, you are fortunate that I am not one of the people for whom cilantro tastes like soap, which according to experts may be as much as 14% of the population. I just don't care for the flavor. Therefore, overlooking my personal taste preferences, I can appreciate your work today. It is pleasing to the eye and uses a smart combination of texture and colors. Just be careful about overuse of ingredients, such as cilantro, that are commonly disliked."

Whew! I thank the judges for their feedback. Amy thanks me and tells me to return to the kitchen while the judges finish evaluating the other finalists' appetizers.

As I enter the kitchen, the room quiets and I'm met with focused stares from the other finalists, who are obviously trying to glean how the judging went from my expression and body language. I'm guessing they are reading me as relieved because overall, that's exactly how I feel. The judges seemed to like the concept of my appetizer and the flavor combination. Fortunately, even Judge Indigo was reasonably positive given that he hates cilantro. I know some people think it tastes like soap, but I didn't realize that 14% may have that reaction. I'll keep that in mind in the future and have an alternative option available, such as parsley. I'll also heed Judge Holden's advice about using more salt, but I don't know about "a lot, lot more." I noticed Judge Indigo grimace at Judge Holden's comments, so maybe a balance between what I like and what Judge Holden likes will work.

I smile, sit down at the table they've set up for us, and say, "Glad that's over."

CHAPTER TWENTY-NINE

CASSIE

When Round 1 is complete, as the crew and finalists leave, I realize this is my best chance to investigate. It's risky, but I want to know if they keep hummus in the walk-in refrigerator, which could have been substituted for Leon's bean dip. I hang back and sneak into the fridge unnoticed to check it out. As I'm searching, I hear voices out in the kitchen and tiptoe toward the fridge's door to see who is talking.

I recognize Jayden's soft, Texas drawl, as he says, "I need to get out of here. Why did you summon me back?"

A second deeper voice says, "Do you want another advantage in the competition?"

What?! *Another* advantage? In shock, I lean closer to the door, pressing my face against the cold metal.

"I can use all the help I can get, but it depends on what I have to do to get it," Jayden replies.

Deep Voice responds, "You will simply sabotage one of the other finalists in the next round."

"Was my first advantage connected to Leon's death? I don't want anyone to get hurt."

"Of course, not. Don't worry. It'll just make a finalist to do poorly in Round 2."

"Ok. If you're sure no one will get hurt. What do you want me to do?"

"When the time comes, I'll let you know. Don't forget, when you win, you'll owe me."

"As long as no one gets hurt, I'm in. It's not a problem."

I'm frozen in place by more than just the chill of the fridge as the deep-voiced man says, "It better not be. Now let's get out of here."

"Where are you headed? The door is in the opposite direction."

"I don't want to be seen by the cameras or seen leaving together, so I'm going to use the Maze. But you need to head out the front door," Deep Voice instructs.

Just when I think they are about to leave, I hear Jayden again. "Hey, it looks like someone left the fridge door ajar again. I better close it." I quickly take off my shoes and move into a corner behind some crates. Crouching down as low as I can, I hide my face.

Deep Voice asks, "Is anyone in there?"

"Nah. Everyone left earlier. Someone was probably just careless."

"Check it out before you close the door to make sure. We don't want any eavesdroppers."

"You're being paranoid, but I'll check."

Then I hear footsteps approaching the fridge.

"Ok. I'm out of here," says the unidentified man, I hear a click followed by what sounds like a door opening and closing.

From the fridge door, Jayden calls out, "Is anyone in here?" I hold my breath as he wanders inside and quickly looks around. Then he turns off the light and shuts the heavy door behind him.

At first, I panic hearing the loud thud as the fridge door closes. I'm stuck inside a fridge without a cell phone. I could send a message to someone via the TekCuff, but I don't want to risk a message going to the bad guys, whoever they are. I start taking deep breaths so I can think.

Then it hits me, in today's litigious environment, the manufacturer must provide a way out. With the faint light from my TekCuff, I move toward the door and feel for the light switch. Relief floods through me when I find a safety knob that will open the door. As my hand grasps it ready to open the door, I pull back. It will be safer to wait a little longer to make sure Jayden and Deep Voice are long gone.

Now that my pulse has slowed a little, I can't ignore that I'm shivering all over. It's about 38 degrees Fahrenheit in here, and I don't have a jacket. I look at the time on the TekCuff and decide to wait five minutes. Hopefully, that will be long enough for it to be safe but not cause hypothermia. I'm lucky. No telling what would have happened if they had found me.

While I wait, I think about what I can do with this new information. I should call the police. But technically, the two guys didn't mention an actual crime. In fact, Deep Voice denied having anything to do with Leon's death.

I wish they hadn't taken my phone. I could have recorded the conversation. Instead, I go back over what they said. Do I have any reason to believe Deep Voice? Was the prior advantage actually related to Leon's death? Or was it something simpler, such as Jayden knowing ahead of time that we had to use our dip in our appetizer. That information would have given Jayden more time to decide what to make, which would be an advantage. The fact that Deep Voice has access to the Maze and knows where the cameras are located means that at least one Athena employee wants Jayden to win this competition. But why?

Maybe I should tell Cynthia or Amy what I heard since they are in charge of the competition. The problem is that I can't prove that the conversation actually happened, so Cynthia and Amy may not believe me. They will think I'm trying to get another chef tossed out of the competition. I could tell Evan what I heard, but can I trust him? What do I know about him other than he's Sean's friend from college and works in his family's business? He hasn't even told me what that business is. I could keep quiet about this a little longer and see if I can get some proof of what is going on. I have time to decide; I'm not meeting Evan for another hour or so.

Slowly opening the fridge door and exiting, I find the kitchen is dark and quiet. I audibly exhale the breath I didn't know I was holding, I realize two things. Now, I need to figure out who wants Jayden to win this competition, and who I can trust with the information I discover.

CHAPTER THIRTY

SEAN

I was supposed to have the financial information for our F&B suppliers this morning, but my team didn't get it to me until this afternoon after I returned from watching the judging of the chef's competition. Now I am going to be up all night sorting through the data. Based on my initial review, it looks like we have been slowly dumping all our old suppliers and going with new ones. I will do a more detailed analysis, but first, it's time to grab a large coffee!

After caffeinating myself and analyzing the information for a while, I call my friend Wes when I see we quit using his company several months ago, hoping he can shed some light on what is going on. Someone must have told him why we quit ordering from him, and I'm surprised he didn't reach out to me directly when we dumped his company. I also want to know what he was doing at the pool the day Leon died.

Wes answers hesitantly, "Hello Sean. What's up?"

"Wes, I just learned we quit ordering from your company," I say, jumping right to the point. "Can you tell me what happened?"

"Don't you know?"

Hearing the disbelief in Wes' voice, I slowly respond, "No. I wouldn't be asking if I knew the answer. It recently came to my attention that we have made a number of changes in our F&B department that don't make sense to me, so I'm following up."

Sighing, Wes says, "Sean, I should have known you weren't involved, but I assumed you knew. I don't have all the answers, but we should talk in person."

"Ok, Wes. Do you have time for lunch tomorrow?" I say, mystified.

"That works, if we can make it a late lunch."

"Sure. Do you want to meet me at the VIP lounge here?"

"Definitely not. Let's meet at our favorite Mexican place downtown at 1:30. It's been a long time, but you know where I mean, right?"

Why is he being so mysterious? Why not name the stupid restaurant? But I go along and say, "Of course, I know. See you then."

Hmm. I've known Wes for much of my life and that's the strangest conversation we've ever had. He usually can't wait to get past business to discuss the latest sports news, but he didn't even mention how his favorite baseball team is doing. Even more out of character, he turned down lunch in our VIP lounge. I can't remember him ever doing that. Something is seriously wrong.

CHAPTER THIRTY-ONE

CASSIE

After escaping the walk-in fridge, I hurry to my room to warm up with a hot shower and trade my nondescript white shirt and black pants from the competition for a more cheerful, purple and white sundress. As I step out of the shower, I hear my TekCuff ding with a message from Evan, indicating he will pick me up at 8 p.m., which gives me enough time to apply fresh makeup, detangle and dry my hair, and dress.

As I start dressing, I notice the maid left a copy of today's newspaper on the bed. My eyes go wide when I see my photo on the front page. I grab the paper and start reading. The headline declares, "Lawyer Suspected of Murdering Chef at the Athena." Shit! Shit! Shit! I'm shaking as I continue reading the article that outlines my fingerprints were found on the bowl of hummus that "poisoned" Chef Boucher due to his food allergy. The article quotes an unnamed source as speculating that "Cassie must have wanted to eliminate Chef Boucher so she could take his spot in the competition." No! This is a complete disaster. My reputation is destroyed. I must find a way to clear my name and make the newspaper print a retraction. Of course, papers don't usually put retractions on the front page, so I don't know how much good that will do.

As I'm worrying about losing my job, Evan knocks on my door, right on time, and I show him the newspaper. "It's going to be ok, he tells me. "We were meeting tonight to go over strategy anyway. Bring what you need and let's go to my room, so we will have more space to work."

I grab my clutch, and we walk toward the elevator. Stepping inside, I turn my head to watch Evan, who is acting aloof. No hug, no hand holding, just two people silently riding in an elevator after I shared that devastating article with him. I wonder if he is rethinking his continued association with me in light of the negative publicity.

After we walk through the door of the Monarch Suite, he finally pulls me into a reassuring hug. I'm surprised after the cool treatment in the elevator, but relieved to know he may still be on Team Cassie. It feels so good to be held that I sink into his arms, and thankfully he doesn't let go.

The simple hug reaffirms that the chemistry between us is off the charts. I can't believe my body is reacting to his after seeing that horrid article, but my heart is racing, goosebumps cover my arms, and my skin tingles from his touch. I can't get close enough to him. I want to rip his shirt off and slide my hands over the peaks and valleys of his warm, muscular chest and forget about everything else. I don't care what he said about wanting to help me because I'm his friend. I want more than friendship. With that thought, I pull my head back and look up into his eyes. He meets my gaze with an intense stare. Then he captures my lips like he can't get enough of me either, erasing any friend-like thoughts.

After a couple of minutes, he pulls away, places his hands on my shoulders, and rests his forehead against mine. "Cassie, I should apologize for kissing you, but I can't say I am sorry. However, now we need to focus on the real reason we are here."

Still panting, I manage to say, "Evan, you're right that we need to focus, but no need to apologize. After that article, I can't wait for the police to figure this out. I have to find a way to prove my innocence and piece my reputation back together, but first I need to know something. Why do you believe I'm innocent when no one else does? Even

Sean wouldn't return my smile during the judging, and now the newspaper has put the allegation in print."

"Cassandra, I doubt I am the only one who believes you."

"Right now, it feels like you are the only one. So why?"

"First, you and I were in the same room most of the time on the
day Leon died. I can't recall any time you had an opportunity to
tamper with Leon's food. Second, you were calm throughout the day.
If you were planning something like that, I would have sensed your
mind was somewhere else. Third, and most importantly, I may not
have known you long, but I am a good judge of character, and unless I
am horribly mistaken, it would be out of character for you to harm
someone."

Shaking my head, I confirm, "You're not mistaken. I would never
do anything like that."

"Ok. Let's sit down on the sofa and make a plan to clear your
name." Evan takes my hand and walks me to the sofa. After we sit, he
scoots closer so our knees are touching and hands me a pad of paper
and pen off the coffee table, saying, "Let's start by making a list of
what we remember each finalist doing at the prep session. Who went
near Leon's station and who went into the fridge after Leon put his
cart in there?"

With our heads together, I write down the name of each finalist.
Pointing to Jayden's name, Evan says, "He was the most nervous of
any finalist when Detective Fielder interviewed him, but that may not
mean anything."

Realizing it's time to share what I learned, I say, "I think Jayden has
reason to be nervous, but I'm not sure it has anything to do with
Leon's death. I stayed in the kitchen after I thought everyone had left
so I could check whether they stock hummus in the refrigerator.
Jayden returned to the kitchen while I was looking around, and I
overheard him talking to someone who had such a deep tenor to his
voice I gave him the name Deep Voice. Deep Voice offered Jayden an
advantage in the competition."

Grasping my thigh, Evan says, "Cassie, what were you thinking?

Sneaking around the kitchen alone was dangerous. You need to be more careful. What if they had found you?"

"Evan, I knew it was a little risky, but it's driving me insane that I'm a murder suspect. I had to at least figure out where the hummus may have come from."

Evan closes his eyes and drags his hands down his face. "I understand your stress, but please promise me you won't put yourself in situations like that again."

Trying not to be mad at his bossiness, which is admittedly a little sexy, I place my hand on his shoulder and agree, "I'll be careful, but you don't have the right to tell me what to do. My whole future is on the line, even more so after that article, and I can take care of myself. That said, I appreciate you are concerned about my safety. It's sweet. Now, can we talk about what I overheard?"

"Ok," Evan acquiesces with his hand back on my thigh, "but I'm not sweet. Pick another descriptor next time. And yes, I want to hear the details of what you overheard. What advantage did the guy you call Deep Voice offer Jayden? Did Jayden agree to take it?"

I tell Evan every detail of the conversation I overheard, including that Deep Voice exited via the Maze.

When I finish, Evan, deep in thought, murmurs, "Interesting. Someone is trying to manipulate the outcome of the competition. But who and why?"

"Evan, if Deep Voice has access to the Maze, doesn't that mean he works for the Athena?"

Evan nods. "Likely. Cassie, we need to tell Sean about this."

"Not yet. First, we need proof. Aren't there cameras in the kitchen? Can't you check with security to see if they have video from this afternoon? Also, won't they have records of who used the Maze door in the Trendz kitchen? Shouldn't we check that data before bothering Sean? Besides, it's not clear this has anything to do with Leon's death, and I'm worried Sean, Cynthia, and Amy will think I'm trying to get another chef kicked out."

"We need Sean's help to accomplish most of those things." When the doorbell rings, Evan says, "I hope you don't mind, but I ordered dinner. I gave Eduardo the evening off, so we could have privacy for this discussion, but I suspected we both could use some food."

"You're right. I haven't eaten much of anything all day."

"I assumed as much. Let me get the door. We can talk more while we eat."

Evan opens the door and directs room service to set dinner up on the dining table. As the server is readying the table, it occurs to me that someone could live here full time. The two-story suite is enormous. There's a kitchen, a dining area adjacent to the living room with a table for eight, and who knows how many bedrooms and bathrooms there are, not to mention the curved marble staircase that leads to an open loft-like area with a pool table that is visible from the lower level.

After the server leaves, Evan ushers me to one end of the modern, glass and chrome dining table where our dinner awaits. My mouth waters as my eyes feast on the offerings before I even sit down. An avocado, heirloom tomato, cucumber, and watermelon salad glistens from a light dressing flecked with lime zest, and grilled halibut topped with pico de gallo is served with a side of steamed asparagus. Sitting down, a whiff of the warm, yeasty dinner rolls draws a moan from my mouth. They smell like they just came out of the oven, reminding me of my grandmother's kitchen. On weekends, she always made the best homemade bread. Yum.

Evan pours us glasses of a lightly sparkling Vinho Verde wine from Portugal. The crisp white wine with its tiny bubbles is a perfect match to the halibut and will, hopefully, lower my stress level a notch too.

After I take a sip of the soothing beverage, I say, "Evan, this is delicious. It's just what I needed."

"Glad you like it. I usually drink red wines, unless I am celebrating something with champagne, but I figured that a chef such as yourself would give me a hard time for ordering red wine with fish."

"That's funny, I usually prefer red too, but I also like a crisp white wine. I must confess though, I've only had Vinho Verde once before, but I loved the hint of fizz that reminded me of champagne. It's a great choice, but don't worry, you can order a red wine with any meal, and I'll be happy too. And I promise not to give you a hard time." When I realize what I said, I add, "That is if the occasion to share another meal arises."

Evan laughs softly and replies "I like the way you think. I will make sure the occasion arises. Now let's ban talk of Leon's death for a few minutes and enjoy our dinner before we pass out from lack of nourishment. Then we can discuss clearing your good name."

"Ok, but I'll need a distraction, so while we eat, I would love to learn more about you."

"Same here," Evan nods. "First, tell me why you signed up for this competition when you already seem to have a great career."

"It's complicated," I sigh. "Until now, I've taken the safe route to ensure I could pay my own way. Sometimes even when family plans to have your back, they can't. After law school, I thought I would be happy when I secured the job my parents always wanted for me at a well-respected firm. It's stable and pays well, but it's monotonous, and my boss doesn't show any consideration or respect for any of the younger attorneys. He expects us to be available 24/7, and anything less crushes any chance for a promotion."

As I place my napkin on my lap, I continue explaining. "I'm goal-oriented, so I've been laser-focused on exceeding those expectations, which means I haven't had much time for fun or for seriously exploring my passion for cooking. When I saw the application for this competition, I was burned out. I was truly craving an adventure and a chance to regain my zest for life, so with a little nudge from my best friend Lowri, I took the plunge and applied." After a short pause, I add, "Sorry, I didn't mean to go into such a long explanation, but as I said, it's complicated."

Evan places his hand on my forearm and gently squeezes. "Cassandra, I admire that you took the initiative to explore a new path. Most people aren't willing to take chances or make changes unless they are forced to. It is important to be passionate about your endeavors."

"Thanks for the support. What are you passionate about?" I ask as I butter a roll.

"A number of things, but if I had to pick one, it would be the charities that my family is actively involved with. We have a foundation whose goal is to make sure no family in our country goes to bed hungry."

"That's a noble and worthy cause. How successful have you been?"

After finishing a bite of the halibut, Evan lays his fork on the plate. "Moderately successful, but we have a lot more work to do. We are hoping to expand our efforts to improve employment opportunities, education, and training to make sure the next generation will be less likely to suffer from hunger or homelessness. However, it is a difficult and complicated problem to solve," Evan says, scrunching his brow.

"I'm sure it is. Tell me something else about yourself. What do you like to do for fun?"

"As I mentioned before, I love to travel. I particularly love visiting new places and experiencing different cultures. What about you?"

"Other than cooking new creations for friends, I've always wanted to travel, but I haven't had too many opportunities to do so yet. Growing up, my parents were workaholics who rarely took time off. Even when we traveled, it was usually somewhere they needed to go for work. That meant I spent most of my time at the hotel while they went to meet their clients. I can't wait to be able to go sightseeing when I travel. What were your favorite trips? I would love to hear about them. I've been making a list of my top 10 dream vacations," I tell him.

Dabbing his napkin to this mouth, Evan smiles and enthusiastically responds, "I would love to describe my favorite places. That sounds like a good excuse for another dinner. For now, tell me about your top 10 list. Is there a common theme to the places on your list?"

"Actually, there is. During our lunch, I think I mentioned I love beaches. I also love sipping a fruity, frozen cocktail while reading a good book. However, my list also includes trips to some of the countries that influence my cooking, so I can take some cooking classes to learn more about their food. Of course, I would also want to have time to see the major sights in each place. What about you? Do you prefer warm weather or cold weather?"

"Warm weather, unless skiing is involved. Do you ski?"

"A little. I could use some lessons and definitely more practice. I've only been skiing a couple of times."

"I can help with that," Evan says with a mischievous glint in his eye.

Laughing, I admit, "Sounds like fun. When you aren't playing, what type of work do you do?"

"I help manage the family business, which is a full-time job," Evan explains as his eyes turn somber. "With my father retiring, I don't want to let the family down, so I will be busy supporting my older brother, who will be taking over for my father." Finishing the explanation, he stares into infinity as though transported somewhere else.

Noting the seriousness in Evan's voice, I put down my utensils and gaze at him. Hoping to pull him back to the present, I say, "It sounds like you have a close family. Do all your siblings work in the family business?"

With a quick shake of the head, the trance is broken, as Evan turns to face me. "Yes, we all work in the business." Pushing back his chair, he says, "I hate to cut this conversation short, but if you are going to get any rest tonight, we probably need to get back to our work for the evening. Let's take our chocolate-covered fruit over to the sofa."

"I know you're right, but I wish we didn't have to return to the topics of murder and sabotage." As we walk back to the sofa, I realize I've enjoyed learning a little more about Evan. He's so easy to talk to, and I'm pleasantly surprised that we have shared interests. It's a little strange that he hasn't shared more about what type of work his family does, but since I'm not ready to share more about my parents yet, I didn't push for fear he would push me.

As we sit on the sofa, Evan directs the conversation back to the main topic of the evening, saying, "We need to talk with Sean about the conversation you overheard, but I understand your hesitancy and wanting more proof. Let me call Sean to see if we can get access to the video from this afternoon without sharing too much of your story."

Pulling his cell phone from his pocket, Evan contacts Sean. After ending the call, Evan shares, "Good news. Sean is going to get me access to the video from the kitchen camera and access to the data showing who used the kitchen's Maze entrance. The bad news is we must wait until tomorrow morning."

"Thanks, Evan, but I wish we could get the videos and data now."

He pulls me tighter against him as we stare out the wall of windows that face the Strip with its neon lights and parade of cars and people. "I know, but you asked me not to share more with Sean, and I couldn't push the timing unless I did."

"I know. Thank you for respecting my concerns." Evan pulls me even closer and reaches up, brushing the back of his hand against my cheek. Gently turning my head toward him, he captures my lips with his. I melt into his warmth as his hand wanders down the side of my torso with gentle but firm strokes. At my hip, he reaches underneath to grasp my ass and pulls me onto his lap, deftly positioning his warm hand on my inner thigh. I ache for more as my hand grips his strong bicep.

When our kiss breaks, he nuzzles my neck and nips lightly at my skin as I softly moan for more. I feel his warm breath tickle as he moves his lips up toward my ear. He uses his tongue to lightly tease my earlobe before he sucks it into his mouth. His teeth barely graze it as he continues to taunt me with his talented attention. I'm squirming on his lap as he tightens his grip to firmly hold me close, whispering in my ear, "Stay with me tonight."

"Evan, I already told you that I'm not used to moving this fast," I tell him, but I'm conflicted. He feels so good, but I don't want a Vegas-only fling. The problem is I don't do casual and I don't do serious, so I haven't been doing much of anything in the relationship department since my parents died. Lowri's right, I need to get past my fear that if I get close enough to love someone, I'll lose them like I lost my parents. I just met Evan, but he's making me want to deal with my fear, something no one has made me want to do before.

Evan peppers my neck with soft kisses, as he murmurs, "You cannot tell me you do not want to stay."

Breathing heavily, I gasp, "You're right, our chemistry is the most intense I have ever experienced, but for me, staying the night implies I'm in a relationship. You travel the world, dress like a male model, clearly come from money, and are best friends with the owner of a major Las Vegas resort. Therefore, I'm sure you are accustomed to women just throwing themselves at you and begging for even one night with you. But that's not me. I'm sorry."

"Cassandra, you have nothing to apologize for. I like that you are different. And I want to be with you tonight. We will not do anything you do not want. I promise. But at least let me hold you all night."

"That sounds so tempting. I spend a lot of time alone, which is usually fine, but I don't want to be alone tonight, and it feels so good to be in your arms. I just can't promise everything I know you want. Are you sure you still want me to stay if I'm not ready for more?"

Moving me off his lap, Evan says, "Then it's settled. For now, let's sit here and finish our wine and fruit while we take in the neon extravaganza on the Strip. Would you like me to tell you about the trip I have planned to New Zealand?"

After learning about Evan's love of sailing and his plans to go to New Zealand to watch the America's Cup yacht race, I fall asleep on Evan's sofa with my head snuggled against his chest. At some point, I am vaguely aware of him carrying me to a big bed and sinking into the softest mattress ever. Then he crawls in beside me, spoons me against his warm, hard body, and covers us up with a fluffy comforter. It is heavenly.

I don't recognize the dark room. But it feels like someone is staring at me, so I jerk away. A warm hand pushes the hair off my face, and a familiar voice says, "Calm down. You're safe." Then I remember I'm in Evan's bed.

OMG! I'm in Evan's bed!

He is propped up on his elbow looking at me with a soft affection I haven't seen in his eyes before. He pulls me closer and kisses me.

I'm still fully dressed, but his torso is bare. I wonder if that's all that's bare as I feel his hardness press firmly against my lower half. Cautiously I explore, slowly turning toward him and moving my hand down his back until I encounter the elastic waistband on his shorts. I'm not sure if I'm relieved or disappointed.

"I'm at a disadvantage," Evan says. "You are wearing far more clothes than I am. What do you think about evening the playing field?"

I laugh softly and say, "I think we can work on that." Then his hands gently nudge my torso up so he can lift my sundress over my head. I'm surprised when he doesn't immediately try to remove my bra and underwear but, instead, starts exploring the part he uncovered, lavishing each area of exposed skin with kisses. Evan's hand finds its way between my legs and his fingers trace tiny circles over the lace covering my most sensitive area, causing my core to throb in anticipation. As he works his magic, my hand finds its way down his torso until it reaches his bulging boxer briefs. An involuntary gasp escapes my mouth, which draws a chuckle from Evan. Given my relationship issues, I don't have as much experience as most women my age, but he's big, and it's been so long …

Before I can ponder that concern further, Evan's talented fingers have me wound up so tight I'm about to go over the edge. But at the last second, he pulls his hand away. What the fuck?! I grab his hand to put it back where it belongs when he whispers, "Just a second," and reaches for something from his nightstand. Showing me the foil packet in his hand, his eyes silently ask permission. I remember promising Lowri I would give the right guy a chance, and Evan is definitely the one who makes me want to keep that promise. For the first time in almost five years, I'm ready to take this chance. I'm sure this is what I want, so I nod in assent and soon am filled to the brim, and we are soaring to the stars. Floating back to earth satiated, I fall asleep wrapped in Evan's arms, thinking I need to rest before dealing with reality again tomorrow.

CHAPTER THIRTY-TWO

CASSIE

The next morning I wake spooned against Evan's warm body. It brings a smile to my face. Maybe I should have regrets, but I'm bathing in my new mantra, so I will not look back. Evan stirs and starts stretching. Then he pulls me closer and kisses me hungrily. "Cassandra, I could get used to having you in my bed. Let's order breakfast and stay here the rest of the morning. Last night wasn't enough."

My body agrees. It wants to stay under the covers with Evan. But the image of the newspaper headline flashes in my head, and I know I must find a way to clear my name. "Evan, last night was absolutely fantastic, and I would love to spend the morning in bed with you. But we need to start reviewing the videos, so I can clear my name."

"I know, but we still need to eat. I will order breakfast and check in with Sean to see if the videos and Maze entry data are ready, but stay in bed for now."

When breakfast arrives, we eat in bed. I feel so pampered indulging in croissants with apricot jam, thick slices of bacon with brown sugar and coarse black pepper, old-fashioned hash brown potatoes, blueberry pancakes with pure maple syrup, and hot tea with lemon. How did he know my favorite breakfast splurges without even asking? Then the light bulb goes off. Christian! He must have asked Christian to send up one of everything I've ordered for breakfast since arriving at the Athena. Of course, I never ordered them all at once. Tapping my index finger against my lips, I think to myself, "Thoughtful and clever. Bonus points for Evan."

After we've finished eating, Evan says, "If you want a shower, you can use the one in the adjoining bathroom. I will shower in one of the other bathrooms. As much as I would prefer joining you in the shower, I know we don't have time for where that would lead."

Stepping into the shower, I have mixed feelings. On one hand, meeting Evan and spending last night with him was like a fairytale. He makes me feel like a princess. On the other hand, I have this constant uneasiness and fear from the cloud of being a murder suspect that is hanging over my head and the concern that the Firm will let me go if, and more likely when, they see the news article. I highly doubt the negative publicity will be overcome by the truth that I'm innocent, but I hope otherwise. With that thought, I turn the shower to scalding, trying to clear my head.

As I grab a fluffy white towel to dry off, the doorbell rings. After throwing on my clothes from last night, I hurry to the suite's living room where Evan is already loading the files onto his laptop. "Cassandra, Sean sent the data we wanted, along with a printed layout of the kitchen showing where the cameras and Maze door are located."

"Great. Let's look at the layout first so we can get a sense of what the cameras cover. I think the Maze door was not too far from the walk-in refrigerator, but I don't remember ever seeing it."

We both start looking at the layout. Evan says, "It's probably hidden like the other Maze entrances."

"Let's see. The fridge takes up a large portion of the back left corner of the kitchen. I heard Deep Voice's footsteps pass along the front side of the fridge. That means the Maze door must be somewhere along the left side of the layout, not too far from the fridge."

"Ok. This must be it. See the little circle with a small, capital M inside?"

"Evan, that has to be it. Hmm, let me think. I believe there's a door in that area with a sign that says 'Electrical Room. Danger. Keep Out.'"

"Then that's it. Now that we know where to look, we need to search the videos."

We fast forward the video to the time I was stuck in the fridge. The video is grainy, so we both lean in close to his laptop screen. When I see Jayden's mouth start moving, I get excited and say, "See Evan, Jayden is talking to someone. We just can't see who it is. Do you believe me now?"

Evan puts his arm around my waist, pulls me close and presses a sweet kiss to the top of my head. "Princess, I never doubted you."

"Evan, that is the polite thing to say, but you wouldn't be human unless you had at least a little doubt. My unexplained fingerprints on Leon's bowl would be enough to make anyone question my innocence."

"Cassandra, my only doubts were caused by Sean. My gut always told me he was wrong. I never questioned your story about what you heard while trapped in the refrigerator, so please believe me when I say, I don't doubt you. We are past that now. Let's get back to the videos and figure out who is the real villain of this story."

After watching all the videos, we realize none of the cameras captured anyone but Jayden. And unfortunately, the videos don't have audio. "Evan, do you think Deep Voice knew where the cameras were and purposefully stood where he knew he wouldn't be captured?"

"That is quite possible. You said he mentioned cameras before leaving the kitchen. Let's check the Maze entrance data. He should show up there."

We pull up the entry and exit data for the Maze door. It shows the door was only accessed and opened a few times during the whole day, with only one access at about the time I remember being in the fridge. Getting excited again, I point to the screen and exclaim, "There Evan, that entry has to be the guy who was talking with Jayden. But there isn't a name, only a number. Is it an employee number?"

Staring at the screen, smiling, Evan says, "Finally some progress. It is probably an ID number. We need to find out whom it belongs to, so I need to call Sean."

Grabbing his cell, Evan dials and puts it on speakerphone. Evan holds his finger over his mouth indicating that I should stay quiet, then says, "Sean, if I know the number for a person who entered or exited the Maze, how can I match that to a name?"

"That's easy, give me the number."

"7583928."

I'm wringing my hands with impatience as we hear typing. Then Sean says, "That is Mitch Hendricks. He works in security. Why are you asking? Did he turn up in the data I sent you?"

My mouth falls open. Why would a security guy be trying to sabotage and rig the competition? It doesn't make sense.

"Yes, he did. What type of security does he do? Would he have reason to be in the kitchen in Trendz?"

"According to our records, he is a mid-level employee in the security department, so he could be anywhere at almost any time. However, he may have gone there to check that everything was secure after the competition today."

Agitated, I push my chair back, scrapping it against the marble floor, which causes Evan to remind me to be quiet so Sean won't know I'm listening. I nod in understanding but start pacing around the room while I listen. Sean won't hear my bare feet meet the cold marble.

Evan responds, "I see. So, it wouldn't surprise you that he was in the Trendz kitchen late yesterday afternoon?"

"Not particularly."

Pushing for more information, Evan asks, "What do you know about him?"

"Not a lot. He has worked for us for a couple of years. I recognize his photo. I've run into him on occasion when he was working an event. Evan, you clearly have learned something. Tell me."

Returning to my chair and sitting on my hands, I nod, indicating that he has my permission to share more. "Sean, I have reason to believe that Mitch offered an advantage to one of the finalists yesterday, and it may not have been the first offer of this type."

Sean almost screams through the speaker, "What? Where did you hear this?"

Evan wraps his arm around my shoulders. "That's not important. What is important is that Mitch offered Jayden 'another advantage' in exchange for Jayden sabotaging one of the other finalists. Even more disturbing is that Jayden accepted the offer saying that he just didn't want anyone to get hurt."

"Do you think Mitch and Jayden had something to do with Chef Boucher's death?"

"I don't know, but maybe."

"This whole thing doesn't make sense. Mitch isn't in a position to give someone an advantage."

"Maybe Mitch is working with someone else who is."

"Maybe, but why? What would he gain?"

"I don't know, but we need to keep a close eye on Jayden and Mitch, and I don't know how you are going to do that given that Mitch works in security."

After a long pause, Sean concedes, "Whether I like it or not, I need to share this with Detective Fielder. Then I will deal with Athena's security team."

"Also, Sean, we don't know who Mitch may be working with, so I wouldn't mention this to anyone else involved in the competition."

"You are probably right, Evan. But I need to know where you got this information. I need to know how credible the source is."

"I can't tell you yet."

"I see. You didn't heed my warning to stay away from Ms. Edwards. How do you know she didn't make this up?"

Deflating, my shoulders sag as I realize Sean still doesn't trust me or want Evan near me. I'd hoped this new information would change his opinion.

Squeezing me closer, Evan says, "We'll talk later. Goodbye." Evan ends the call and looks at me with apologetic eyes as he pulls me from my chair onto his lap, pressing my head into his chest as I fight to hold back tears of frustration, sadness, and fear for what the future holds.

After regaining my composure, I say, "Evan, I'm not surprised. I knew Sean wouldn't believe me, but at least he agreed to keep an eye on Mitch and Jayden."

"Do not worry, Cassandra. We will get to the bottom of this."

Then my TekCuff beeps to remind me it's time to get ready for our photoshoot and interviews at the Olympic Torch Tower. I can't believe it's already 2:15. "I need to go to my room and dress for the interviews at 3:00. Will you be at the photoshoot?"

"Yes, I will see you at the Olympic Torch Bar. It should be fun."

"They haven't given us any details about the photoshoot. They just said to wear a swimsuit underneath shirts and shorts. What are we doing? Are we going sailing on the Aegean?"

"It is a surprise."

CHAPTER THIRTY-THREE

SEAN

"Emily, please have them bring my car to the VIP driveway. I'm going downtown for lunch with Wes."

Wes owns one of the best gourmet food distribution services in Las Vegas, so I don't understand why we aren't using his service anymore. Hopefully, this one-on-one meeting will shed some light on the reason.

Interrupting my thoughts, Emily responds, "Of course, Sean. Your car will be waiting for you."

"Great. I am taking the elevator down now."

As I arrive at the VIP driveway, my prized, red Lamborghini Aventador SVJ pulls around, stopping at the curb in front of me. I thank the fresh-faced valet and get behind the wheel. I love driving this car, but the trip downtown won't let me take advantage of its power, which reminds me I need to find time to drive out to the desert again soon. That seems to be the only place where I can push the limits of this powerful machine. It's been too long. Until then, I still get to enjoy the heads it turns, particularly when they are attached to some of the eye-catching women that grace our city. This car and a wink have sealed the deal for me more than once.

When I arrive at the upscale Mexican restaurant that Wes loves, before going inside, I make sure the valet understands the consequences if my car is harmed.

Spotting Wes in the back corner, I make my way to his table. "Wes, what was it you couldn't tell me on the phone?" I say as I slide into the booth, getting right to business.

Laughing at my having skipped the normal niceties, Wes responds with, "Sean, good to see you too."

Then Wes calls the server over and orders a yellow diamond margarita with an extra shot of tequila on the side.

"What the fuck is a yellow diamond margarita?"

The server explains, "It's our newest and most popular margarita. It's made with premium agave tequila, simple syrup, lime juice, a splash of pure cane rum, and a lemon twist."

"Wes, that sounds like an afternoon hangover in a glass."

He looks at me and says, "Sean, for this discussion, you are going to need at least one."

That ominous statement takes me aback. I thought this meeting was going to make things better by clearing things up. With brows scrunched, I tell the server I'll try the margarita but hold the extra shot.

While we wait for our drinks, Wes insists on small talk, so I comply. But my patience is running thin, so after our drinks arrive, I waste no time reiterating my first question.

Downing his shot of tequila, Wes cautions, "Sean, I didn't reach out to you before because I don't have proof of what I'm going to share."

"Wes, don't play games. We both know it's strange that your company is no longer one of Athena's suppliers. You own the best gourmet food distribution service in Las Vegas, and we'd be foolish not to source from you. Plus, you are not the only one that was cut off. I need to know what is going on, and I need to know now."

He leans back against the booth and narrows his eyes at me, hesitating before saying, "There are rumors that if suppliers don't give kickbacks, the Athena cuts them off."

"What? I force myself not to jump up at the news. Kickbacks to whom?"

"Sean, I'm not even sure the rumor is true. We were never approached for a kickback. Orders from the Athena just slowly decreased until eventually we weren't getting any of your business. When our account manager asked why, he was told that Chef Maurizio was in charge of approving all suppliers and all orders."

"Did your account manager speak with Chef Maurizio directly?"

"No. Apparently, your chef wouldn't return his calls or take a meeting."

"That's strange. You have been one of our suppliers since the beginning. Why would Chef Maurizio suddenly cut you off?"

"Our account manager said he heard your former chef was reaching out to other suppliers, offering them business if they kicked some money back to him."

"So, Chef Maurizio was behind this?" I chug the rest of my margarita as I contemplate the implications of this new information.

"I'm not so sure. Like I said, I heard the story from Eric, our account manager, soon after we lost Athena's business. If he hadn't been with us so long, I would have questioned whether Eric made the story up to cover for a mistake that caused him to lose your business."

"Did Eric tell you anything else?"

"Yes. The other suppliers told him their conversations with Chef Maurizio were awkward, like the chef wasn't comfortable asking for the kickbacks. I'm not sure what that means."

"After Chef Maurizio left, did you try to get our business back?"

"Of course, but we were told that the Athena was not looking to change suppliers at the time."

"Who told you that?"

"I'm not sure. I can check with Eric. But rumors are circulating that the kickbacks are still a requirement to do business with the Athena. That makes me think your former chef was not the only one involved."

"Shit. I think I need that shot now." Wes must be communicating with our server telepathically because a shot mysteriously appears in front of me. I down it. "Wes, I wish you had come to me about this."

"I was planning to talk with you, but it was awkward, and then Chef Maurizio left shortly after we were cut off. Like you, I assumed we would be able to get the business back when you got a new chef. Besides, it's not in my nature to beg a friend for business. If you didn't want to use us, I figured it was your choice."

"But we've known each other almost our whole lives. Surely, you didn't think I would put up with someone skimming or taking kickbacks."

"I didn't have any proof about the kickbacks, so the conversation I needed to have with you was going to be awkward. But when we didn't get the business back and rumors continued about the kickbacks, I decided we had to talk. I was planning to corner you at the reception for the Guest Chef Competition."

"Why didn't you?"

"Well, this is another awkward part. I noticed the food at the reception was lower quality than what we had been supplying you in the past. I decided that maybe we lost the business because you needed to save money and were cutting corners where you could."

"No, that is not the case. I must admit that I didn't have a chance to sample the food at the reception, so I didn't notice its quality. Now I'm also embarrassed that we served our VIPs crappy food."

"The differences in quality were small. Your guests probably didn't pay much attention."

"Can you give me examples?"

"Sure. For example, the cheese was not top end. They served a lower quality Gouda instead of an aged Gouda. Instead of caviar, they served salmon roe, which is much less expensive. Instead of champagne, they served prosecco. Nothing was wrong with the food, but it wasn't up to your past standards."

"But I was served champagne. I saw the bottle."

"Of course, you were served champagne. Everyone knows you could tell the difference. But the guests were served prosecco, which was nice, but less expensive."

"I see." I remember thinking my first glass of champagne at the reception tasted off.

"Sean, have you spoken with Chef Maurizio?" Wes leans in and asks.

"Not yet. First, I'm trying to gather as many facts as I can. I had hoped the problems left with him, but it looks like that may not be the case." I pause to think. "Wes, I have another question for you. What were you doing at the pool the day of the cooking demonstration?"

"My wife and I had friends visiting from New York who were staying at the Athena. They invited us to have lunch with them at the pool. Why do you ask?"

"No real reason. I was just curious why you didn't stop by to chat."

"That's simple. As you entered the pool area, we were being hustled out because of the accident. It wasn't the time for a friendly chat."

"That makes sense." I slide out of the booth to leave. "Sorry to rush out and not stay to eat, but I better get going now. Thanks for your help."

"No problem. When you get this sorted out, we would like an opportunity to get your business back. And next time let's enjoy a good meal and actually catch up without all of this ..." He waves a hand in the air to indicate the unpleasant business.

"Of course. I hope to get this sorted out soon, and I promise we will make it right with you."

"Thanks, Sean."

"Wes, please reach out to me if you hear anything else," I say as I turn to leave.

"Will do."

I need to talk with Chef Maurizio as soon as possible. I would prefer to talk with him in person, but I don't have time to fly to Europe until after the competition, so a call will have to do. Until then, I need to figure out who else was part of this kickback scheme.

Sliding into my car, I tell my phone to call Evan, but I get his voicemail and leave a message. "Evan, I have some new information I would like to share with you. Let's meet as soon as you finish with the promotional event."

CHAPTER THIRTY-FOUR

CASSIE

"Please be seated," Amy says, gesturing to four high-top tables in the Olympic Torch Bar, as her assistant Cameron hands out pens and notecards.

"I am going to tell you the theme for Round 2 of the competition. You will have 15 minutes to write down your entrée and a list of any key ingredients you need us to have on hand for you."

What? Only 15 minutes? That's insane. I thought I had another full day to figure out my ideas for a special entrée that will wow the judges. I should have been giving it more thought. Instead, I've been focused on clearing my name, and of course Evan was a significant distraction last night. I take a few deep breaths and remind myself that while I would prefer to be fully prepared, I tend to perform well under pressure. Let's hope that works for me today.

Surveying the reactions of the other finalists tells me they are just as surprised. Trenton looks pissed, and Kai looks perplexed as to what he will do. Interestingly, Jayden looks smug. Does that mean he received the advantage he was offered? Hmm.

My thoughts are interrupted when Amy says, "Are you ready?" We all nod like robots. What else can we do, right? Sean did say this competition would require us to think fast on our feet and tackle unexpected challenges with a smile.

"Ok. As a word of caution, I will not answer any questions about the theme. You must interpret what it means to you and come up with an entrée that reflects that meaning," Amy says. "Be sure to also write down a one-sentence description explaining what the theme means to you. The theme is 'Comfort with a Flair.' Your 15 minutes start now."

What is "Comfort with a Flair"? It could mean a lot of different things. It could be comfort food with an unusual twist. It could be comfort food plated in a fancy way. Hmm. But neither of those seems quite right for the Athena. The Athena is about luxury in everything, so maybe we are supposed to create an upscale experience that is based on a comfort food. What if I can deliver a little of all three?

I start racking my brain for ideas. When I think upscale, I think lobster, crab, shrimp, filet mignon, and fancy sauces, but those don't scream comfort food. I picture mac and cheese or beef stew on a cold winter night. That's comfort food. That's it! An upscale version of beef stew, but instead of a traditional stew, I will make beef in a red wine sauce. I can serve it with mashed potatoes and puffed popover rolls. Roasted rainbow carrots would also add some nice color to the plate and fit with the idea of a stew."

Amy calls out, "You have only three minutes left."

How did the time go so quickly? I wonder as I scribble my list of ingredients.

When time is called, Cameron picks up the cards, and as Amy starts interviewing each of the finalists, the room grows warmer and a tingling sensation runs down the back of my neck. Turning my head, I notice Evan behind us, discreetly watching everyone. I should have known where the warmth came from. I always seem to sense when Evan's in the room even when he's not in my line of sight. He looks great in his dark blue swim shorts and taut red and blue polo shirt with designer sunglasses tucked into the front. We still don't know why they had us wear bathing suits and cover ups, but I won't complain if I get to see Evan shirtless soon.

After the interviews are over, Amy announces, "It's time to go to the Olympic Tower for the photoshoot." We follow her toward the balcony overlooking the Aegean and walk down the wide staircase that leads to a pathway at the edge of the water, where a security officer opens the gate, allowing access to the path to the Olympic Tower. As we approach the Tower, I gaze at the staircase that winds up its exterior like a clinging vine, my fear of heights rapidly rising to the surface.

We round the base of the tower, and another security guard holds open a hidden door in the back. Peering inside, I exhale a relieved breath when I see an elevator. If we have to go to the top of the Tower, an elevator sounds much better than the outdoor, open staircase. I squeeze into the small elevator with Amy, Evan, and the other finalists. When we reach the top and exit, I'm handed a helmet and some other gear and directed to step out onto a balcony encircling the Tower that overlooks the Aegean Sea and the Olympic stage.

A warm hand caresses my back and Evan whispers, "Are you ok?"

"No. I hate heights. What is this harness for? Why do I need a helmet?"

Before Evan can answer, Amy says, "Welcome to Athena's Thrill Ride. While this is a cooking competition, the Athena is also using it as an opportunity to show off some of the fun activities guests can enjoy when they visit. Therefore, today we are going to highlight Athena's Thrill Ride. We have drones ready to take videos, and we also have camera crews here and on the other side of the Aegean to capture you ziplining across the water. Since you will land in the water, you'll want to be wearing only your bathing suits, so you can hand your other clothes to one of the crew members. The Athena is excited to be able to show off this exhilarating experience, so please remember to smile for the cameras."

I can't believe I never noticed the zipline connected to the Tower. I'm really freaking out now. I can't do this. I'll admit, it looks like it could be fun, but heights terrify me. I don't think I can take that first step off the platform. What if the wire breaks or I fall off?

I can't be the only one who is scared. However, Kai and Jayden are excited and ready to go, and Trenton merely looks annoyed, as though this is a waste of his time. As I peel off my shirt and shorts, I ask myself "What is wrong with them?"

Evan whispers, "It's going to be ok. Breathe slowly and deeply." He is peeling off his polo shirt revealing ripped abs that I want to run my hands over. My pulse was already high, but staring at him not only distracts, it also causes my pulse to skyrocket further upward. His gaze fixes on my black and gold bikini. His eyes tell me he wants to devour me right here and now. We are in big trouble. If we don't quit staring at each other this way, everyone will figure out something is going on between us.

Fortunately, Amy breaks the spell when she asks, "Who wants to go first? We would also like to show off the tandem option for couples. Cassie would you be willing to do a tandem ride with Evan? We would greatly appreciate it if you would."

I choke out a strangled "Sure" as Evan whispers in my ear, "See, it will be fine. I'll hold you the whole way down." I shudder. I'm not sure I can do this at all.

"That would be perfect. You two will go last," Amy says. "Now everyone, put your helmets on. The instructor is going to show you how to put on the harness and go over the safety information. Have fun."

We watch everyone else take their turn soaring through the air and landing on the platform submerged a foot or two under the water on the far side of the Aegean Sea. Kai was the most relaxed, signaling "Hang Loose" with his left hand as he hurtled through the air. Jayden is naturally meeker but was pumping his fists right before he left the platform. I guess this brought out some inner, adventurous beast in him. As for Trenton, he still looked annoyed but unfazed. For me, what was important was that they all survived, so I guess it's safe enough, and maybe this experience will help me overcome my fear of heights. Las Vegas certainly is making me face my fears whether I wanted to or not. That said, I'm still scared to take that first step.

When it's our turn, Evan and I are connected to the zipline cables with me in front of him. The ride operator tells Evan to put his arms around my waist. I'm relieved when I feel his muscular arms encircle me. The next thing I know, we are hurtling through the air. Rather than scream, I close my eyes tightly, tense my body, and hang on; it's how I handle scary drops on roller coasters, so maybe it will get me through this too.

Almost immediately, I hear a ripping and cracking sound. Then I scream, "I'm going to fall! My harness is tearing! I don't want to die!" as I feel myself dropping farther below the zipline cable and slipping out of Evan's arms.

Evan shouts "Stay still. I've got you."

"Please don't drop me," I cry.

Evan's arms tighten around my waist so much that it's hard to breathe. "I won't. My arms are locked around you. Just hold as still as possible."

But just then I hear more tearing as more of the webbing on my harness gives way as he tries to hold onto me. Tears run down my cheeks as I scream, "I can't hold still; I'm falling!"

I continue to slip down Evan's body, and he grabs under my arms with his hands locked together across my chest. Evan commands, "Cassandra, reach behind and grab onto my harness. We're almost to the landing platform. Try to hold your legs up and get ready for the splash."

Hoping his harness isn't tearing too, I reach behind and try to grab hold, but my arms aren't long enough. I give up and, instead, grasp his swim trunks as best I can as my harness completely disconnects from the zipline. My whole body is dangling, held up only by Evan's arms and my grip on his shorts. I hope he can hold me the final few yards because I'm not sure the water is deep enough to survive a fall onto its concrete bottom.

As the gear smashes into the block designed to stop us, my shins drag across the rough underwater platform as we simultaneously are splashed with water and jolted to a stop. We are quickly surrounded by workers shouting instructions and freeing us from the zipline, handing us towels, and checking us out to make sure we aren't seriously hurt. I hear one call for medics.

Evan lifts me out of the water, cradling me in his arms as he carries me to a dry area of the platform. "You are going to be ok," Evan reassures.

Trying to catch my breath, I manage to say, "I thought we were going to die! Are you ok?"

He assures me he is fine, and as the medics arrive, he lays me down on the dry platform.

I stare into his eyes, whispering, "Thanks for holding me the whole way. I could have been killed if I'd gone by myself. Thank goodness we did the tandem ride." It's good I'm not the fainting type or I would be out cold by now.

"You are safe now, but we need to let the medics look at your legs."

Raising my head to look down at the front of my legs, I realize they're covered in blood. Now that the initial shock is wearing off, they are starting to burn. "Evan, did someone just try to kill me?

"Cassandra, to be honest, I am not sure."

After evaluating my wounds, the medics explain that the bones are bruised with protruding bumps, and both shins are covered in floor burns and scrapes from being dragged along the platform. Fortunately, the injuries are not serious even though they hurt like hell. It could have been so much worse. However, it's going to take a while for the medics to clean and bandage the wounds to prevent infection, so I have no choice but to lie on the platform and let them do their job. I hear Evan demand the zipline supervisor shut down the ride and check all the equipment immediately. He also tells her to set aside my gear for Mr. Cartwright to see.

With both legs bandaged from knee to ankle, I am instructed to take an over-the-counter pain reliever as needed. Evan helps me to my feet, and we are directed to a little boat beside the platform. We ride back to meet the other finalists and crew on the pathway near the stairs leading up to the Olympic Torch Bar.

In the boat, Evan and I decide to be careful what we share with the others, but once our group is back together, we are peppered with questions about what happened. Pointing out that we have had two outdoor events and two "accidents," Kai questions whether the competition is being sabotaged or whether it's just bad luck. I'm thinking sabotage, but I don't share that thought. Trenton wants to know if I unclipped myself. Really? Does he think I'm that stupid? Jayden is quiet and just asks if I'm ok. I will be, but I need a shot of something strong to drink, and the sooner the better. Maybe some ice on my legs would help too.

Amy, on the other hand, shocks us all when she glibly says, "Glad you're going to be ok, Cassie. We shot some great videos and photos. Mr. Cartwright and Cynthia will be thrilled. Thank you, everyone. Now you have less than 24 hours to get ready for Round 2. We will meet at the Trendz kitchen at 2 p.m. tomorrow. You will have four hours to prepare your entrée. Then you will meet with the judges for their evaluation. See you tomorrow." She bounces off.

My jaw hangs open. Really? I almost die and all she can say is that they shot some great video and management will be thrilled? Is she clueless? We all stare dumbfounded, watching her walk away as if nothing unusual happened.

CHAPTER THIRTY-FIVE

EVAN

After the group disperses, I say, "Cassandra, we need to find Sean now and have him put more security in place. I don't think he was particularly worried about the event today because it wasn't a cooking event, but clearly, all of you finalists need security at all times."

"We don't know that my equipment was sabotaged. Besides, anyone could have been given that harness."

"I wish that were true, but it is not. Did you notice that all the helmets had names on them and were connected to the harnesses when they handed them out? More likely than not, someone wanted you to get that harness."

"You're right, but it could have been an accident. Maybe I was just unlucky and was given faulty equipment."

"That is one explanation, but we cannot take that chance. We have to assume this may have been the sabotage that Mitch mentioned to Jayden. Having you out of the competition would be an advantage."

"But Jayden said he wasn't willing to hurt anyone."

"True, but maybe others have also been offered advantages, and they may not have been so worried about the safety of their competitors."

"This whole thing is nuts. I'm tempted to quit the competition and go home. It isn't worth my life. But if I quit, Detective Fielder might arrest me to keep me from leaving town and that would follow my name forever."

"The competition is not worth your life, but I agree that Detective Fielder will insist you stay in Las Vegas until Chef Boucher's case is closed. And if you are here, you might as well continue with the competition. We just need to ensure there is more security."

We rush to Sean's office to tell him about the zipline "accident." Sean promises someone will be looking out for Cassie, but he refuses to tell her who it is. He does share that they have undercover police in place but thought it would be better if Cassie didn't know who they were. That way she would not accidentally expose their identity.

Leaving Sean's office, Cassie asks if I'll walk her back to her room. When we arrive at her room after crossing the hotel, I start to follow Cassie in, but she says, "Evan, thanks for walking me back. I'm going to try to get some rest now."

Leaning against the open door, I nod in understanding. "Ok. Why don't you pack up your stuff, so we can move it to my room? You can rest there."

"I can't do that," Cassandra responds with a firm shake of her head. "I need some time alone to process everything."

Baffled, I spread my arms, palms up. "Why not stay with me? You will be safer in my suite."

"I'll be fine here," Cassie implores as she pats my chest, and I wrap my arms around her, pulling her tight. "I cannot thank you enough for keeping me close when I felt alone, but now I need some time to clear my head and get some rest. If I stay with you, I suspect there won't be much time for rest. I'll lock my door and stay in for the evening. I'll see you tomorrow."

"Are you sure?" I do not want to leave her alone, but ultimately, it is her choice.

"Yes, I'm sure. Also, don't forget, Sean activated panic codes on my TekCuff that will directly alert you, Sean, and security if I'm in trouble. Sean promised that Mitch is not part of that aspect of security, so I will be fine."

"Ok," I acquiesce. "I will call the concierge desk and ask Christian to escort you to the competition tomorrow afternoon. Please do not open the door for anyone else unless it is me, Sean, or Christian. Right now, we do not know whom else we can trust."

"That seems like overkill. I have the panic code now, so I feel much safer. Besides, I'll need meals between now and then, so I'll need to open the door for room service."

I give Cassandra a final squeeze and step aside. "Christian or I will bring you food. Please respect my request to not let anyone else in. You've become very special to me. You need to be careful." I lean back and push a strand of hair out of Cassandra's eyes. Then I resist the urge to kiss her luscious lips, and instead, gently kiss her forehead and tell her to lock the door. As the door closes between us, I murmur, "Stay safe, Cassandra."

What I chose not to share with Cassandra was the insane fear I felt when she almost fell 40 feet to her death today. First, I didn't want her to realize how close I came to dropping her. Our bodies and arms were slick with sweat from the sun's heat, so she kept slipping further and further. Second, I am confused about my feelings. The thought of losing her was shattering. I wonder, am I falling for her and want to hold on forever, or would I have felt that same way about anyone in that situation? Given that I have never been the type to fall in love in the past, I assume it's the latter. Cassandra is different, but I am not ready for a forever someone. It is my brother who is looking for that now. Not me.

CHAPTER THIRTY-SIX

CASSIE

At 1:45 p.m., Christian knocks on my door to escort me to the competition. I thank him profusely for delivering dinner last night and brunch this morning. Along with dinner, he brought me ice packs to soothe my swollen legs and reminded me to take some Tylenol before going to sleep because I would be on my feet a lot during Round 2. Then with brunch this morning, he handed me a bag with antibiotic cream and new bandages. After he left, I read his note that said, "I made sure the cream is the one with pain reliever because we want you to be able to concentrate on cooking today rather than on your aching legs. I'm rooting for you. Good luck today! *Christian.*" I make sure to let him know how much I appreciate all the extra work he is doing to look after me and acknowledge that I know this is not part of his job. The true professional, he tells me that it's his pleasure.

As we walk to Trendz, we talk about the competition and what I'm planning to make this round. He offers sincere words of reassurance and support, which I find soothing. He must be an amazing person to have as a friend if he can provide a relative stranger like me such comfort. Looking after people seems to come naturally to him. No wonder he's head of Concierge Services. It's the perfect job for him.

When we arrive at Trendz, I thank Christian for taking me through the Maze's shortcut, and he wishes me good luck and says goodbye. I should be nervous about the competition, but I've been too busy trying to stay alive and clear my name. When I look around, the other chefs seem wound up tighter than a spring though. In a funny way, that may give me an advantage because the idea of cooking for a few hours surrounded by Sean's undercover security team sounds like a relaxing break from my real concerns. But where's Evan? I'd hoped to receive a smile of encouragement from him before we get started, but he isn't anywhere in sight.

When the cameras and lights are in place, Amy directs us to our stations and reminds us of the four-hour time limit. At exactly 2:30 p.m., Sebastian cues the crew to start filming. Then Amy explains Round 2 to the camera. She stops at each of our stations and has us explain what we're making and how it fits with the theme. This time, I go first. I explain that I'm transforming a comforting beef stew into an elevated meal with a flair. My entrée will be braised beef with red wine mushroom sauce, mashed potatoes, and roasted, baby carrots. It will be served with my favorite, homemade rolls, called popovers, which are airy rolls made from an egg, milk, and flour batter. They are similar to England's Yorkshire pudding.

I'm working as fast as I can because I know the four hours will go by quickly, but I'm still a little distracted by the interviews. Trenton explains he's stuffing manicotti with roast beef, spinach, and béchamel sauce. Then he's topping the manicotti with marinara sauce and baking it in the oven. I hear him tell Amy, "Nothing is more comforting than pasta, right?" She agrees and asks what he considers to be the flair to his dish." He explains the flair is using roast beef instead of a more traditional ground meat mixture. Sounds good to me.

Kai is serving a macadamia-coated fish filet on top of pineapple fried rice. As Amy asks Kai to explain how it fits the theme, someone turns on a food processor, so I can't hear his answer.

Jayden explains he's making Texas comfort food with a flair. He says that enchiladas are comfort food where he comes from, but for a flair he's making seafood crêpes filled with crab, shrimp, and spinach, topped with a cream sauce, and accompanied with a side of wild rice. I give him credit for using the similarity to enchiladas as his explanation for why it's a comfort food.

My beef is in the oven braising, and my popover batter is ready. It's almost time to put the carrots in an oven to roast and the popovers in another oven to bake. I just need to time them right so that the carrots and popovers are ready at the right time to plate. Too early and they will be overcooked or cold. Too late and the carrots will be raw, and the popovers will deflate. Double checking the clock, I realize I have 10 minutes to wait, so I use that time to select my plates and get my parsley chopped for garnishing.

As I walk toward the racks with the dishes, I hear Kai call out "Jayden, watch where you're going. You could have been badly cut." Looking toward Kai's station, I see he's holding up a long, sharp knife for fileting his fish. Jayden must have bumped into him when he passed by, but why would Jayden be walking by Kai's station. Jayden's station is closer to the pantry than Kai's station. Was this an attempt by Jayden to sabotage Kai? Hopefully, security is watching closely. Regardless, I better grab my plates and get back to guard my food.

Throughout the three hours, Amy has distracted us by asking more questions about how things are going, which makes it difficult to concentrate. To stay on track, I repeatedly run through my mental checklist as I continue watching the clock. I also keep looking around, trying to figure out if there is any security here other than the two guys standing near Cynthia and Amy. Evan still hasn't shown up, which doesn't make sense. Maybe he's upset I turned him away last night. But that wouldn't keep him away from the competition, would it?

Amy pulls my attention back when she calls out, "You have five minutes left to plate your dishes."

I chose plates that are a cross between a plate and a shallow bowl to keep the red wine sauce from running all over the place. First, I slice a popover in half, place one half on the bottom of the plate, and spoon mashed potatoes into its hollow center. Then I carefully place tender chunks of beef on top making sure that some of the mushrooms and pearl onions are visible. I add three whole, baby carrots so the tops rest on the rim of the plate and the tips rest on top of the beef. I angle the other half of the popover on the edge of the plate. I lay the last popover in place as Amy says "15 seconds," and quickly start sprinkling parsley on top of each plate. I barely drop a little parsley onto the last plate when Amy says, "Stop. Step away from your stations." Whew! The last few minutes flew by. I wish I had time to clean up the rims of the plates a little, but they don't look too bad. I just hope my entrée has enough flair. I'll find out soon.

CHAPTER THIRTY-SEVEN

CASSIE

I'm about to enter the judging room as Kai exits. As our paths cross, I hear him mumble, "How could my entrée have been so salty? I didn't add any extra salt because the macadamia nuts were already very salty. It doesn't make sense."

"Kai, are you ok?" I ask, surprised to see Kai so distraught.

"No. My entrée was ruined, and I don't know how," he says.

"That's terrible." But since we aren't supposed to discuss the judge's comments, I don't inquire further. Then it hits me; I didn't have time to taste my food before I plated it. Mine may not taste right either.

Kai is about to say something else, but Amy's assistant tells me to hurry into the judging room, so I do. I'm surprised to see Evan standing at the side of the room after having been absent all day. His presence makes it easier to remember to smile as Amy announces my name and describes my entrée. As the judges lift the silver domes from their plates to reveal my creation, I hope it's still warm enough.

The judges lift their forks as Amy asks me to explain how my entrée fits with the theme, so I say, "A warm beef stew is very comforting on a cool winter's evening or any evening for that matter, so I started with that concept in mind. To add my flair, I transformed the basic ingredients of a stew—beef, potatoes, and carrots—into what you have before you. The beef was braised with mushrooms, pearl onions, and red wine. For a special touch, I served it nestled inside a popover with mashed potatoes and roasted rainbow carrots. I hope you enjoy it."

Not a smile crosses one of their faces, as their eyes squint in judgment of me and my food. Watching closely as they first close their eyes and take in the aromas of the stew and then taste their first bites, I can't tell if they're enjoying it or not, but I catch a hint of a smile on Evan's face, which is reassuring. It also reminds me that I'm supposed to be smiling whenever the camera is running. At least that's what Amy and Cynthia have told us.

The judges set their forks down, and Amy asks Judge Gerard for his comments. He says, "Overall, I like the idea of transforming stew into something more interesting. The red wine sauce is subtle, the beef is tender, and the popover is a nice, light addition. However, I would have preferred more salt, and perhaps a little more flair. For example, you could have used medallions of tenderloin instead of the cubes of beef. Your entrée is closer to comfort than flair." I'd worried about that.

To my relief, Judge Holden chimes in, "I disagree. I would be happy to order this dish at an upscale restaurant and would find it the perfect balance between comfort and flair. However, I agree it could have used a little more salt. Did you taste it before you served it?"

"Unfortunately, I ran out of time and didn't have a chance to taste it to make a final adjustment to the salt."

"I see. Don't make that mistake again. Never serve food you haven't tasted."

He's right. "Understood. Thank you for the feedback."

Amy turns to Judge Indigo and asks, "What are your comments for Cassie?"

"I agree with Judge Holden. Personally, I would not braise tenderloin. It would be a waste of that cut of meat, so Cassie you made the right choice. And I like the sauce and flavors you developed from the slower cooking method. The dish Judge Gerard proposes would have had to be prepared entirely differently to work. That said, you could have elevated the mashed potatoes with some add-ins, but overall, good job."

Nodding, I respond, "Thank you for your feedback."

Not too bad. I know people hate under-salted food, but I will take that over Kai's situation.

When the judging is over, Amy, Cynthia, and Evan return to the kitchen and tell us we have tomorrow off except for a one-hour, promotional event in the afternoon, and then Round 3 is the following day. After yesterday's Thrill Ride fiasco, I'm not too excited about another promotional event. My legs are sore and aching even with the pain reliever cream and Tylenol, but at least Sean promised security for all the events.

As we prepare to leave, Cynthia reminds us that the Final Dinner is black tie. I love an excuse to wear a long flowing formal dress, but I'll need to find one. Then Cynthia explains that we each need to stop by the Tux & Tiara Chalet tomorrow to arrange for the proper attire. It's located in Aphrodite's Way, the shopping area. Tux & Tiara will be loaning us clothing for the event. Thank goodness. I brought a cocktail dress for the Opening Reception, but they didn't tell us to bring anything formal.

On my way out of the kitchen, Evan surreptitiously slips me a note. When I start to say something, he barely shakes his head and keeps walking, so I wait a minute or two before walking out the door with the note hidden in my fist. In the nearest restroom, I enter one of the stalls before reading the note. It says *Meet me at my suite at 8:30 p.m. Sean arranged for your handprint to give you access to my floor now.* I check my TekCuff and see it is 7:30 now. That gives me time to change clothes first. As I'm about to exit the bathroom stall, I turn back and decide to flush it down the toilet, like I've seen in spy movies. Over-dramatic? Probably, but at least I stopped short of eating it.

CHAPTER THIRTY-EIGHT

EVAN

I look at my phone. Cassie is already 15 minutes late, which is long enough to worry me, given all the incidents with the finalists. As I'm about to have Sean track her location, the doorbell rings, and Cassie is leaning against the doorframe out of breath.

"Are you ok?"

"Yes, I just didn't allow enough time to get here. When I left the competition, I went to my room to change clothes, which took longer than expected. Then I only had five minutes to get here, and the casino is packed. No wonder they need the Maze to get between places. It took me 20 minutes to make my way through the crowded casino, get to your hotel tower, and then wait for an elevator."

Reaching for her hand, I gently pull her in for a hug. "No problem. I'm just glad you are safe. Come in and sit down. Let me get you something to drink."

As I walk toward the bar, Cassandra settles on the sofa and says, "That sounds good. Do you have some sparkling water?"

"Sure, but what about some champagne? It sparkles."

"That sounds great, but the water first, please. By the way, where were you today?"

As I open a bottle of San Pellegrino and then pop the cork on a bottle of Louis Roederer, I explain, "I was remotely watching the live video. Sean had extra video cameras set up in the kitchen overnight and had some larger monitors delivered here. By watching the live video feeds here, I could monitor the competition from several angles as well as pause and rewind when something interesting happened. I hoped I would learn more than I could standing in one place watching in person."

"How did you listen? I thought the cameras didn't have audio?"

Pouring champagne into crystal flutes, I share, "We have audio now. The tech company installed microphones as well as additional cameras last night."

Cassandra turns to face me, with her arm resting on the back of the sofa. "Good move. Did anything out of the ordinary happen?"

"Yes. Did you happen to notice when Jayden bumped into Kai's station?" I say as I balance two champagne flutes and Cassandra's sparkling water and walk carefully toward the sofa.

Meeting me part way, Cassandra takes her drinks as she explains, "I didn't see what happened, but I heard Kai tell Jayden to be more careful or he could get hurt. It was strange though. I couldn't figure out why Jayden was near Kai's station in the first place."

As we sit beside each other on the sofa, I solemnly confirm, "It was sabotage. When Jayden bumped into the station, he grabbed the top of Kai's food processor to balance himself. But the video shows him opening his fist and releasing a handful of granules into the food processor where Kai had his macadamia nuts."

Cassandra places her hand on my thigh and squeezes. "Oh no! I was afraid of that. Could you tell what the granules were? Was it salt?"

Nodding as I take a sip of my champagne, I watch her over the rim of my glass. "Yes, but how did you know it was salt?"

"As I was entering the judging room, Kai was leaving. He was extremely upset and talking to himself. He said something about not knowing how his food could have been too salty."

"I see."

After downing the rest of her water, Cassandra picks up her flute and asks, "Evan, how could you tell from the video that it was salt rather than something more dangerous, like poison?"

Wrapping my free arm around her shoulder, I explain, "I went back and looked at the video of Jayden's station right before the incident. Jayden poured a bunch of salt into his hand. He put a sprinkle of salt in his food as he looked around the room to see who was watching. Then instead of throwing out the leftover salt, he closed his fist and walked toward Kai's station."

Abruptly pulling away and perching on the edge of the sofa, Cassandra chastises, "What if you were wrong and it wasn't salt? Regardless, why didn't you do something about it? Evan, it's unfair to Kai."

I know better than to tell Cassandra to calm down. I learned that lesson from my sister getting upset with me. Instead, I lean forward to explain, "First, I was absolutely certain it was salt. Second, once I figured that out, I knew it wouldn't hurt anyone. Given that we still do not know whom else Mitch is working with, if anyone, I thought it was better to let it play out."

"But Kai's chances of winning are probably destroyed."

"When the time is right, I promise I will make sure everyone knows what happened. Just not yet. Have you picked up any more clues as to who is working with Mitch?"

Cassandra sits back and nestles against my shoulder as she says, "No, but maybe your new cameras and audio will give us some insight if Mitch meets up with Jayden again. Did you learn anything else?"

I give her shoulder a squeeze but hesitate before responding. I am not sure how much Sean wants me sharing with Cassandra. To buy time, I take a long sip of champagne and excuse myself to the bar to retrieve the bottle. After weighing my options, I decide she deserves reassurance that Sean has made some progress. Back at the sofa, I refill our glasses and share, "Sean learned a little more about how someone is skimming profits, but he doesn't know who is involved or if it is connected with the competition's accidents and sabotage."

"Evan, something tells me all these things are connected," she says, looking into my eyes. "And if there is money involved, that would be the motivation. Do you think Mitch is the one skimming?" Before I can respond, she is shaking her head and continuing, "But that doesn't make sense. Mitch works in security. How could he have any connection with the F&B suppliers?"

Setting my glass on the coffee table, I agree, "Good points. Maybe they are connected. That would tie all of this together, but Mitch's involvement is a mystery." After a brief pause, I ask, "You have tomorrow off, right?"

"I have most of tomorrow off, except I need go to the Tux & Tiara Chalet to borrow a dress for the Final Dinner, and remember, we have a short promotional event tomorrow afternoon. I also need to decide what I want to make for Round 3 of the competition. They told us it's a dessert round, but I'm sure there will be a twist." Before I respond, Cassandra starts asking one question after another. "Do you think learning the twist early will be Jayden's advantage? How will you know if Mitch meets Jayden in the kitchen? You can't watch the video feed all the time, so you might miss their meeting. Do you think they will ask Jayden to sabotage Round 3 too?"

Patting her leg, I implore, "Slow down. Let me take your questions one at a time. First, you could be right about the advantage. That would make a lot of sense. Second, Sean had a motion sensor installed, so I will get a notification on my phone if someone goes into the kitchen. The video will be recorded, and I can watch it any time. Besides, Detective Fielder also has access to the videos and gets the same notifications. Finally, as to whether they will ask Jayden to sabotage another chef, I have no way of knowing, but it is possible, if not probable."

"Who is privy to what the twist is going to be?"

"Good question. No one was discussing it behind the scenes today. I would assume that at least Cynthia, her assistant Cameron, and Amy know. For that matter, the whole crew may know. I can ask Sean if he knows how those details are being handled, but I don't think I want to ask anyone else at this point."

"That makes sense, Evan. I have no idea whom we can trust."

"Neither do I, but I do have a great idea. Stay here tonight. We can order dinner and wait to see if anyone enters the kitchen. If they do, we can watch the video together."

Laughing for the first time this evening, Cassandra retorts, "You're just looking for an excuse to convince me to spend more time in your bed. Besides, you said the police are watching the videos, so why do we need to watch them too?"

"Can you blame me for wanting you in my bed again? And while the police are watching the videos and will follow up, I highly doubt they will watch them tonight. This is not their only case. But you will be safer the sooner we have more information, so I want to know if Mitch and Jayden meet again tonight and, if so, what they say. I don't want to wait a day or two for the police. So, what do you say? Will you stay?"

"Another evening with you is sounding pretty good, so yes, I'll stay. You are wearing me down, in a good way."

Smiling, I stand up and reach for Cassandra's hand. "Fantastic. Let's take our drinks to the hot tub on the balcony. Dinner should be here within an hour."

Following me to the balcony, Cassandra teases, "You already ordered. A little over-confident, huh?"

"I call it optimistic. Now let's get into the hot tub and work up an appetite for the steak and lobster I ordered." After making our way to the hot tub, we strip off our clothes and do just that.

By the time the doorbell rings, we have left the hot tub and are intertwined on a double lounge chair cooling off in the dry night air. I grab my robe and hand one to Cassandra before making my way to the door. Room service quickly sets up a beautiful candlelit dinner on the balcony table, and the inviting aromas draw us to the table where we quietly devour the food.

After dinner on the balcony, I pick Cassandra up and carry her into the dimly lit bedroom, my lips never leaving hers. Lowering her so she can stand, I untie the belt of her robe and push it off her shoulders, revealing her beautiful curves. My fingers trace her pebbled nipples, as my mouth worships her neck on a path to her perky breasts. She quickly frees my robe, wrapping her arms around my waist and pulling me closer, arching against me, as she murmurs, "Oh my God, Evan."

My hands roam down her soft curves, caressing each one. I ease a hand between her legs, finding her soaked and ready, so I gently ease her onto the bed. Parting her thighs, I hover above her as I grab a condom from the nightstand. "Do you want all of me?"

She gasps, "Absolutely!"

Wanting her more than I remember ever wanting any woman, I push my hard-as-steel manhood into her channel of ecstasy. My God, she feels amazing. I'm using every trick in the book not to lose it instantly because Cassandra deserves the best I have to give. I move slowly so as to rub just the right spot, and then I flip us over, so she is on top. Reaching between us, I circle her sensitive nub as she rides me harder and harder. When her eyes close, I know she is close, so I add a little pressure and watch her barrel over the cliff just before I join her.

When she rolls off me, I pull her against my side and whisper, "Princess, that was incredible."

"Evan, that wasn't just incredible, that was a thrill ride."

Then she nuzzles her head against my chest, and we doze off. Rolling on my side and resting my hand on her bare torso, I say, "Did you know you are a truly special woman? Unlike most of the women I have dated, I find myself letting my guard down around you. I am not constantly worried that you are looking to convince me you would be the perfect wife or that I should fly you around the world on an all-expenses-paid luxury vacation. You seem to enjoy a mere dinner on the balcony with me."

Pulling away, Cassandra bolts up wide awake now and starts jabbing her finger in my direction, "Evan, right now is not the time to talk to me about how happy you are that this is not serious, about what a cheap date I am, or about the other women you have dated. If I wasn't having second thoughts before, I certainly am now!"

I rub my hand through my already tousled hair. Fuck! I am an idiot. I was trying to tell her she was different in a good way, but boy did I blow it if that is how it came out. "That is most definitely not what I meant! What I was trying to say is that being with you feels comfortable and real. I can be myself with you without feeling like you are trying to take advantage of me. Most women see a blank check or a black AMEX card when they look at me. I was trying to thank you for being different."

"And I certainly was not implying this is some unimportant fling. Neither of us knows where this will lead, but I look forward to spending more time with you, and I am truly sorry it all came out wrong. I realize I am probably making it worse. I just have never wanted to have this type of conversation with a woman before, so I clearly do not know how to express my feelings properly. Please, forgive my ineptitude and stay."

Letting me pull her close again, I sigh in relief. Then in a soft voice, Cassandra says, "I am sorry other women have made you so jaded. We don't all pick our friends or dates based on their bank accounts. But I have my issues, too, that make me hesitant to get close romantically; they're just different. You see, money is replaceable. People and memories aren't."

Sensing that Cassandra wants to share more, I spoon her and ask, "What happened?"

"I grew up with successful, driven parents who made sure I had everything I needed growing up, but when I went to college they cut off financial support, explaining they wanted me to be financially responsible and earn my way in the world. I wanted to make them proud, so I took out student loans, made a budget, and lived frugally like most college students."

"Then when my parents died five years ago, I found out they had lost most of their savings, including our home, to a Ponzi scheme. The rest was left in trust to charity. Don't get me wrong, my parents had always told me they were planning to leave most of their estate to charity, so that wasn't a big surprise. I admired their generosity, but they had also said that they would quote 'make sure I could always come home to our family memories.' I thought that they would protect our family home. Instead, I barely had time to retrieve a few mementos before it was gone.

"Cassandra, that is terrible."

"Most people assumed I was taken care of for life because of my parents' success, so other than my best friend Lowri, no one understood the pain I felt from first losing my parents and then our home. It wasn't about the money; it was the loss of the only family left in my life and the lifetime of memories I had with them. Everyone thought I decided to sell the house, and I was too emotionally wrecked to explain. To make matters worse, they died in a car crash on the way to my law school graduation, so in a twisted way, I've always blamed myself for their death. You see, they were workaholics and never took time off, but I wanted an extra-long weekend with them before I started my new job. If I hadn't guilted them into coming a couple of days early, they would still be alive.

Stroking her arm, I respond, "Sweetheart, I am so sorry for your pain, but wanting extra time with your parents does not make you responsible for their car accident."

"The rational side of my brain knows that, but on lonely nights, it's sometimes hard to be rational when it hurts. Through everything, I learned it was easiest to portray myself as strong and try to hide my vulnerabilities, including my fear of getting close to someone and then losing them like I lost my parents. That's part of the reason I've had trouble letting myself get close to you. Over the last few years, I rarely went on a second date, much less a third date, to protect myself. If I didn't let anyone get close, I figured I wouldn't feel the pain of loss again."

"For some inexplicable reason, I find myself wanting to share more with you, but it's still hard," she continues. "You have no idea how hard it was for me to admit the other night that I didn't want to be alone. It made me feel weak to admit I needed someone. I'm not typically the damsel in distress, but that doesn't mean I don't sometimes crave a hug and someone to care and hold me. It just scares me to get close."

Turning her to face me and holding her tight, I say, "We are quite the pair. We both have found we want to get closer to someone for the first time in a long while, if ever, but our pasts are in the way. I say we help each other, which leads me to the reason I started this conversation. I want to raise the issue of my father's retirement party again. I am not sure you took my prior invitation seriously, but it was real. It is going to be rather stressful for me and my family, so would you be my date? There is no one that I would rather have with me, and I will admit I do not want to attend it alone, so please say 'yes'."

In a hushed voice, Cassandra asks, "When did you say the party is?"

"At the end of next month."

"Didn't you say it will be in Europe?"

"Yes. You can fly over with me on our private jet. It will be a very special celebration. I would like to share it with you."

"I would love to go to Europe and to have more time with you, but I don't know how I'll get more time off from work. I already had to take unpaid leave to be here, and now you know why I need a job."

"If you win the competition, you will win the prize money and will be quitting your job to work here, right?"

"True, but that is beyond unlikely. At best, I have a one-in-four chance of winning the competition. And it looks like the competition is rigged for Jayden to win, which is not fair, but it also means my chances of winning are practically zero. In fact, I'm certain that if the other finalists knew about Jayden's advantages, they would have quit by now."

"Trust me, Sean will find a way to make the outcome of the competition fair. Now please reconsider my question. If you win and Sean agrees to give you the time off, will you go with me to my father's celebration?"

"Evan, even if I were to win, which is a Las Vegas long shot, Sean will not give me the time off because I would need to start as guest chef for Trendz. But I have nothing to lose by agreeing that if all those things were to happen, then I will happily go with you."

"Excellent. Goodnight, Cassandra." I say, as I close my eyes and smile, relishing the possibility of more time with her.

CHAPTER THIRTY-NINE

EVAN

Waking up to a new day, Cassandra goes to her room to change, which gives me time to ask Christian to arrange a few things for me. Assured he will take care of my requests, I hop in the shower, daydreaming about what we would be doing if Cassandra were joining me. To cool off the need that arises, I turn the knob to the coldest setting and rush through the rest of my shower.

After dressing in khakis and a linen shirt, I meet Cassandra at her room, and we follow the signs to Aphrodite's Way. Stopping along the way, we peer in the windows of various shops, and I attempt to casually steer her toward the boutique where I had Christian arrange an appointment. Walking in, we are greeted by an elegant, silver-haired woman who says, "Welcome. We have everything ready for you."

Cassandra looks at me with brows raised. "What is she talking about?" The woman backs away, sensing we need some privacy.

"I want you to have a special dress for the Final Dinner, so I had Christian arrange an appointment for you to try on a few gowns," I tell her.

"Evan, I make a good salary, but I'm still paying back a small fortune in student loans. I can't afford to shop here. These gowns will be thousands of dollars."

"I completely understand your need for independence and how hard it is for you to let anyone help you. But you have already proven you are quite capable of taking care of yourself, and I know you do not expect anything from me in terms of money. However, I have lots of money, and it would make me very happy if you let me spoil you today. Besides, they have gone to a lot of trouble to select things specifically for you, so please at least try them on. I would love to see you in one of the gowns."

Cassandra smiles as she says, "Thank you for understanding how I feel. I will try them on for fun, so you can see how they look on me. How's that for a compromise?"

"I can live with that for now."

Just then another woman approaches us carrying a silver tray with two flutes of champagne. I hand one to Cassandra and take one for myself. The woman then escorts us to the back of the shop where there is a large dressing room for Cassandra and a separate sitting area with a comfortable love seat where I can wait. As I clink my glass against Cassandra's, I hope this will relax her a little so she will enjoy letting me pamper her. I cannot help but shake my head and grin. No other women I have dated — even titled, royal ones — had any problem letting me spend insane amounts of money on them. Cassandra is refreshing.

CHAPTER FORTY

CASSIE

Silvia, the first woman we met, shows me four gowns they have selected. One is black with thin spaghetti straps and crystal accents embellishing the entire gown. There's also a deep royal blue satin gown, a red chiffon gown, and a white gown. They are gorgeous dresses a princess would wear. I hate to admit it, but I could get used to his pampering.

But it's not about his money — it's him and the way he makes me feel like I'm a treasure. Dare I say, he makes me feel loved? Even though Evan said this isn't just a fling and we will see where it leads, I still need to prepare myself for the inevitable sadness when he heads back to Europe and I return to my life in California. I also remind myself he said he is accustomed to pampering his dates because they expect it, so I may be reading too much into the attention he is paying me.

I try on the black dress first. It fits perfectly but shows a lot of skin. While there is an inch-wide strap across the back at bra level, the rest of the back is open and plunges so low it barely covers my backside. I step out to show Evan, and of course, he loves it. Next, I try on the royal blue dress, which is elegant with sequined lace overlaying the top and a tasteful slit in the skirt. The red dress has too many layers of chiffon for my taste. Fortunately, Evan also gave it a thumbs down.

Then I try on the white dress. I gasp. OMG! It looks like a wedding dress. It has a pearl and crystal encrusted bodice that flows into a beautiful skirt that is adorned with more pearls and apricot-colored crystals. I can't let Evan see this dress. It will scare him off.

Evan calls out, "When do I get to see the fourth dress?"

I can't resist a quick twirl to see how it looks in the three-way mirror before I respond. "It doesn't look right, so we should skip it." Silvia asks my shoe size and says she is going to bring me shoes to try and leaves the room. Right after she leaves, Evan steps in.

Pushing my hand against his chest, I exclaim, "You can't come in here."

"Why not?" Evan questions as he takes my hand and leads me in a dance-style spin while eyeing me from head to toe. "That dress is gorgeous. What do you mean it doesn't look right? It looks fantastic on you."

"I don't think it is right for the Final Dinner. I don't want to wear white. I'm sure I'll spill something and ruin it."

"Ok, but it is gorgeous. You look beautiful in white." Evan reaches for me and brushes a strand of hair from my face as he leans in for a kiss that makes me blush.

I breathlessly murmur "Thanks" as Sylvia returns with not only shoes, but also skimpy, paper-thin, lingerie that deepens my blush. She also has a few small clutch purses. I try to tell her I don't need all those things, but Evan quickly assures me that I do.

He then tells Silvia that we will be taking the black and blue gowns and all the appropriate accessories. He asks that they be delivered to his suite as soon as the gowns are hemmed to the proper length for the shoes. Holding my hand up to stop Evan, I tell Sylvia to give us a minute alone.

After she leaves, I remind Evan, "First, you don't get to boss me around and pick for me. Second, remember, I only agreed to try the gowns on for fun. I can't afford them, and I don't plan to let you buy them. We need to thank Sylvia for her time and efforts, and then go to the other shop so I can borrow a dress for the Final Dinner."

"Cassandra, please at least let me buy you the black dress. You look amazing in it."

"No."

"Has anyone ever told you that you can be stubborn? Consider it a birthday present. According to your application, you had a birthday a little over a week ago. Please do not tell me you turn down birthday presents. Besides, I know you love the dress."

"What if you give me half for my birthday and I splurge and pay for the other half?"

"How about half for your birthday and an interest-free loan on the other half? You can pay me back after your student loans are paid off and not before."

"Deal."

A bit lightheaded as we are leaving the store, I realize I have a little buzz from the champagne. It's a good thing we aren't competing today. I hadn't realized until it was too late that Silvia's assistant kept refilling my glass. I think that was Evan's plan for talking me into letting him pay for the outrageously expensive dresses, but I held my ground — well, at least somewhat held my ground.

Evan suggests we walk through the casino on our way back, which sounds like fun. Before I came to Las Vegas, I read up on the basic strategy for blackjack. Essentially, you can even the odds a little by making certain decisions about when to take another card and when to double your bet based on the cards you see in the dealer's hand. I've been planning to try the strategy but haven't yet, so I ask Evan, "Would you mind if we stop and play a couple of hands of blackjack? I've never actually played in a real casino."

"I love blackjack, and the high roller lounge is not too far."

"Evan, I can't afford to play in the High Roller Lounge. I can barely afford to play a few hands at the $20 tables here."

"You can play with my money."

"Evan, that would take all the fun out of it for me. Let's play here."

"Ok. My apologies. Do you know the rules for blackjack?"

"I think so."

We sit down at the nearest table, and I hand over the $100 chip I drew during the competition and ask for smaller denomination chips. Waiting for the dealer to count out the chips, I chew my lower lip as I struggle to remember all the rules I studied. Maybe Evan will help me if I get stuck.

The dealer pushes a small stack of chips toward me. In exchange for my black $100 chip, he gives me ten red $5 chips and two green $25 chips. The minimum bet is $20, so I place four red chips into the circle. For the first hand, I'm dealt two 8s, and the dealer is showing a 10. I know I should take another card, but I also remember reading that I'm supposed to split 8s and aces. But that's scary because I will have to bet another $20 to split the 8s and play two hands at the same time. It sounds like a way to lose faster. As the dealer patiently awaits my decision, I whisper to Evan, "I think I'm supposed to split the 8s."

Evan replies, "You are correct."

"But that will cost me another $20."

"You shouldn't play unless you are going to play correctly. Playing by the strategy, you will win more often in the long run, but it is ultimately your money and your choice as to how to play."

I hesitantly push forward four more red chips and tell the dealer I want to split the 8s. The dealer then adds a Jack of clubs to the first 8 for 18, so I don't take any more cards on that hand. Then the dealer adds a 3 to the second 8, giving me 11 against the dealer's 10. Oh no! I think I'm supposed to double my bet. I look at Evan who knows what I'm asking without my having uttered a word. He just nods and pats my back.

My heart is starting to pound, but I stick to the strategy. I double down and add another $20 to my bet on that hand, so I am dealt one card face down. Now the dealer flips over his down card revealing a 7 for 17. I get excited because that means my 18 in the first hand beats his 17, so I win that hand.

He flips the card in my second hand revealing a 9 for 20. Yes! I jump in my seat and clap. Turning around, I'm met with Evan's broad grin and a high five. My $60 bet just turned into $120!

Evan watches me play a few more hands, squeezing my shoulders in support, but none is as exciting as the first one. My winnings go up a little and down a little, and soon I'm back at the $100 I started with, so I decide to stop while I'm even.

I decide to reread the basic strategy rules before I play again because I know I made a few mistakes.

The nice thing was that Evan, who apparently is an expert player, didn't make me feel like the amateur I am. He seemed to truly enjoy watching me play and learn, only giving advice when I asked. Unlike most of the guys I've dated, he didn't seem to show off.

I collect my chips, and as we walk toward the elevators, Evan's phone dings. He glances at the screen and says, "Let's hurry. We have a video to watch."

When we arrive at Evan's suite, he logs into his computer to access the video feeds from the kitchen in Trendz. Sure enough, Jayden is in the kitchen talking to someone. This time we have audio and better camera angles that cover the entire kitchen. That means we can see that Jayden is talking with Mitch. Jayden says, "I took care of Kai's dish, so give me the advantage."

Slapping a white envelope in Jayden's outstretched hand, Mitch says, "Relax, buddy. Here's your advantage. Use it wisely. We need you to shine in the last round to ensure you win this competition."

Jayden responds, but we can barely make out what he is saying, so Evan cranks up the volume and replays it. We re-watch the grainy video and move closer to the laptop, straining to hear Jayden ask, "Do you think this advantage will be enough? I think Trenton has been doing well. His food always looks great. Hell, I even think that amateur Cassie has done okay based on how her food looks, and rumor has it she has the inside track because of her relationship with Evan."

I grab Evan's leg, worrying what the rumors entail. Staring at the computer screen, we watch Mitch lean against a counter as he inquires, "What have you heard about Cassie's relationship with Evan?"

"Well, one of the crew said they seem really close. Some think she is probably sleeping with him in exchange for a good word with Mr. Cartwright."

I gasp, and Evan hits pause on the video and wraps his arm around my shoulder. "Evan, I would never sleep with anyone to gain an advantage! That's appalling."

"I know," Evan reassures. "You would not do that. Let's keep watching."

When the video continues, Mitch says, "Don't worry about Cassie or Trenton. They won't be a problem. Just make sure you take care of your dessert."

"Ok. Do you need me to do anything else?"

"Not now. But when you win, we expect a few other favors from you."

"Understood."

"Ok. We won't be meeting again. After the contest, my partner will be your contact."

"Who is your partner?"

"Win first. Then you will find out." Then they both leave, and the video goes silent.

Wow. "That confirms he has a partner, but Evan, what do they mean by 'They won't be a problem?' I had convinced myself that the panic code on my TekCuff was enough, but after hearing this conversation, it's scary and creepy to know that someone wants me out of the competition."

"I will call Sean to make sure he watches the video and keeps security on you at all times."

"Good."

Just then my TekCuff chimes, and within seconds, Evan's phone beeps with the same message. We need to be at the Olympic Torch Bar in 30 minutes for a mixology promotional event. I'm always up for tasting new cocktails, and it would be a fun event under other circumstances. Instead, a cold chill runs through me knowing I'm walking into an event where someone may be scheming to eliminate me from the competition.

CHAPTER FORTY-ONE

EVAN

"We are here for a fun afternoon of mixology," Sean announces as the cameras roll in the Olympic Torch Bar. "As you all know, my college friend has been helping me with this competition, and I wanted to do something as a thank you to him, so we are all going to learn how to make Evan's favorite drink, a Boulevardier."

There is mumbling among the finalists and the crew, indicating no one has heard of the drink, much less has a clue how to make it. Sean continues, "It is a somewhat unknown drink here in the States, but it is my best friend's favorite, so he will also get to be the judge of your efforts today. To get started, Ray, the head bartender for the Olympic Torch Bar, will give you a quick demonstration of how to make a Boulevardier. Then you will each have 10 minutes to make your version. Any questions before we start?"

Kai asks, "Will the competition judges also be tasting it? Do we need to make extra drinks for them?"

"No, this is just for fun. You only need to make one drink. However, I would suggest making two, so that you can taste your drink and make any desired adjustments before serving it to my buddy. I should add that while this mixology event doesn't matter in the overall competition, there will be a small prize for the chef who makes the winning drink today. If there are no more questions, let's get started. Ray, show them how it's done."

While Ray starts talking, I approach Sean and whisper, "Thanks for the tribute to my drink of choice, but please do not show me on camera. It is a miracle that no one has recognized me yet, and I would like to keep it that way."

"Don't worry, I brought you an Athena baseball cap and told Amy to have the crew film from behind, so your face will never be shown. Regardless, they are going to concentrate on filming the finalists. Are you ok with your voice on the video?"

"That should be ok."

"By the way, when are you going to tell Cassie who you really are? I'm told that she has moved into your suite."

"Soon. I am waiting for the right time. It is nice getting to know someone without them knowing who my family is, so I am not in a hurry to tell her. It would also be best for the police to close the murder investigation first."

"So, what you are saying is you don't want your family to know you are sleeping with a murder suspect? I warned you to stay away from her. She is adding unnecessary complications to your life."

"She isn't guilty, and you know it. By the way, we need to talk. Mitch met with Jayden again today. You need to watch the video because Mitch essentially threatened Cassandra and Trenton. He also gave Jayden an envelope that supposedly contained an advantage for tomorrow's competition."

"I'll look as soon as this is over. We already have security on Cassie and the other finalists, but I will increase Trenton's security."

Applause draws our attention to Ray, who is putting on quite a show of making the Boulevardier. Tossing a drink shaker in the air and catching it behind his back, he then strains the amber liquid into a glass and adds a twist. Wrapping up the show, he reminds the finalists that the drink has 1-1/4 ounces of Bourbon, 1 ounce of Campari, and 1 ounce of sweet vermouth shaken with ice and strained into a glass with a large ice cube. He cautions not to forget to garnish with an orange peel.

Taking over as host, Amy says, "Let's thank Ray for that great show. Now it is time for you to make your versions for our judge to try, but guess what? There is a twist. You must add or change an ingredient to make it your own. Your goal is to convince Evan that your drink is even better than his favorite version. You have 10 minutes, and the time starts now!"

While watching the bedlam of everyone scurrying to the bar to pick up their ingredients and return to their tables, Sean asks me, "So, I assume Cassandra has this one in the bag, right? You must have shared your favorite add-in with her."

"No, this will be completely fair. Until now, she did not know this is my favorite cocktail. We've mainly shared champagne or other wines."

"Then this should be interesting. Have you seen the unusual choices the finalists are making? Is that rosemary that Trenton is adding?"

"It looks like rosemary. That doesn't sound very good. Are you sure this is a thank you, or are you punishing me?"

Amy calls time, and I taste each of the drinks in turn. Trenton's sprig of rosemary overpowers the orange twist, giving the drink a strong herbal scent that effectively kills my taste buds. Jayden decided that Texas tequila would be a good substitute for the bourbon. It wasn't. Kai and Cassandra had better ideas. Kai added a cinnamon stick along with the orange twist, which provides a note of warmth. Cassandra added a pineapple spear with the orange twist; it is a little acidic but still good. After tasting them all, I write down the winner's name on a slip of paper and hand it to Sean.

"Well, first, I'm told it was a close call, but the winner is Kai with his cinnamon Boulevardier. However, none of you added the extra ingredient that Evan always requests, which is three Luxardo cherries, not to be confused with the bright red, maraschino cherries. And yes, for some undisclosed reason, it must be exactly three. Now for the prize, Kai please come accept your gift certificate for a day at the spa.

Congratulations! We will see everyone for Round 3 tomorrow at 2 p.m."

Cassandra's drink was great, and I would have loved to give her the win. But Kai's creation was just a tad better, which was not a bad result. After what Jayden did to him with the salt, I was happy to see Kai triumph.

CHAPTER FORTY-TWO

CASSIE

I'm disappointed Evan didn't pick my drink. I thought it tasted great, but I wonder if he didn't like it or didn't think he should show favoritism by picking mine. Maybe he didn't want to fuel the rumors about us after hearing Jayden's comments to Mitch. I still don't understand where those rumors came from because we've tried to be professional when we're in public. We haven't held hands or done anything else in public other than have a few conversations at events. We did do the zipline in tandem, but that was Amy's idea, not ours.

Regardless, I can't let rumors worry me if I'm going to truly embrace my newly adopted mantra of "don't look back." If I'm truthful with myself, I don't regret taking a chance on Evan, and I know I haven't been given any inside info on the competition as a result. It's not me the other finalists need to worry about, it's Jayden, Mitch, and Mitch's partner. And instead of questioning my decisions regarding Evan, I need to move forward and finally deal with how the loss of my parents has caused me to worry so much about the possibility of losing others in the future that I don't allow myself to enjoy the present enough. Not only should I not look back, but I should be actually adding more goals, such as *carpe diem*, live in the moment,

239

seize the day, and all the other mottos that will compel me to just enjoy today and not worry so much about tomorrow.

With all my new adventures in Las Vegas, I feel like I've already started this process. In the past, I would have found an excuse to skip the Thrill Ride because of my fear of heights, but I managed to take the leap and experience ziplining. Although the broken harness may have reinforced my fear of heights and falling, at least I tried. I also took the full leap with Evan and ended my multi-year dry spell, which was a huge step for me in the relationship department. Perhaps, hardest of all, I shared my past with him, which was hard.

As I'm leaving the bar, Evan slips me a note. *Deja vu*. The note says he needs to talk with Sean, but he hopes I will meet him at his suite at 7 tonight. That gives me time to think about what dessert I want to make tomorrow. I know there will be a twist to the dessert round just like the other rounds. I wonder what it will be. Could Jayden's advantage be learning the twist early? It's annoying that Jayden has an edge, but I hope that won't matter in the end. However, since I don't know the twist, I need to have two or three ideas that are flexible and can be adjusted to fit whatever twist they add to the challenge. With that in mind, I head to my hotel room to work on ideas.

CHAPTER FORTY-THREE

CASSIE

W hen I arrive at the kitchen for Round 3, Cameron asks me to draw a chip from the chef's hat. Today, we will use the station adorned with the color that matches our chip. I draw the green $25 chip, so I take my place at the green station as I pocket the chip, thinking it will pay for another hand or two of blackjack when I have a break.

I examine all the ingredients that are on my table to make sure no one swapped the salt and sugar or messed with the equipment. I don't find any problems. Trenton and Kai are double-checking their ingredients too, so I'm not the only one concerned. Meanwhile, Jayden is assembling his ingredients before even hearing the requirements for our desserts, which makes me even more suspicious that he already knows what to expect.

When the crew is ready, Sebastian signals for the cameras to roll and Amy asks everyone, "Are you ready for the final round?" We all smile and respond that we are ready. She says, "Then let's get started. As you all know, this is the dessert round. But as we have said from the beginning, the Athena is looking for a guest chef who can think on his or her feet, deal with last-minute changes, and present beautiful plates of food to the guests. Therefore, we have had various twists that you have had to deal with in each round to keep you on your toes. Therefore, it's probably no surprise that the same is true for this dessert round. In this round, you must make a dessert that includes both chocolate and fruit. You have three hours, and time starts now! Good luck."

Relief washes over me. Prepping for this round, my imagination ran wild. I feared the twist would require me to use something savory in my dessert, like mushrooms or olives. I also worried they might tell us we couldn't use chocolate or some other key dessert ingredient like sugar. But I can deal with this twist.

As I begin assembling ingredients, Amy stops by and asks, "Cassie, I see you are melting butter? What are you making?"

"I'm making mini molten chocolate cakes in small ramekins," I say as I turn to grab a bowl and whisk.

"That sounds delicious. How are you going to incorporate fruit?" Amy asks as she steps closer.

Moving the pan of melted butter off the heat, I look into the camera and answer "Strawberries will be hidden in the molten center."

"Chocolate and strawberries are a fantastic combo, but I have another twist for you. This hat is filled with four chips. Each chip has an additional ingredient written on it. You must draw a chip and use the additional ingredient in your dessert. And you cannot change what you have just told me you are going to make. The final twist is that you will have 30 seconds after you draw the chip to tell us how you will be using the additional ingredient, so think fast."

Attempting to hide my panic, I keep smiling as I draw a chip.

"Cassie, show us what ingredient you drew."

I take a deep breath and read "Almonds." Whew! That was a lucky draw. I know exactly what to do.

Amy walks to the other side of my station and inquires, "How will you use almonds in your dessert?"

"Well, I should thank my gluten-free friends because they led me to experiment with almond flour, so I know from experience that the molten cake will be just as delicious made with almond flour in place of regular flour."

Amy wishes me good luck and moves on to talk with Trenton. He is making individual chocolate swirl cheesecakes with orange rind. I listen for which extra ingredient he draws. I hear him say it is cinnamon, but the whir of Kai's food processor drowns Trenton's explanation of how he plans to use the cinnamon.

Kai is making chocolate coconut tarts, and he reminds the camera that coconut is a fruit. His extra ingredient is mascarpone, which will work just fine to stabilize whipped cream topping or maybe as an addition to the chocolate filling.

I can't resist a quick pause to watch as Amy interviews Jayden next. He must use rum with his chocolate and raspberry ice cream. While he may have had an advantage in knowing that we had to use chocolate and fruit, there is no way he could have known that he would draw rum as his extra ingredient. However, to my surprise, Jayden immediately says he will make chocolate rum ice cream with raspberries and almonds.

Then it hits me. At first I thought ice cream was a lame choice, but it's the perfect base and can be easily adjusted to accommodate any of the twist ingredients. His response was too quick to be a coincidence.

Shaking off the distraction, I return my focus to my own dessert, knowing I better pay attention if I want to have any chance of winning. I'll need to be extra careful with the cooking time, or it will be a disaster. Too little time and it will be soup; too much and it will be dry rather than molten.

As I place the last ramekin on a plate and garnish it with a strawberry, the timer goes off and Amy announces, "Time is up. Step away." Wiping my damp brow, I smile because the molten cakes look perfect.

When I look up, Detective Fielder's glaring eyes erase my smile and elevate my nerves. While I know there is plenty of evidence pointing to others, I still can't explain my fingerprints on Leon's bowl, so I'm not off the hook yet. Finally, Sebastian yells, "Cut," and filming temporarily stops so they can reset for judging in the main area of the restaurant. The detective uses this time to corner various crew members and ask questions, but I can't hear what they are talking about.

I'm up first for judging, so I walk into the restaurant, hoping my molten cakes are still warm and gooey. Amy announces, "Cassie has presented you with a molten chocolate cake."

"Why didn't you turn it out of the ramekin for a more elegant presentation?" Judge Gerard asks. But before I can answer he adds, "And merely putting fruit on top doesn't impress me as a creative use of that requirement either."

That's right, he is the presentation-centric judge. Staying as calm as I can, I politely address his concerns by explaining, "Unlike a standard molten cake, I not only garnished with fruit, but also hid fresh strawberries in the center for a special twist, which I hope you will find enjoyable. However, I did not believe it would work to remove the cake from the ramekins given the weight of the fruit in the center. I was concerned the cake would collapse."

Returning my smile with a huff and intense stare, Judge Gerard sinks his spoon into the warm chocolate and scoops up a combo of cake, strawberries, and to my relief, runny chocolate. Placing the spoonful of dessert in his mouth, he never takes his eyes off me. After a long pause, he says, "I rarely admit it, but I was wrong. I am impressed with your use of the ingredients. However, I would have garnished the plate with some chocolate drizzles."

"Thank you for the feedback. I'll do that next time."

After tasting the dessert, Judge Holden then says, "Please remind us which extra ingredient you drew."

"Judge, it was almonds."

Rather sarcastically, he asks, "Where are the almonds? Did you forget to sprinkle some on top?"

Boy, this is a tough crowd. They are looking for anything to criticize. "To incorporate almonds into my dessert, I decided to use almond flour, so you are sampling a gluten-free dessert," I answer, trying to keep any annoyance from my voice.

"I must say, I had no idea this was gluten free. Great job," Chef Indigo compliments.

Turning to leave, I am smiling from ear to ear, barely holding back on doing a fist pump, excited I nailed the dessert.

When the judging is over, all the finalists are smiling, so I guess the judges universally liked our desserts. No disasters or sabotage this time. Now, we must wait until the Final Dinner tomorrow night to learn who will be the guest chef. That also means Detective Fielder needs to hurry up and solve the murder because most of the suspects will be clamoring to leave town soon after the winner is announced, and I need my name cleared.

CHAPTER FORTY-FOUR

EVAN

The morning light streaming through the windows nudges me awake but Cassandra is still sleeping peacefully. I hope today will be good to her. Tonight the winner of the Guest Chef Competition will be announced. Based on what I have watched, Cassandra has done quite well, but I know she thinks her chances of winning are low given that the other finalists are professionals, and someone is handing out advantages to one or more of the others. However, she does not know Sean the way I do. Having dealt with cheaters in the casino industry, he loathes them, so I have no doubt he will ensure the result is fair. Regardless, I have told Sean I do not want to know the outcome before it is announced. My goal for today is to take Cassandra's mind off the competition, so I planned a little surprise for her.

I hate to wake her when she looks so beautiful snuggled next to me with one arm splayed across my torso and the other hugging her pillow. However, for my surprise to work, I must, so I kiss her gently on the cheek and then pull away. She slowly opens her eyes and finds me propped up on an elbow staring at her. "Good morning," she whispers.

"Good morning, Princess. Remember that I asked you to let me spoil you a little?"

"Yes, you said that. And thank you again for the birthday dress. It is beautiful."

"Well, it was only half a dress. You are paying for the other half. And while I understand it is against your nature to accept gifts, it gives me great pleasure to do special things for people I care about. Therefore, I am hoping you will let me do one more thing for you today. I made appointments at the spa this morning for you to have a massage and then have your hair and nails done. You will be relaxed and look like a shining star at the Final Dinner tonight."

"Evan, that is too much. Besides, we need to figure out who else is behind the sabotage. I'm running out of time to clear my name."

"It is not too much. I understand your need to prove you can take care of yourself, and I respect you for it. From what I can tell, you have already proven you are successful and independent. But you have been under a lot of stress with the competition and the murder investigation, not to mention the newspaper article. A morning at the spa is my way of letting you know I care and want to see you relax for a few hours. And even strong, independent people let others do nice things for them from time to time, so please let me do this. It's not like it's a diamond necklace. It's just a morning at the spa. Besides, Sean is going to talk with Chef Maurizio this morning, and I plan to listen to the call to see what we can learn."

"You're right. It's a lovely and thoughtful gift, and I need to learn to just say 'thank you' sometimes. Will you tell me what Chef Maurizio says?"

"Of course. You can meet me when you are done, and I will give you an update. How about lunch at the Blue Ramen Bowl at 1:30? I will send you a message if we need to change plans after our call."

"Sounds good. I better get ready if I'm going to be on time for the spa appointments."

As soon as we are both dressed, we leave the suite and walk toward the elevator. When we arrive at the spa level, Cassandra carefully peers out the elevator doors despite the hallway being empty except for a couple of maids and a guy on a ladder with his head stuck up into the ceiling repairing something.

"What are you doing?" I ask.

"I want to make sure no one is listening," Cassandra whispers. "I feel like I've missed an important detail or forgotten something that happened during the competition that is key to solving this mystery. I keep thinking that I know the key to how my fingerprints ended up on Leon's bowl, but it's like I almost have it and then the memory slips away before I can make sense of it. It's stressing me that I can't figure it out, and my future probably depends on it."

"If you saw something important, I am sure you will remember it. Sometimes it helps to first clear your head, so let your mind rest while you are at the spa. Then you can think back over the last few days to see if you remember any new details."

"You're probably right."

"Don't forget, meet me at the Blue Ramen Bowl at 1:30 unless I send you a note with a change of plans."

"Sounds great."

I do not want Cassandra worrying, but I hope Chef Maurizio can fill in the missing pieces of the puzzle. If he knows why Jayden, Mitch, and Mitch's mystery partner are trying to rig the competition, I suspect the rest of the pieces will fall into place.

CHAPTER FORTY-FIVE

CASSIE

Stepping into the spa's circular reception area transports me to a peaceful indoor garden. Soothing music plays in the background, interrupted only by the sound of trickling water from a cherub-topped, multi-tier fountain that rises almost to the ceiling in the center of the room. Green ivy trails over the edges and down the sides of each tier, and white gardenias float in the water, filling the air with their sweet fragrance. A domed skylight is surrounded by hand-painted clouds and birds. I close my eyes and take a deep breath to enjoy the floral scent and peaceful feeling that washes over me for the first time in forever. My shoulders start to fall as tension slowly releases. Evan was right. This will be good for me.

The receptionist has an attendant show me to the women's locker room, where I change into a fluffy white robe. After wandering into an adjacent relaxation lounge, I stretch out on a cushy lounge chair and sip herbal tea while I wait for my massage. I'm not usually one to sign up for massages, so I'm not quite sure how comfortable I'll be having a stranger rub oil all over my naked body. But my arm and shoulder muscles have been so tight, I'm ready to give it a try.

As I finish my tea, Ava introduces herself and walks me to the massage room, which is lit with a soft, warm glow from candles and sparkling pinpoint lights in the dark ceiling, simulating a starlit night sky. The room is much larger than I expected with a massage table and a cozy sitting area with an oversized chair and fireplace.

As Ava gives me time to get settled on the table, the scent of lavender and something else permeates the room. I'm trying to determine whether the other scent is eucalyptus when Ava starts working on my shoulders, causing me to abandon all thought. Between the stress of the competition and having my reputation brought into question by essentially being called a murderer, my muscles have been constantly tensed up. Even if this relief lasts only a few minutes, it's amazing to let my muscles relax as I drift off.

The next thing I know, Ava is gently waking me up to tell me it's time for my pedicure and manicure. I slowly climb off the massage table and, clad in the luxurious Athena robe and slippers, follow an attendant to another private room. The attendant helps me onto an elevated heated chair, and I let my feet dangle in a pool of swirling, lavender-scented water. I think I'm going to fall back asleep. This is pure heaven.

As they are finishing my nails, an attendant walks in with an envelope for me. A note inside says

URGENT! CHANGE OF PLANS. WE ARE HEADED TO THE LOADING DOCK VIA THE MAZE. THE POLICE ARE ON THE WAY. SHOW CHRISTIAN THIS NOTE AND HAVE HIM LET YOU INTO THE MAZE AT THE OLYMPIC TORCH LOUNGE ENTRANCE. WE'VE FIGURED IT OUT, BUT YOU NEED TO HURRY IF YOU WANT TO WITNESS YOUR NAME BEING CLEARED.
EVAN
PASSWORD: ARES (NER)

They must have reached Chef Maurizio earlier than expected, and he must have been the key. I wonder if they are about to catch someone in the act of stealing high-end wine and food at the loading dock. I better hurry if I want to see the police catch the bad guys, so I tell the attendant to cancel my hair appointment and scurry to the women's changing room, where I quickly yank on my clothes. I wish I thought to bring sandals instead of tennis shoes. My toenail polish is still wet, so these shoes are going to ruin my beautiful pedicure. Oh well. Watching handcuffs snap onto the people that tried to ruin me is much more important. Besides, I already messed up the wet polish on my fingernails while getting dressed. Now I must quickly find Christian.

I arrive at the concierge lounge out of breath, gasping as I ask for Christian. Fortunately, he's on duty and appears in front of me. I thrust the note at him, and after reading it, he tells me he isn't supposed to let anyone into the Maze without Mr. Cartwright's approval. I tell him we don't have time and point out that not only is Evan Sean's best friend, but Evan also included a password. Christian acknowledges that the password is the correct one for today. Reluctantly, he admits he may get into more trouble if he doesn't follow Sean's instructions, so he finally agrees to take me.

As he is about to walk me down the stairs, he gets a call that causes him to scrunch his forehead and rub his eyes. "I'm sorry. There is an urgent problem that I must attend to. The note included NER, which means no escort required, so I suppose you can go ahead on our own." He unlocks the Maze entrance, and I thank him before darting down the stairs.

That's when I realize I don't know where I'm supposed to meet Evan. Should I wait here or try to find the path to the loading dock? I had assumed he or someone he sent would be waiting for me at the entrance.

As I'm looking around for a sign of where to go, the Maze's hospital-like smell hits me, an antiseptic aroma that permeates the halls. The cleaning crew must be exceedingly diligent, but they could learn from the spa and pick a more pleasant-smelling cleaner. Then, I hear the click of a door opening behind me, and the antiseptic smell grows stronger. As I turn my head, a cloth is pressed against my mouth and nose, and an arm encircles my neck. I reach up to pull the constricting arms away, but they are too strong.

I begin to feel dizzy, and the familiar Deep Voice says, "You aren't going to cause us any more trouble now." Knowing that fighting is futile, I relax my arms and try to unobtrusively reach for my TekCuff to enter the panic code. But I can't see the screen, so I go by feel, hoping I entered the correct 555 panic code. Then the attacker's left arm tightens even more against my neck and everything goes dark.

When I come to, I'm under a blanket on some sort of cart that is moving quickly. The cloth that was around my mouth has fallen off. I check my TekCuff to see if the panic code went through and stifle a groan when I see 222 displayed on the screen. Shit. I sent the wrong code. I quickly delete the digits, enter 555, and press send, hoping the panic code works this time.

Then the cart screeches to halt. I close my eyes, pretending to still be knocked out, but someone grabs me, and I feel a sharp prick on my upper arm.

Fuck! Lights out. Again.

CHAPTER FORTY-SIX

SEAN

"Evan, you got here just in time. I'm about to call Chef Maurizio, but I would prefer if you don't let him know you are here and listening."

Settling back into a guest chair, arms resting on the side arms, Evan confirms, "Understood."

After a few rings, Chef Maurizio answers with the Italian greeting, "Pronto."

"Chef Maurizio, this is Sean Cartwright from the Grand Athena. Thank you for taking my call. I hope you and your family are doing well. I have a question for you related to your work at the Athena. During the last couple of months that you were here, you changed a lot of our suppliers. I am trying to figure out why you decided to change to more expensive, lower quality suppliers. Could you help solve that mystery for me?"

After a long pause, Chef Maurizio coughs and then hesitantly responds, "Mr. Cartwright, no mystery. We were trying out new options."

Huh? An experienced chef doesn't randomly decide to try out new options for an operation as large as the Athena. "I'm sorry, but that doesn't make any sense. We are now receiving lower quality products at a higher price. For the love of God, please tell me why someone with your excellent reputation and training would do something like this?"

Silence fills the phone connection. In a hushed voice, Chef Maurizio says, "I don't think I can answer your questions."

"Chef, you are now at the helm of your family's business, so I'm sure you understand my position. This hotel is my family's business and legacy. I protect it just as I assume you are now protecting what your family built. I'm sure if you were in my position, you would do whatever is necessary to resolve these problems and determine the cause, so please just be honest with me."

"I understand, but it's not that simple," he says, regret in his voice.

Mystified, I ask, "Why not? You made the change to the new suppliers, correct?"

"Yes, that is correct. I made mistakes that I regret, but at the time I had no choice. It would have been dangerous for me not to make the changes."

Raising my voice in bewilderment as well as frustration, I practically scream, "How could it possibly have been dangerous? Please tell me why you changed suppliers. Otherwise, I will have no choice but to send the international authorities to question you and your family." Evan muffles a laugh, knowing that I have no power to have Chef Maurizio questioned, much less his family.

But Chef Maurizio falls for my bluff, responding, "Please don't do that, Mr. Cartwright. I don't want my family involved. I'll explain what I can. As I said, I had no choice, and I'm very sorry, but I was being blackmailed. I never wanted to take anything from you or the Grand Athena, but I feared for my career and my safety if I didn't go along. Then when my father became ill, I saw an escape path. I could return home to take care of him, and if I kept my mouth shut, I would be safe. It was my chance to get away. I will try to pay what you require for me to make restitution to you, but please don't tell anyone you spoke with me."

Evan raises his hands in question, mouthing "Blackmail?" He is as stunned as I am. Lowering my voice, I ask, "Why did someone want you to change suppliers?"

"For the kickbacks. I was only allowed to use suppliers who paid us kickbacks. The suppliers would raise the prices of the food and wine and give us a cut of what the Athena paid them. I only got a small portion, but I understand the masterminds got a much larger portion. Please believe me that I didn't want to be a part of the scheme. I just didn't know how to get out of it when they kept threatening me."

"What were they holding over you? Who was blackmailing you? Who is behind this mess?"

"Mr. Cartwright, I cheated on my wife, for which I am sincerely regretful. That served as the basis for the blackmail, but I have already said too much. I want to avoid further risk to the safety of myself and my family. All I can say is remember to look up." Then the line goes dead.

I'm appalled, stunned, and confused. I can't believe blackmail and theft took place under my watch, even if for only a few months. "Evan, what the hell does *look up* mean? Does he think the cameras in the ceiling in Trendz recorded something important?"

Leaning forward and shaking his head, Evan replies, "I have no idea. Do you even have video from that far back?"

"Not unless it was archived in our backups. Do you think Chef Maurizio is telling the truth?"

"I think he is, Sean. He sounded remorseful but afraid of someone."

"If we believe him, then we know a little more. Unfortunately, it looks like our problems did not leave with Chef Maurizio. I had hoped the problem was that without a new chef in charge of ordering, we just hadn't changed back to the old suppliers yet. I also had hoped the sabotage in the competition was unrelated, but if Chef Maurizio was being threatened too, it may be all linked together. Now, I need to figure out what the next step should be."

Looking at his phone, Evan stands as he says, "I am supposed to meet Cassandra at the Blue Ramen Bowl for lunch. Do you want to join us? We can discuss what to do next."

An alert goes off on both my phone and Evan's phone, interrupting our conversation.

"Fuck! Sean, that's Cassandra's panic code. Where's her security?"

"If she's at the spa, then security would be waiting nearby. Let me text them to see if they have eyes on her."

EVAN: WHERE IS CASSIE EDWARDS?
SECURITY: PANIC CODE WENT OFF. SHE LEFT THE SPA. DIDN'T SEE HER LEAVE. MAY HAVE LEFT WHILE I WAS IN THE RESTROOM.
EVAN: FIND HER NOW!!!

"Shit! Let's go. They lost her, but we can track her TekCuff using the app on my phone.

As we leave my office, I call out, "Emily, it's imperative we find Cassie Edwards ASAP. Please ask our IT department to text me her last known location and have security search all video feeds to locate her. Tell them to start with the spa exit. Tell them this is a Code Red Alert."

Emily's head pops up from her work, jaw slack and eyes practically popping out of her head. We never have Code Red Alerts, so she knows this is serious, but like the true professional she is, she quickly gathers her poise and calmly responds, "Will do."

CHAPTER FORTY-SEVEN

CASSIE

Where am I? I try to open my eyes but am met with intense pain when light enters the narrow slits between my eyelids. My head spins, and I think I'm going to throw up. I take a couple of deep, cleansing breaths, trying to remember what happened.

Without opening my eyes, I carefully take in my surroundings. I'm sitting on a hard, cold floor, probably concrete. My hands are bound in front of me. My ankles are tied together too. My right arm is sore, like after a flu shot; that sharp prick I felt must have been an injection of some kind. I wonder why they chose to keep me alive when they killed the others?

I take a few more deep, but quiet, breaths in case someone is watching me, hoping more air will ease the nausea. Vomiting would be a clear giveaway that I've woken up, which would kill my only hope of getting an upper hand.

Again, I crack my eyes open a sliver to check things out and push past the searing pain as my eyes adjust to the brightness. I'm between crates in a back corner of a warehouse that has rows and rows of metal shelving 40-feet high. There are costumes and props with the

Athena logo, indicating this must be where they store supplies, holiday decorations, and props for the various shows.

I'm relieved I'm still at the Athena, and I wonder if Evan and Sean got my panic alert or if the signal wouldn't transmit through the thick concrete and steel of the Maze. I hang onto the hope that even if they didn't get my signal for help, maybe Evan will look for me when I don't show up for our lunch.

The sound of footsteps and someone talking on a cell phone nears, so I close my eyes tightly and still my body as much as possible. Deep Voice, who I'm now sure is Mitch, says "Don't worry. I got her. She won't cause any more problems." After a pause, Mitch continues, "No, she's safely hidden out of sight and still knocked out cold. I gave her enough meds to keep her quiet for hours, so we have plenty of time to deal with her a little later. Besides, Mr. Cartwright and his friend have no idea what is going on. They probably think the chefs are cutthroat enough to take each other out. When Jayden is the last viable option left standing, they will be forced to pick him. Besides, with Cassie gone, they will think she sabotaged Leon, got scared, and took off. They already found her fingerprints on the bowl of food that killed Leon." After another pause, Mitch responds, "No. Cartwright's friend won't care. She was just a fling." Following another brief silence, Mitch says, "No. They haven't connected Chef Bernard's death to the F&B increases, so we are in the clear. Besides, I planted opioids at Chef Bernard's restaurant. The police just haven't found them yet. I guess I hid them too well, but an anonymous tip will take care of that loose end."

Mitch listens longer this time and then says, "Stop worrying, Sis. There's no need to abandon our plan. The competition will end soon, and Jayden will be in place as the chef." After another pause, Mitch reassures, "Yes, I'm sure. I heard they loved his dessert. After all, they should have. He was ready for the twists. We've got this. I need to go now."

I open my eyes just enough to see that Mitch is staring at my ankle bindings. I quickly clamp my eyes shut and freeze. Then, most likely satisfied that I'm still sufficiently bound and asleep, he walks away.

After the footsteps have faded into the distance, I open my eyes. The nausea and dizziness threaten to overwhelm me, but after a couple of deep breaths, I'm able to use my teeth to pull my long sleeve up so I can look at my TekCuff. More time has passed than I realized. It's already 2 p.m. I was supposed to meet Evan half an hour ago. Hopefully, he's searching for me.

Glancing back at the screen on the TekCuff, I see that the signal bars are missing. Shit. No service. Did Mitch disable it, or is the signal blocked in the warehouse? And will the built-in GPS still work? I decide I can't risk waiting and must save myself.

Thank God Mitch had no way of knowing I have a super high metabolism when it comes to knock-out drugs. With me, they wear off so fast the dentist can't even do a simple filling without stopping to give me a second, and sometimes third, deadening shot.

I roll over and crawl from behind the crate, looking for something to cut the zip ties binding my ankles and hands. There is a thin metal sign on a nearby shelf, and I use the sharp edge as a knife on the ankle zip ties. The zip tie cuts into my already scraped-up legs, bringing more pain. The process is slow and I begin to panic, moving my ankles against the metal in a faster sawing motion. Finally, the zip tie snaps. My legs are starting to bleed, but I'm free.

I shake as I hold the metal sign with my knees and start working on the zip tie that is binding my hands. When I hear someone coming, I quickly return to where Mitch had me hidden, barely tucking myself behind the crates before a couple of guys walk by. Fortunately, they keep walking and don't notice the drops of blood I left behind, so I go back to the shelf with the metal sign and work to free my hands until, eventually, the zip tie breaks and my hands are free.

I look for a safe path out of the warehouse, remembering Emily mentioned everything is color-coded. We followed the blue lines on the floor and signs on the walls to get to Sean's office, but I don't see any blue lines now, and I don't know what the other colors mean. If I head into the Maze's corridors, I may run into Mitch, and if I run into someone else, well, I don't know whom I can trust.

But I can't stay here, so I take my chances and head to the nearest door. Testing the doorknob, I'm relieved to find the Athena doesn't lock doors in areas restricted to employees. Easing the door open, I enter an empty Maze hallway, and walk until I'm forced to turn right or left at a dead end. I pick right. As I near the next intersection, I hear voices, so I approach the corner slowly and take a quick look before pulling back. But strong arms yank me back and turn me around. Mitch seethes, "So you thought you could get away. I'll make sure you don't get away this time."

I scream and try to kick Mitch, but his arms are too strong for me. I try again. This time aiming my knee toward his crotch. I guess I connect because he squeals, but he still doesn't let go. He yanks my arms behind me and throws me onto the floor. Then Mitch kicks me in the side, knocking the air out of my lungs as Evan, Sean, Christian, and a bunch of security guys round the corner. Then before Mitch can kick me again, the security guys tackle Mitch, throwing him to the ground.

Evan is quickly kneeling and pulling me toward him asking if I'm ok and saying, "I have you. It is over. You are going to be ok," in a moment of *déjà vu*.

Struggling to get air into my lungs, I mouth, "They got Mitch, right?"

"Yes, they got him. Are you ok?"

"It's a little hard to breathe and everything is still fuzzy," I gasp in spurts.

"Sean, get medical help here fast. I think Cassandra was drugged. She may have broken ribs, and her wrists and legs are bleeding."

"They are already on the way," Sean responds.

Examining my arms as he cradles me, Evan asks, "What happened to your wrists?"

"Mitch used zip ties on my wrists and ankles. He injected me with something. I don't know what, but I still feel dizzy and nauseous. My head is throbbing like the worst hangover ever."

"Fuck. Just close your eyes and rest. Medical help is on the way."

"Evan, Mitch was talking to his partner on the phone. He called his partner 'Sis'. Please tell Sean and the police. They need to find out who his sister is," I plead as I grasp onto his shirt.

"Will do," he assures, stroking back my sweat-slicked hair.

"Evan, did you get my panic alert?" I ask.

"Yes, but then your GPS wasn't working. The tech guys said that someone had disabled your device, but they knew Christian had let you into the Maze. By the way, I didn't write that note you gave to Christian. We figured it was Mitch, so we started tracking Mitch's movements through his cell phone."

"Thank you. You saved my life." I reach up to touch his cheek, but the EMTs arrive and pull Evan away. I hear them talking about transporting me to a hospital, but I beg, "No hospital, please. Just take me back to my room."

"Is anything broken?" Evan asks the EMTs, and they tell him they don't think so. My ribs are badly bruised, and my wrists and ankles are raw from the zip ties. The chloroform and the injection, which they are fairly certain was ketamine, will take time to wear off, but I should be fine. Hearing that and looking at my pleading eyes, Evan agrees I can stay at the hotel.

Evan yells to Sean, "I am going to take Cassandra to my suite. Are you going to interrogate Mitch?"

"We've called the police. They are on their way, but that won't stop me from asking him some questions while we wait."

"I want to hear what he says first-hand. Who can stay with Cassandra?"

Christian steps from the background and says, "I will."

Evan narrows his eyes. "I don't know if I trust you."

"Please let me make it up to Ms. Edwards, Mr. Cartwright, and you. When the note was typed instead of handwritten, I knew something seemed off. I should have double-checked before letting her into the Maze, but the note indicated time was of the essence, and Ms. Edwards had the password, along with the NER designation. I had planned to accompany her into the Maze, but I was called away for what turned out to be a crank call. I feel horrible. I could have been responsible for her being killed. I know I am going to lose my job over this, but please let me help keep her safe until then."

"Sean, what do you think?" Evan asks.

"It's the least he can do after leaving Cassie unescorted when he knows we were keeping close watch over her. And his story checks out. Security just confirmed it was a crank call they traced back to Mitch. Besides, he followed protocol by verifying the password. However, we will be tightening our procedures even more going forward."

"Ok, but I am going up to the suite with them to make sure Cassandra is comfortable. Then I will come back. Where should I meet you?"

"Take a couple of the security guys with you. I want one posted outside your suite. Another one can bring you to Holding Area C."

CHAPTER FORTY-EIGHT

CASSIE

I must have been in a deep sleep because I slept until noon today, finally waking up thirsty, hungry, and grateful the horrible headache from yesterday is gone. My ribs are still sore, and my wrists and ankles are tender from the cuts and bruises, but otherwise I feel a lot better. Evan must have been exhausted too because he is still asleep.

Watching Evan sleep, I can't help but relive yesterday's scary events. Thanks to Christian and one of Sean's long-time security guards, I was able to rest last night while I waited for Evan. Not knowing whom to trust, Evan insisted two people stay with me to ensure this didn't turn into a real horror movie if one of the two turned out to be a bad guy. I told Evan he was being too paranoid, and thankfully, I was right. If anything, they were overly protective. Neither would leave the other alone with me.

When Evan returned last night, my head was still throbbing, but I was starting to feel a little better. I was eager for him to tell me what Mitch revealed, but he just said the police had everything under control. I'm not very patient, so I didn't find that answer acceptable. However, I was too exhausted and my head hurt too bad to argue.

When I try to slip out of bed, Evan stirs, so that is my cue to re-ask,

"Evan, what did Mitch tell you? Do we know who is behind the killing and sabotage?"

Rolling toward me as he rubs the sleep out of his eyes, Evan says, "Yes, we know."

"Who?"

"I can't say. Let's get some food."

"Yes, let's get some food, but why can't you tell me who's behind everything?" I ask, nudging Evan's shoulder.

"I made a promise to my best friend and the police," Evan says while giving my hand a reassuring pat. "Sean and the police are taking care of everything. It will all be clear soon, so let's enjoy today. The police have it under control and don't need our help. Besides, Sean delayed the Final Dinner until tonight when he plans to announce the winner of the competition."

My eyes pop. "You're kidding, right? Sean is still going to pick a winner after everything that happened? I had assumed he cancelled the competition."

Nodding, Evan explains, "Sean says he knows the outcome of the competition and assures me the finalists will agree it is fair. Do you think you will feel like going?" Evan asks, concern in his voice.

"I'm not sure how he is going to pull that off, but you couldn't keep me away from it tonight regardless of how I'm feeling. However, the good news is that I feel much better today," I say, waving off his worry with a flick of my wrist.

As Evan props up on his elbow, a smile replaces his concern. "Great. I will have the spa send someone up to fix your hair. By the way, what happened to your fingernails and toenails? They look like they were painted by a 5-year-old."

I splay my fingers in front of me and laugh as I stare at the smeared polish. "You're right. They are a mess. When I got the note to meet you in the Maze yesterday, the nail polish wasn't dry yet. But the note said it was urgent and to hurry if I wanted to witness my name being cleared, so I ignored the wet polish and rushed to find Christian."

"That explains it. I will have the spa send someone to fix your nails too," Evan says as he grabs his phone and starts texting.

Remembering Mitch's phone call with his sis, I frown and hug myself to fend off the chill running down my spine. As I pause to contemplate the dose of potential reality the call dispensed, I know I need to clear the air. "Evan, Mitch said I was just a fling to you and you wouldn't care what happened to me. Is that true?" After all, we haven't known each other long, and I know Mitch's comment shouldn't bother me so much, but thinking about it now is like being in the shadow under a dark cloud. As the days have passed, deep down I've been hoping Evan and I would find a way to stay connected even after I go back home.

Dropping his phone and jumping out of bed, Evan tugs me against his chest, exclaiming, "Cassandra, that is absurd. I do care what happens to you. I was worried sick."

"That doesn't mean this wasn't just a Las Vegas fling to you," I say with a shake of my head. Burying my head against his neck so he won't see the tears threatening to overflow, I admit, "Regardless, I know this is all coming to an end. After tonight, I'll be headed home to look for a new job, and you will be headed to Europe."

Evan pulls back, hands holding my face. "Wait a minute, why do you need to look for a new job?" he asks as his eyes search mine for answers.

"Oh, I haven't had a chance to tell you. The Firm required me to contact the human resources department to confirm my return date, so I called yesterday. With the competition over, I assumed it was ok to use a phone again."

"At this point, no one would care you called into work. But you still have not told me why you need to look for a new job."

"I'm getting to that part. When I called HR to let them know I would be returning next week, they told me I've been laid off. The Firm is making cuts and realized that they could cover my workload without me. However, I wonder if someone saw the news article, intertwining me with the murder, and this is their excuse to let me go, wanting to distance themselves from the drama."

"That is terrible," Evan consoles as he nestles my head to his shoulder. "When your name is officially cleared, they will want you back. But you may be better off looking for another position at a firm that is not so quick to judge, if that is the career you want to return to."

Arms wrapped around Evan's warm torso, I dig my fingers in tighter as Evan rubs comforting circles on my back. He continues, "I am still confident that the beautiful dishes I saw you prepare have you in the running to win the competition tonight, so let's enjoy every minute together. Tomorrow we can deal with the problems, if any remain. Besides, this means you can join me at my father's retirement party, and we can have more time together."

"Oh, Evan, I wish I could, but now I definitely can't afford to go with you to Europe. I need to find a new job to pay my bills. However, I agree with you that tomorrow I will have certainty as to my career path. If I don't win the competition, I have decided to look for another job in law."

Unwrapping our tangled arms, Evan steps back as he says, "It is your choice, which I respect, but I hope you are able to pursue your real passion. I would also like to clarify another point. I do not want what we started here to end here."

"I don't see how it continues with us in two different countries," I say with a disappointed shake of my head.

"I have a few ideas, but please give me some time to see if I can work out the details."

"What do you have in mind?" I ask as I tilt my head to study the twinkle making his eyes smile.

"I don't want to get your hopes up just yet, so please be patient for a day or two," he says, squeezing my shoulders. "I will know more later this weekend when I hear back from my parents about some issues with the business. We can talk more after that, ok?"

Grasping his upper arms, I stare intently into his captivating eyes as I say, "It means more than you can know that you want us to continue, but you know patience is a tough one for me. I also don't like to be left out of the loop. Look how it has been driving me insane waiting for my name to be cleared. But if it involves your family business, I'll respect your request and not push for now. On another topic, who do you think will win the competition? How will Sean make it fair?" I ask, as I step away and wander toward the bedroom window.

"Well, I'm pretty sure it won't be Jayden, which will go a long way in the fairness department. But the other three of you have done a great job based on the look of the dishes you prepared and the judges' comments. I guess we will find out tonight."

Resting my hand on my chin, I contemplate the possible outcomes as I take in the scene outside. "While I can't help but want it to be me, my money is on Trenton. Sean promised you that all the finalists would find the result fair, and it would be hard to argue with that choice. He's a top New York chef who has years of experience and exudes confidence. He would fit in perfectly here."

Nevertheless, I hold out a modicum of hope for a different outcome. Exhaling a deep breath, I turn back toward Evan, crossing my fingers behind my back and silently wishing for my version of a fairytale ending.

CHAPTER FORTY-NINE

SEAN

Detective Fielder and I watch in anticipation as the blue dot blips across my screen, tracking Jayden's TekCuff. When the dot stops outside Cynthia's office, we know it's time to move in.

In minutes, Detective Fielder, his backup officers, and I stealthily fall into position outside Cynthia's door. Hearing muffled voices inside, I press my ear against the door while temporarily holding back the officers with an outstretched hand. Barely audible, I hear Jayden saying, "Cynthia, I still don't understand why you wanted to talk with me."

Without waiting to hear the answer, I turn the knob and shove the door open, causing Jayden to flinch in the guest chair across from Cynthia's desk. To conceal the other officers' presence, I partially close the door after Detective Fielder follows me in.

Hiding my anger, I calmly say, "Hello, Cynthia. Sorry to interrupt, but we wanted to share some information. Jayden, you will want to hear this as well. We have learned one of the finalists received advantages in the competition in exchange for what they thought were harmless pranks." A glance out of the corner of my eye, reveals Jayden slumping in the chair while white knuckling its wooden arms.

Cynthia palms her cheek in shock. "No way! That can't possibly be true."

"It is. Unfortunately, one of the pranks was to substitute hummus for bean dip." Jerking my head toward Jayden, I hiss, "Right, Jayden?"

"What are you talking about?" Jayden barks in defense. "I didn't do that."

"Oh, but you did. We have video of you in the Trendz kitchen discussing sabotage in exchange for advantages in the competition, so don't even try to deny it."

"There aren't any microphones in the kitchen. You're making that up," Jayden scoffs.

"Wipe that smug look off your face. While originally there weren't any microphones in the kitchen, after we saw a video of you talking with Mitch, we added microphones and more cameras."

Jayden bolts from his chair, screaming, "Cynthia, is this why you called me to your office? I don't have to take this. I didn't do anything wrong. I'm leaving."

But before he can escape, one of the officers slips through the partially open door and pushes Jayden back into the chair, firmly planting his hands on Jayden's shoulders. I command, "Sit back down and stop lying. You're not going anywhere. You knew sesame seeds were a banned ingredient, but you still substituted hummus for the bean dip. You are responsible for Chef Boucher's death. You also sabotaged Kai's food in exchange for an advantage. The evidence is clear. But why did you do it?"

Deflated, nervous sweat beading on his forward, Jayden stares down at his lap, wringing his hands. Finally breaking the silence, he says, "He promised I would win the Guest Chef Competition if I went along with some harmless pranks. I didn't know anyone would get hurt. I thought Chef Boucher died from his head injury when he fell. I thought it was an accident."

"Who promised you would win?" I ask. My question is met with silence as Jayden refuses to look me in the eye. Staring a hole through his downturned head, I repeat my question louder and add, "Was it Mitch's partner in crime. Tell me now!"

Jayden's voice shaking, he reluctantly answers, "Mitch told me I would win. I don't know who his partner is."

"I see. Well, Mitch doesn't even work in the Food & Beverage department. He works in security and certainly doesn't control who wins. Therefore, it shouldn't come as a surprise that you are officially disqualified from this competition. I would also like to introduce you to the police officer who is currently restraining you. His name is Ken. You may recall seeing him in the kitchen during the competition. He was the dishwasher who saw you sabotage Kai's food. He will make an excellent witness at your trial."

"Shit," Jayden mumbles as Ken pulls out handcuffs.

"Stand up. Hands behind your back." As he slaps the cuffs against Jayden's wrists, Ken recites, "You are under arrest. You have the right to remain silent."

Turning toward Cynthia, I ask, "Cynthia, did you know about this?"

Rising from her chair, hands on her hips, she indignantly responds, "Are you kidding? Of course I didn't know. This is appalling."

Gritting my teeth, my anger rises by the second. Incredulous, I raise my eyebrows halfway up my forehead. "As head of F&B at the Athena, you expect me to believe you didn't know anything about the supplier kickbacks?" I say, sarcasm lacing my words.

Closing the distance between us, Cynthia throws her hands in the air. "Kickbacks? What are you talking about? This is the first I'm hearing about it."

After taking a deep breath, I approach the matter from another direction with a calmer tone. "The kickbacks are the reason for the unacceptable increase in F&B expenses. Did you ever talk with Chef Maurizio to find out if he knows anything about the changes in suppliers and increased costs?"

Cynthia shrugs. "I wasn't able to get hold of him."

I squint in question and retort, "That's strange. I didn't have any problem reaching him when I called."

A flash of fear briefly flickers in Cynthia's eyes at the news that I've spoken with Chef Maurizio. If I hadn't been watching her intently, I would have missed her tell because she instantly hides her concern. And with a wave of her hand, she explains, "To tell the truth, I didn't bother trying to find Chef Maurizio. Based on my experiences with him, it would have been futile. Chef Maurizio is a liar. You can't believe a word he says."

My skin heats with fury. I face the betrayal head on, unleashing my pent-up anger and disgust over the pointless loss of life. "Oh, but I do believe everything he says. You see, Mitch told us the same story as Chef Maurizio. And the suppliers I spoke with this afternoon identify you as the mastermind behind the kickback scheme. The authorities also got a warrant and searched your home today. They found extremely interesting bank records. It appears you are a very wealthy woman as a result of your thefts from the Athena."

Perplexed, Jayden asks, "You mean it was you all along? You are Mitch's partner?"

I turn to answer. "Yes, Jayden, it was Cynthia." Turning back to Cynthia, I demand, "Tell me why."

Cynthia seethes, responding with venom in her voice, "You bastard. How dare you accuse me of such things?"

I pull a piece of paper from my pocket and wave it toward Cynthia. "My father left me a note about you, but I didn't figure out what it actually meant until yesterday. It says

SON,

I PROMISED CYNTHIA SHE WILL ALWAYS HAVE A JOB, AND YOU WON'T FIND A BETTER F&B MANAGER. BUT IF SHE TRIES TO SAY SHE DESERVES MORE, SHE IS SADLY MISTAKEN. SHE OVERESTIMATES HER PLACE AT THE ATHENA AND HER PRIOR RELATIONSHIP WITH ME.

FATHER

"I only wish he had realized how fucked up you are," I say, shaking my head.

Tears running down her face, Cynthia jumps up and screams,

"That's a lie! Your father and I were in love. He would have never said those things. His heart attack took him before we could marry."

"Cynthia, you are delusional. I had IT search for emails between you and my father. Shortly before he died, he broke up with you, but you clearly refused to accept his decision. Let me tell you what I think happened based on our little talk with your half-brother Mitch and the facts we have pieced together. First, you offered Chef Bernard money if she would use her position as a judge to ensure that the right person won the competition. But she refused and was going to tell me about your offer as soon as she had the chance. You couldn't let that happen, so you made sure you were the one who handed champagne to the judges at the press conference. Her champagne had a little something extra so she wouldn't have the chance to tell me about the conversation. Did I miss anything?" I say, balling my fists, barely containing my rage that this trusted employee murdered my good friend, Chef Bernard.

Like a caged animal, Cynthia's face contorts, eyes flickering between me and the door. Suddenly, she darts toward the door and flings it wide open, yelling, "You don't have proof of anything. I won't stay here and take this." But before she makes it through the doorway, Detective Fielder and another officer lunge toward Cynthia, each grabbing one of her arms, yanking her back.

Shouting obscenities, Cynthia thrashes in their hold and stomps her spiked heels on their shoes, struggling to free herself. But with his free hand, Detective Fielder successfully snaps handcuffs tightly around her wrists.

I shake my head in disgust and shout over her outbursts. "We also know you killed Chef Boucher. Just like Chef Bernard, he didn't want to play your game. You made him the same offer before approaching Jayden. You promised to rig the competition so he would win in exchange for him sabotaging other finalists. But instead of grabbing the opportunity, he was going to report your offer, so you decided he had to go too. What do you have to say for yourself?"

Cynthia fumes, "I want a lawyer."

Nodding toward Detective Fielder, I say, "I think you need one.

Detective Fielder, she is all yours. Let me know if the Athena can be of further assistance."

"Mr. Cartwright, thank you for your assistance." As the police drag Cynthia and Jayden away, I hear them reciting in unison, "You have the right to remain silent ..."

I stand frozen in Cynthia's office as the reality of the situation soaks in. My blood is still boiling from Cynthia's betrayal, but the anger is mixed with regret that we didn't uncover it before she orchestrated to two senseless deaths.

CHAPTER FIFTY

CASSIE

I feel like I'm in a fairytale with my low-cut, black dress that shimmers when the light hits. The spa's hairdresser worked her magic on me, weaving shiny crystals through my long wavy hair so my hair sparkles against my almost bare back. She even gave me some lotion with glitter to make my neck, arms, and back shimmer, which Evan was more than happy to help apply. Based on the hunger in Evan's dark, piercing eyes, he's torn between wanting to tear my dress off or show me off at dinner. Either way, he makes me feel incredibly appreciated.

As I admire my finished look in the mirror one final time, Evan surprises me by draping a spectacular diamond necklace around my neck. I bring my hand to my throat touching the gems; this must be 30 carats of diamonds. "Evan, this is too much. I can't possibly accept it."

"Cassandra, don't worry. I borrowed it from my favorite jeweler."

"But what if it falls off my neck or I lose it?"

"It's insured. Quit worrying," Evan says, but he doesn't stop with the necklace. He locks onto my eyes and silently wraps a diamond-studded, white gold cuff around each of my wrists, saying, "These will cover and protect your wounds from the zip ties." I can't muster a response, as tears well up in my eyes.

"Enjoy the evening as my princess. I hope this will be the first of many formal evenings we will have together."

I nod without requiring further persuasion, and as we walk out the door and make our way to the Final Dinner, I do feel amazingly special.

When we enter the Grand Athena's Wine Cave, I stop and take in the scene, overwhelmed by the warm and inviting atmosphere. The ceiling is low, the walls are made from rough-cut stones, and the floor is concrete, which gives the feeling of being in an underground cave. Dim lights with a yellowish glow dance off the various surfaces. The scent of oak and wine fills the air from the barrels that line one wall. A long, formal, table with flickering candles graces the center of the room. Nothing could be more perfect.

I pause, wanting to remember every moment of tonight, but Evan places his hand on my back and urges me further into the Wine Cave where we are handed glasses of champagne. Then a white-gloved server presents shrimp appetizers on a shiny silver tray.

I had no idea there would be so many people here: the film crew and photographers, Sean, Trenton, Kai, some of Athena's management, the three judges, and several other people I don't know. Even Christian is here as a guest. I hope that means Sean isn't going to fire him for falling for the fake note and letting me into the Maze unescorted. Then I notice Detective Fielder, which is interesting.

We stop to chat with Trenton and Kai. Greetings exchanged, Kai asks, "Have you seen Jayden?"

Cautiously, I simply say, "No," rather than share my thoughts that Jayden may have been kicked out by now.

Trenton chimes in, "He doesn't have a chance at winning, so who cares if he shows up?"

"That's rather harsh," Kai retorts.

Hoping to diffuse the situation, I interject, "I am so excited tonight. This is such a beautiful setting for the final event. I can't wait to hear who the winner will be."

"Me, of course," Trenton says with a huff.

Inserting a little diplomacy, Evan points out, "You all three did a great job. The Athena would be lucky to have any one of you."

Kai admits, "I agree, we all have a good chance, depending on exactly what type of guest chef the Athena is looking for."

"You're right," I add, silently noting the difference in Trenton's and Kai's personalities is certainly shining through tonight.

A bell rings, indicating we are to take our seats, so Evan and I part ways, and oddly, it feels rather lonely without him by my side.

Trenton, Kai, and I are sitting directly across from Sean and Evan, but with an empty seat between each of us. When everyone is settled, Sean gets our attention, saying, "Tonight, we have assembled key people who have been involved in this competition. Unfortunately, Jayden will not be able to join us tonight, but I want to offer my congratulations to all the finalists!" The announcement about Jayden brings raised eyebrows and low murmurs around the table.

But Sean calmly raises his magic hand that always silences a crowd. He continues, "As a surprise, we have invited someone special to join each finalist for this dinner. Trenton, your father is here. Kai, your girlfriend is joining us. And Cassie, your best friend, Lowri is here. Welcome!"

We simultaneously turn around and jump out of our seats in surprise. Trenton's father is slapping him on the back as the two giant men embrace. Kai swings his girlfriend in circles as he plants a kiss square on her lips. Lowri and I hug as best friends do. "I can't believe you are here," a smile plastered on my face.

She exclaims, "We have a lot to talk about!"

I nod in return and whisper, "No kidding, but there are microphones and cameras everywhere, so now is not the time."

As the exuberant greetings subside, Sean instructs, "Everyone, please take your seats. There will be plenty of time for catching up later." After we are all seated, Sean continues, "I also would like to thank our staff and the film crew for their hard work. Please raise your glass and join me in a toast to everyone who made this competition possible. Cheers!"

We all raise our glasses and then take a sip of the exquisite champagne. Given the presence of cameras, Trenton, Kai and I are resisting the opportunity to discuss Jayden's absence and what it means, but raised eyebrows and quick looks between each other indicate we are dying to discuss the implications of his absence.

Sean explains, "Our worthy finalists have been working hard in the kitchen during the competition, so it is now the Grand Athena's pleasure to present the finalists and our other guests with a specially prepared meal to celebrate the conclusion of our competition. I am told our first course is a salad of spring greens, sugar-sweet cantaloupe, and prosciutto, topped with a drizzle of aged balsamic vinegar. It is paired with the Veuve Clicquot champagne we just used for our toast. Enjoy."

Sean then asks Sebastian if the microphones can be turned off while we eat, and Sebastian complies.

With the cameras still rolling, conversation remains limited, but I notice Lowri staring at Sean intently, as she says, "I had the pleasure of meeting Sean and Evan earlier."

I respond carefully, "That's nice."

"It was very nice. Hopefully, I will have time to talk to them again later." But I notice Sean sneaking glances at Lowri too, so I think she really means she is hoping to talk with Sean again later.

After our salads are removed, the microphones are turned on again as a second course immediately appears. This time Evan explains the dish, saying, "For the second course, you have been presented a lobster and ricotta ravioli served with a lemon butter sauce. The ravioli is paired with a crisp sauvignon blanc. *Buon appetito!*"

My mouth is watering. The ravioli is velvety. The lobster has just the right bite. The ricotta adds creaminess, a hint of lemon zest brightens the overall flavor, and the butter in the sauce adds a smoothness that brings the flavors together. I think I'm in love. I know I should slow down, but it's so good I quickly clean my plate.

The table remains silent as servers arrive with the main course, and I wonder if Sean or Amy will start actively engaging conversation to spice things up for the cameras. As I wait for my plate, I look across at Evan and find him staring at me with a smug grin on his face. I involuntarily return his smile and feel a warm glow flow over me. I'm going to miss him when this is over. I wish there were some way we could extend our time together. Evan says he has an idea for making us work, but it seems it would take a miracle. It's also too bad I can't go with him to his dad's retirement party in Europe, but unless I win tonight, I need to start looking for another job before my meager savings are completely depleted. It would be more exciting to look for a culinary opportunity, but with my student loans hanging over my head, that doesn't make as much sense as applying to other law firms.

When a plate is placed in front of me, Sean reads from a menu card. "Our main course tonight features a dry-aged prime filet mignon served with roasted asparagus. To accompany our steaks, I selected a Screaming Eagle red wine called Second Flight, which is from the same winery that makes Screaming Eagle cabernet. Enjoy." With the mention of Second Flight, there is a gasp amongst the finalists. I've never tasted a wine that expensive before, and I can't believe we are being treated to such an extravagance.

I overhear Evan whisper to Sean, "Why did you select this instead of the real Screaming Eagle cab?"

Sean retorts, "Why do you think? The wine alone is costing me about a grand per person for this dinner. That would at least triple the wine costs. I want this dinner to be special, not outrageous."

I knew this was an expensive dinner, but that's even beyond my estimate. Taking a sip of the high-end wine, I let the full-bodied, silky liquid envelope my taste buds. Closing my eyes, I detect notes of blackberries and chocolate with what I think is a hint of black truffles. A second sip confirms it's truly amazing, which reminds me to concentrate even harder to make sure I enjoy every sip and every bite of tonight's meal. I'm not sure when, if ever, I'll be at another dinner that costs thousands of dollars per person.

After the plates are cleared, Sean signals to Sebastian, who yells,

"Cut!" Sean demands everyone's attention, saying, "I have asked for the filming to stop temporarily because we have a little business to take care of before we enjoy a wonderful dessert." I assume Sean is about to announce the winner now, but why would he want to do that off-camera. Instead, he says, "Before we announce the winner of the Athena's Guest Chef Competition, I want to deal with the sabotage and cheating that has plagued this competition."

Murmurs engulf the space before Sean taps a wine glass with his knife to regain everyone's attention. Continuing, Sean explains, "We have learned one of the finalists received advantages in the competition in exchange for what that finalist thought were harmless pranks. For example, this finalist added extra salt to someone's dish."

Kai exclaims, "That explains it!"

Sean confirms, "Yes, Kai it does. Unfortunately, one of the other pranks was deadly and designed to frame another finalist. The saboteur made use of a bowl Cassie touched when she offered to help during a prep session. I doubt she even remembers touching the bowl."

Face palming my forehead, I exclaim, "So that's how my fingerprints got there. I did move some bowls on that table before Amy told me I wasn't allowed to help. That's what I kept trying to remember."

"Yes, Cassie. Sometime after you touched the bowl, Jayden retrieved and saved it. Later he filled the bowl with hummus and replaced Mr. Boucher's finished dip with the hummus. But Chef Boucher was highly allergic to sesame seeds. It turns out that tahini, which is made from sesame seeds, is a key ingredient in hummus, so when Chef Boucher tasted the dip on camera he went into anaphylactic shock and died. We have confirmed that Jayden didn't know that Chef Boucher would die from the hummus, but he thought Chef Boucher would be disqualified for using a banned ingredient: sesame seeds."

The room collectively gasps, but instead of feeling shock, I'm relieved. I finally know how my fingerprints ended up on the bowl. It's also sad to learn about Jayden. I knew he was given advantages in exchange for sabotage, but I hadn't been sure it was so directly related to the murder.

Continuing his revelations, Sean explains, "I am sure you will all hear the details from the press, so I will share a few more with you tonight. Cynthia through her half-brother Mitch, who was one of our security guards, promised Jayden that he would win the Guest Chef Competition in exchange for performing these pranks."

Turning and gesturing toward a large man seated a few chairs to my right, Sean says, "I would also like to introduce and thank Chef Maurizio, the former chef of Trendz, for joining us tonight and agreeing to share his part of the story as well."

Chef Maurizio stands, dabbing his mouth before placing his napkin on the table. "Mr. Cartwright, thank you for giving me this opportunity to clear things up. Cynthia and her brother were blackmailing me into helping with their scheme to take kickbacks from suppliers. When my family needed me at their restaurant back in Europe, I saw an out, so I left the Athena to get out from under their control. That's when they decided to rig the Guest Chef Competition to get someone else in place that they could control. Mr. Cartwright, let me apologize to you again. I am very sorry for my actions that financially harmed you and the Athena. I should never have been in a position to be blackmailed in the first place."

Sean nods in Chef Maurizio's direction. "Thank you, Chef Maurizio. In exchange for his help resolving this matter and for his agreement to repay the kickbacks he received, we will be forgiving what we will call his missteps. Chef, I cannot think of another instance where we have offered this level of forgiveness, so please do not make me regret the decision not to turn you over to the authorities and press charges."

Chef Maurizio responds, "Mr. Cartwright, I will be forever grateful for the opportunity to make things right with you and the Grand Athena."

Questions are flying at Sean, with one common question dominating. "Why did they have to kill Chef Boucher to rig the competition?"

Sean explains, "Before they approached Jayden to act as saboteur, they first approached one of the judges, Chef Bernard, offering her money in exchange for help rigging the competition. When she wouldn't agree and planned to tell me about the plot, Cynthia spiked her drink, which caused her to have the fatal car accident."

Oh no! She killed Chef Bernard? I thought Chef Bernard got drunk and killed herself in the car accident.

Continuing, Sean says, "Then they approached Chef Boucher for help with their plan, promising he would win the competition. He refused, intending to report it to me, so they decided he had to go as well. Rather than drop the plan after two murders, Cynthia and Mitch were emboldened and approached Jayden, who agreed to help. Cynthia, Mitch, and Jayden are all in custody now, and I understand they will be charged with murder."

Evan asks, "Sean, I have one question, if you don't mind. Did Cynthia sabotage Cassandra's zipline equipment?"

Shaking his head, Sean responds, "Mitch took care of that. According to Mitch, Cassie wasn't supposed to be competitive. That's why they picked a home cook as the alternate in the first place. They were hoping to knock out the best chef early through a disqualification, and substitute someone who wouldn't threaten their intended winner, but then Cassie turned out to be too good of a chef for their purposes. They were afraid she might have a chance at winning. A zipline accident was supposed to get her out of the way, but fortunately, Amy had you ride tandem with Cassie and ruined that part of their plan." Turning to Detective Fielder, I ask, "Do you want to add anything?"

Detective Fielder responds, "I would like to thank you and the Athena for your cooperation on this matter, but it would not be appropriate for me to comment further at this time."

With open arms, Sean says, "Understood. We have all suffered great losses. First, my friend Chef Bernard, then Chef Boucher. We must remember them and honor their memories. However, we should also celebrate the hard work of the three finalists who remain and competed through difficult circumstances. Therefore, it is time to announce the results of the competition, so I'm going to ask everyone to help me make the next part of the filming a happy event. There will be plenty of time for us to honor the lost chefs and discuss the news we just shared after the results are announced. Can you help me?"

Sean meets the eyes of each guest in turn, gaining their agreement. Then he says, "Sebastian, please restart your filming. We still need to announce the results of the competition."

As the cameras roll again, the servers quickly reappear with a decadent chocolate creation. Sean explains, "Our dessert course tonight is a chocolate Grand Marnier crème brûlée. It is accompanied by a 20-year-old port, which should complement the chocolate quite well. Let me know what you think."

It's hard not to discuss Sean's announcements, but I respect his request and take a bite of the dessert. Looking at Lowri, we share a happy moan. It is rich and creamy, and Sean is right, the port is a perfect pairing.

As we continue enjoying our dessert, Sean says "We have kept our three finalists in suspense far too long." Directing his next comments to Trenton, Kai, and me, Sean explains, "You each have a box sitting in front of you." I notice that we are the only ones with the four-inch square boxes wrapped in glossy red paper and tied with gold ribbons.

Sean continues, "The results of the competition will be revealed when you open the boxes. You each selected a name for the restaurant you would run if you won the Guest Chef Competition. If your gift has that name on it, then you have won. On the count of three, unwrap your gifts. One. Two. Three. Open!"

We each reach for our red and gold boxes and start unwrapping. Kai has his open first and reveals a gold bracelet engraved with the name Tropic. He exclaims, "I can't believe it. I won!" Trenton and I stop unwrapping our gifts to congratulate Kai and to try to hide our disappointment from the cameras. I guess I knew I wouldn't win, but I still had a tiny ray of hope. However, after the sabotage inflicted on Kai, I am happy that he won.

Sean says, "Congratulations, Kai. Trenton and Cassie, please do me the favor of unwrapping your gifts as well. I hope you will like them." Of course, we comply, opening ours simultaneously. Trenton shows off his gold bracelet with the name NY Roasted on it. Then I look at mine, and I see that the bracelet says Pinot & Pie. That is the restaurant name I picked to honor my friend who lets me post on her website. She gave me permission to use the name if I won. We are all looking at each other confused and start peppering Sean with questions.

Sean says, "Congratulations, you have all won. It turns out that each of you won one of the cooking rounds, and the judges were very impressed with each of you. Therefore, we decided that you are each worthy of being a guest chef, particularly after the strange circumstances under which you had to compete. As guest chef, you will each plan the menus for one month and be given the opportunity to learn how we run our restaurants here at the Athena. One of you may even be chosen as the full-time chef for the restaurant at the end of your month. We will work out the details tomorrow as to the order and dates. And by the way, you will each receive the cash prize, so congratulations!"

Sebastian yells, "Cut!" Then Sean continues, "For now, please enjoy your dessert and drinks. Afterward, Amy and the crew will be filming interviews with each of you. Also, your cell phones are being returned to you tonight, but we ask that you and all the guests wait 48 hours to reveal your winning status because the video of the last episode will not be released until tomorrow evening." We all jump up and exchange hugs with each other and our friends and family that have joined us. Lowri can't resist saying, "Now, aren't you glad you finally listened to me and applied?" And I smile and agree that she told me so.

I barely remember what happens during the next half hour. It's like a dream. We finish dessert, and Amy interviews us between more hugs and congratulations. The judges stop by to tell me they know my month as guest chef is going to be a big success based on my performance in the competition, and finally, Evan makes his way over and pulls me into his arms. "I am so happy for you. Your name is cleared, and your dream of a culinary career just came true. And best of all, this means we can have more time together. You can come with me to Europe."

I panic. What if Evan rigged this for me? Maybe I didn't win on merit. "Did you have something to do with me being one of the winners?"

Indignant, Evan responds, "Absolutely not! I made it clear from the very beginning that I would have no say in the results, and I didn't. You won this opportunity on your own merits."

"You didn't suggest to Sean that we should all win?" I tilt my head up and ask.

"No. I wasn't part of his decision-making process, and I didn't know until you did. I am hurt that you doubt me." His eyes soften.

"I'm sorry. I just can't believe it's true that I won." I pull him back in for another hug as he whispers, "Believe it," into my ear.

Detective Fielder walks up, interrupting us. "Ms. Edwards, please let me add my congratulations. I would also like to apologize for suspecting you were part of what happened to Chef Boucher. Unfortunately, the trick with the fingerprints led us down the wrong path for a while."

"I certainly understand how it looked. I'm just glad you caught the real criminals in the end."

"Thank you for your understanding. I wish you a very successful tenure as guest chef. Hopefully, I will have the opportunity to stop by the restaurant when you are at its helm."

"Please do."

As Detective Fielder prepares to leave, he first turns to Evan and with a slight bow says "And thank you Your Royal Highness for all your help. It was a pleasure meeting you. Goodbye."

Huh? I turn to Evan. "Why did he call you 'Your Royal Highness'? An inside joke you haven't shared with me?" I tease.

But Evan looks mortified, and for the first time ever, he looks like he doesn't know what to say. I step back as shock takes over. Is that really Evan's title? Is he royalty? The look on Evan's face confirms it's true.

But if Detective Fielder knows, everyone else must too. It's not an inside joke. I'm the only one in the dark. Everyone must think I'm a fool not knowing the true identity of the guy I've been dating.

My mind begins to race and my heart starts pounding as the realization that he lied to me sets in. Before he can respond, I bolt for the door.

"Cassandra, please wait. I can explain everything," I hear him call after me, but I don't stop. I run away from Evan as fast as I can.

CHAPTER FIFTY-ONE

CASSIE

I barely make it out of the Wine Cave before tears are streaming down my face. I rush to the elevators that will take me to my room. Lowri catches up to me asking, "What happened?" as I repeatedly punch the button urging the elevator to open. I need to get to my room before Evan finds me, assuming he even tries.

Once the elevator arrives, I rush in and hit the close door button. As the elevator rises, it occurs to me that I have my cell phone back and can use it to find out who Evan really is. I type "royal Evan Catalinius", and photos of Evan in full royal regalia pop up. Under one photo it says he is Garret Evan Louis Francesco, Prince of Catalinius. I show my phone to Lowri, saying, "Evan's a prince, and I've been royally played. Literally. He invited me to his father's retirement party. But his father is the King of Catalinius. There is no retirement party. What the hell?"

Lowri is rendered speechless, as I fume. As the tears pour out, I say, "He lied to me. He made me look like a fool. I bet everyone but me knows who he is. And even worse, I was falling for him. I can't believe he let me fall for him when all along, he knew there could be nothing real between us. I'm not royalty. I'm a commoner. He probably isn't even allowed to date me. Clearly, Mitch was telling the truth. I was just a fling so Evan would have someone to sleep with while he was in Las Vegas. And like a naïve fool, I fell for the whole lie."

You slept with him?" Lowri asks. "That's fantastic. You finally got past the second date. Don't worry about anything else. We've all been played before, and not many of us can say it was by actual royalty."

"Lowri, you are not helping! I was falling in love with him. He said he would find a way to make us work!"

I take another look at the Google search results for images of Evan. The results sicken me. He always has a beautiful model, actress, or princess on his arm. I guess he was slumming it with lowly me because I'm none of those things. The best night of my life just turned into the worst one. I've fallen for Evan, and it was all a lie. I'm just another of his many conquests. How could I be so dumb?

CHAPTER FIFTY-TWO

EVAN

Sean warned me. Shit! Raking my hands through my hair, I know I should have told her sooner. But it felt so good to be treated like a somewhat normal, albeit rich, guy, so I kept putting off having the "talk" with her. Pacing in front of the wine barrels, I am at a loss as to how I can explain that I enjoyed getting to know her as Evan rather than Prince Garret? How am I going to fix this?

Sean approaches, handing me a drink. "What's wrong, Evan? Why did Cassie take off?"

Taking a quick gulp, I explain, "Detective Fielder referred to me as 'Your Royal Highness.'"

"Shit. Well, I guess that makes ending things easier," Sean replies with a smirk. "Based on the way she ran off, she will end it for you."

Practically taking his head off with my glare, I admit through gritted teeth, "I don't want to end things. I invited her to my father's retirement party and my brother's wedding. I just left out the part that my father is retiring from being king, and my brother is the crown prince."

Holding a hand up in peace, Sean says, "Wow! I had no idea. You are taking her home to meet the family. You actually are serious about her."

"Yes." Grabbing Sean's shoulder, I say, "Now, help me fix this mess."

"I don't know if you can fix it," he shakes his head. "You could try a grand gesture to show her you were not just playing her. That usually works in movies."

"Good idea. I must think of something to get her attention, so she will let me explain everything to her. I need to find a time and place where she cannot run away again."

"One option is to find her now and grovel," Sean grins as though he would love to watch me grovel. Then with a more serious expression, he offers, "If that doesn't work, tomorrow afternoon the chefs are being interviewed for a cooking show on the Food, Fun & Travel Channel. She won't easily be able to run out of the interview."

Hope returning, I say, "Perfect. That gives me an idea. Now I just need to call in a few favors. We will need Lowri's help to comfort Cassandra until then. Can you assist with that?"

With unexpected enthusiasm, Sean responds, "Of course."

CHAPTER FIFTY-THREE

CASSIE

The FFT channel is filming an interview of Kai, Trenton, and me today. I'm excited but sad at the same time. Last night I couldn't sleep. I vacillated between crying because my time with Evan is over and wanting a chance to tell him off for lying to me. As a result, I look horrible today. My eyes are puffy, and I'm exhausted. Now I have the most important interview of my life on FFT's Chef News. Lowri tried to cheer me up and insisted that the show must go on. The makeup artist has also done the best she can to make me look rested, but there is a limit, given what she has to work with.

We drew chips earlier to pick the order for the interviews. I'm thankful that my interview is last. It gives me a few more minutes to pull myself together. I need to forget Evan for an hour or so and concentrate on the next chapter in my life, which begins with this interview and the amazing opportunity to serve as the guest chef at the Grand Athena for a whole month.

When it's my turn, Amy's assistant escorts me onto the stage where I take a seat in a dark blue swivel chair next to the interviewer. After the competition interviews where we had to cook and talk at the same time, I should be ready for this interview. All I have to do is sit in a chair and answer a few questions. The hard part is smiling and pretending my heart isn't broken.

The host begins by introducing me to the live audience and camera. "This is Cassie Edwards. She is the third winner of the Guest Chef Competition at the Grand Athena. Welcome, Cassie."

"Thank you. I'm thrilled to be here."

"What can we expect when you are the guest chef at the Grand Athena?" she asks as she swivels toward me.

Hands clasped in my lap to prevent fidgeting, I explain, "Well, I believe great food and wine bring people together and help them create wonderful memories. Whether it's for a romantic dinner or a celebration with friends or family, we will offer an experience that makes the evening extremely special for everyone who joins us at Pinot & Pie." I turn my head, acknowledging the audience's gracious applause.

"That sounds great," she says, looking up from her notecard. "We understand you were the only finalist who didn't have a professional culinary background. Were you surprised to be selected as a finalist?"

"Yes, I was very surprised, but I decided to seize the opportunity. I didn't want to look back with any regrets."

The host pauses and I detect a hint of tension. Did I say something wrong? Then her smile returns and she continues, "Well, we have another surprise for you today. Everyone, please help me welcome Prince Garret of Catalinius, who wants to say a few words."

Oh no. Not now. I can't handle this. White knuckling the arms of the swivel chair, I attempt to control my emotions and stay firmly planted. I vaguely hear the host saying, "Please welcome His Royal Highness, Prince of Catalinius. Please have a seat next to Cassie. I understand that you have a surprise for her. Is that correct?"

Evan, as I know him, sits in the adjacent chair and swivels toward me, staring intently. My gaze drops to my lap, as I continue digging my fingernails into the upholstery on the chair arms. I hope the mic isn't picking up my ragged breathing.

Without taking his eyes off me, Evan responds, "Yes. That is correct. I suspect that Cassandra is not very happy with me right now, but I would like to share a little story with everyone if I may."

"Please do," the host responds as my mind swirls through the possibilities of what he may have planned.

Speaking softly, Evan explains. "Cassandra and I met during the Athena's Guest Chef Competition. We hit it off and started seeing each other, but I made a big mistake. I never told her I was a prince. She knew me as Evan, which is my middle name. I must admit that it was nice to just be Evan. I knew she liked me for me, not because I was a prince."

"Initially, I didn't think it would ever matter, but my feelings for Cassandra grew to be more than I expected they would. I even invited her to visit my home in Catalinius after the competition. I just didn't mention that my home is a palace." The audience laughs, and Evan continues, "I had planned to tell Cassandra about my family last night, but someone let it slip that I was a prince before I had the chance to tell her. As you would expect, Cassandra was hurt and upset that I had kept my full identity from her."

Loosening the grip on the chair, I let my hands fall to my lap and look up at Evan, wondering if he really planned to tell me last night.

Gazing deep into my eyes, Evan reaches out to touch my arm. "So, Cassandra, I am here today to tell you in front of everyone that I have fallen in love with you, and I, Prince Garret Evan Louis Francesco, Prince of Catalinius want you to come to Catalinius with me to meet my family. While my being a prince complicates the protocol, I am still the Evan you came to know, and I care very deeply for you."

I'm in shock. I can't believe Evan would pour out his heart in front of the world. I'm impressed, but I still don't see how we can work. "Evan, I mean, Prince Garret, it changes everything. I can't imagine your family will approve given that I don't have a royal title."

Evan responds, with a shake of his head and a squeeze of my arm. "Oh, but, Cassandra, you are wrong. My family is looking forward to meeting you."

Evan opens a beautiful, royal blue, velvet box that contains a gold neck chain with a diamond-encrusted key dangling from it. "Cassandra, I am presenting you with the Prince's Key. It was flown over on the royal jet last night for me to present to you. It represents a special invitation requesting your attendance at the upcoming events." A collective "Ah!" rises from the audience. Evan explains, "You will be my honored guest. Cassandra, please say yes. Be my plus one." Giggles erupt from the audience at the prince's use of the casual term.

Overwhelmed by the invitation and the willingness of Evan to go to such lengths to publicly make up for his lie of omission, I can't help but be won over. "I would love to accompany you to Catalinius and be your plus one." Evan smiles and quickly places the beautiful key around my neck. Then he places a reserved kiss on my forehead.

The host then asks, "Does this mean that you will not be returning as a guest chef at the Athena?"

I quickly respond, "Of course, I will be returning."

Evan also weighs in, "Why wouldn't she be returning? She worked very hard and earned that opportunity. I just hope she won't mind if I return with her." It is reassuring to hear him publicly respect my work even if he is a prince. And did he just say he wants to return with me?

The host then concludes the interview and thanks us for joining her, at which point Evan proceeds to pull me up from the chair and into his arms. He leans down and looks into my eyes as he says, "All along I've been calling you my princess because you are so special to me. I was just afraid I would lose you if I told you about my family. I wasn't ready to take that chance. Please forgive me."

"You have to promise me no more secrets."

"I promise. I love you, princess."

"Evan, I assumed the term princess was your standard term of endearment for the women you date. But I love you too."

Then Evan gently kisses me and whispers, "No, only you. I've never thought of anyone else as my princess."

EPILOGUE

CASSIE

A week has passed, and I'm still wondering when I will wake up from this dream. I can't believe it's real. After the FFT interview, Evan arranged for me to speak with his mother, the queen — yes, while in public he is Prince Garret, but in private, he is still Evan to me—to calm my nerves over meeting his family. She was kind, reassuring me that I'm welcome and that they look forward to getting to know me better.

Now I'm sitting on the royal jet with Evan. It's like private planes in movies with polished burled wood that shines like a mirror and plush, cream-colored leather chairs. The flight attendant had our favorite drinks in our hands the second we boarded and presented us with menu options for our long journey to Catalinius. I wonder if she will present a list of onboard spa treatments next, given that this seems like an airborne luxury hotel.

The pilot announces we need to take our seats in preparation for takeoff, and as I wait for the plane to surge down the runway, the corners of my lips tilt upward as I recall my time with Evan since the Final Dinner. At Evan's insistence, we spent the last week in Las Vegas selecting clothes and accessories for me for all the events we will be attending. While I insisted on buying most things myself, it's interesting how the financial security from the prize money made me more comfortable accepting a few gifts from Evan. I think it's because I now have means to reciprocate, such as with the gold cufflinks I bought him. We also have had outrageously great make-up sex, christening almost every surface in the Monarch Suite.

After reflection this past week, I also accepted that my parents would be proud of me even though my career path is deviating from their plan. They wanted me to have a happy, successful career and thought following in their footsteps would guarantee that outcome. But they were wrong. I don't have the passion for corporate law they had. It's not what makes me happy, and they loved me too much to want me to be stuck in a job that was unfulfilling. Finally at peace, I can pursue my true passion and see where it leads me without the guilt that has followed me for so long.

Evan gestures to the window, and I watch us soar into the air, catching a final glimpse of the glitz and glamour of the Las Vegas Strip. Finally on our way to Evan's home for what he keeps referring to as his father's retirement party, I'm still curious about how a king retires. Evan said it's a long story that is part of an old Catalinius tradition. Now that he is captive for hours and we don't have other things we need to do, I want all the details, so I fire off my question. "Why is your father having a retirement party? Kings don't retire."

Evan laughs and responds, "It is a long story, so you will want to get comfortable. In years past, the reigning monarchs tended to live unexpectedly long lives, with some reigning until they were 85 or older. This meant that when the king or queen passed away, the crown prince or princess was typically 65 years old or older. History tells us that several generations of crown princes and princesses were frustrated that they were expected to assume the throne when they were of an age where they wanted to slow down rather than take over more duties. However, the only alternative would be to abdicate and let their oldest child, the deceased king's grandchild, reign. But that would have been frowned upon as shirking his or her duties."

"Then along came King Lorenzo, who had assumed the throne as a teenager due to an accident that led to his father's untimely death.

After reigning for many years, he wanted the freedom he had been deprived of when his time as a prince was cut short. King Lorenzo had the clever idea to allow monarchs to retire, but only under very specific circumstances. He wanted to ensure that the crown prince or princess was at a stable and settled point in his or her life before the reigning monarch was allowed to retire. Therefore, in Catalinius, the reigning monarch is allowed to retire at age 65, but only if the crown prince or princess is married. If that condition is not met on the reigning monarch's 65th birthday, then the reigning king or queen must remain on the throne until death."

Fingering the diamond Prince's Key around my neck, I say, "I gather your father is turning 65 and wants to retire, right?"

Nodding, Evan continues, "Exactly. My father is turning 65 in just over two weeks and wants to retire, but my brother Alexander, the crown prince, is not married, which is a problem. You might ask why my father does not just change the rules to give my brother more time to marry. Unfortunately, that is not a reasonable option. In instituting the rules for retirement, King Lorenzo, clever as he was, made it almost impossible to change the conditions under which monarchs can retire. In fact, my father would be required to abdicate to change the rules, which in our country would put a substantial blemish on his reputation and admirable reign, so he would never do that."

Perplexed, I say, "It's strange that after what you describe as an admirable reign, stepping down would be seen as a significant blemish. In the U.S., people step down from high-ranking positions all the time to retire."

Evan responds, "It's our duty. Everyone born into the royal family is expected to put the interests of Catalinius above any personal interests. We are taught that from birth. But my brother never thought this rule would come into play because my father had always indicated he loved being king and wanted to rule for life. However, he recently changed his mind after a health scare and declared he wants to retire on his 65th birthday.

Reaching out to touch Evan's arm in concern, I ask softly, "Is your father ok?"

Patting my hand in reassurance, Evan replies, "Fortunately, he has fully recovered, but it made him rethink his plans for the future. He and my mother decided it is time to pass the throne to Alexander so they can travel and have some time for relaxation without the weight of the country on their shoulders. Considering my father's unexpected change of heart, Alexander is getting married sooner than he had planned because he does not want to let our father down and prevent him from retiring. Therefore, we are going to attend Prince Alexander's wedding. Then we will attend the king's retirement festivities, which is also his birthday party, followed by my brother's coronation. See, it is a long, complicated story."

I consider what Evan said. "You are right. It is a complicated situation. The concept of retirement for monarchs makes sense because when you think about it, it's somewhat unreasonable to expect someone to work until they die. But the strictness of the marriage rule is nuts. Your brother shouldn't be required to marry just so your father can retire."

Evan shakes his head. "No kidding. My brother was in shock when my father made his announcement."

"I can only imagine. Who is your brother marrying? Do you like her?"

Evan shrugs. "I have no idea."

"What do you mean you have no idea? You don't know if you like her?"

"What I mean is I have no idea who my brother is marrying. He hasn't decided yet, so I have no idea if I will like the woman he decides to marry."

Mouth agape, I ask, "When is the wedding?"

Matter-of-factly, Evan responds, "In two weeks. He is working on it and will figure it out by then. He has to."

"That's absolutely crazy."

Evan reaches for my hand and intertwines our fingers. He laughs. "I agree, but it should be fun to sit back and watch the fireworks. It will also make your first foray into royal life easier. Everyone will be concentrating on my brother rather than us."

Not knowing what else to say to this bizarre scenario, I mumble, "That sounds helpful," grateful the problem is Alexander's, not ours. Thank God!

Wriggling his eyebrows, Evan says "Enough about my family for now. You know there is a bedroom in the back, right? Would you like to take a nap?"

"I don't need a nap. I'm not tired yet."

With a mischievous sparkle in his eyes, he says, "Neither am I, but we can work on getting tired."

"That sounds like a great idea." Hand-in-hand we walk to the back room, where a sign on the door says The Royal Monarch Butterfly Suite. That's weird. His suite at the Grand Athena was the Monarch Suite. As I start to ask about the name, Evan pulls me into the bedroom and makes me quickly decide that my question can wait until we get to Catalinius.

ACKNOWLEDGMENTS

I am extremely grateful to everyone who has supported my efforts to bring the characters and events of *Thrill Ride* to life. Thank you to my husband for his willingness to listen to plot ideas over dinner and proofread early drafts. Thank you to Cece, my editor, for her insightful and invaluable input and critiques. She is truly amazing. Thank you to my cover designer, L.J., who awed me with how perfectly she captured exactly what I envisioned. Thank you to my blurb writer, Deborah, for capturing the essence of *Thrill Ride*. Thank you to my friends and colleagues, especially Audrey and Jeri, who served as early readers and provided extremely helpful feedback and encouragement. And thank you to Cheryl, Michael, and Gloria for sharing their experiences and advice on how to navigate the road to publication.

ABOUT THE AUTHOR

When not consumed by her job as an attorney, J.D. Carothers loves to cook for her family and friends, read murder mysteries and romance novels, eat chocolate, and sip wine watching the sunset in Southern California.

Late at night or early on weekend mornings, she tries to find a quiet place to write her next novel and trade the stress of real life for a fantasy world where murder and romance are on the menu, along with the food she loves.

She just wishes there were more hours in each day!

For more information, visit
www.jdcarothers.com

Made in the USA
Las Vegas, NV
17 August 2022

53469885R00182